Distorted Time: The Hollow Historian

Prequel Book I

H.M. Holzman

Cydonian Works, LLC

Distorted Time: The Hollow Historian is an original work. While it references public-domain elements originating with H. G. Wells' *The Time Machine* (Eloi/Morlocks, time travel), its characters, settings, and technologies—such as the Archway, and ***Malachi Hollow***—are unique creations of H.M. Holzman.

This narrative does not reproduce scenes, dialogue, or plot structures from the 1895 novel *The Time Machine*.

Based on H.G. Wells' *The Time Machine* (1895), a public-domain work. Published by **Cydonian Works LLC**, Florida, United States of America.

ISBN (Paperback): 979-8-9949008-3-3
ISBN (Hardcover): 979-8-9949008-4-0
ISBN (eBook): 979-8-9949008-5-7

Printed in the United States of America.

First Edition – 2026

Contents

Dedication

To AJ: I want to thank you for everything you do for humanity. You are one of the rare, good souls who care deeply for others—even when those people do not yet realize how truly important, they are to the world.

To my Mother and Father, even though you are no longer on this earth to see your son shine in his writing, I love you, and I miss you both every day.

To my readers: To those who bought my first novel and have now returned for my second—thank you. I am grateful for your dedication and the time you spend exploring my world and experiencing the journeys of my characters alongside me.

To my local Starbucks: Your support and good coffee continue to inspire my process.

To everyone: Travel forward, be good to one another, and choose love. Peace is the only true way for humanity to reach the stars and beyond.

To Sabrina—you always bring laughter just when things seem impossible or start falling apart.

To Esther because you are a genuine friend who cares about my writings.

Archival Note

DOCUMENT CLASSIFICATION: ABOVE TOP SECRET CLEARANCE – EYES ONLY
SOURCE: TRIDENT FACILITY ARCHIVAL DIVISION
CHRONOS DIVISION
AUTHORIZED BY: DIRECTOR DEAN FILBY
SUBJECT HISTORICAL RECORD: *The Hollow Historian*
RECOVERED MEMORY LOGS

The following document, classified as **The Hollow Historian**, serves as the official historical record of the Morlock known as Malachi. Readers should understand the severe neurological and psychological toll temporal displacement had on his mind and body.

Originating from **689,789 AD**, Malachi first traveled to **897 AD** before becoming stranded outside his native timeline from **1957 to 2035**. Combined with his age prior to temporal displacement, he was chronologically well over one hundred years old. Though this is considered middle-aged by Morlock standards, the accumulated burden of grief, isolation, and trauma proved devastating.

As a direct result, Malachi developed the condition known as ***"The Hollow."*** In modern terms, it most closely resembles profound melancholic depression accompanied by severe memory fragmentation. It must be noted, however, that the Hollow is not terminal, but reversible when the subject is finally able to confront and process deeply rooted trauma.

Readers comparing this record with the recovered personal journals published under **Distorted Time: The Cydonia Paradox** will note clear narrative discrepancies. Those journals reflect Malachi's fragmented memories while actively suffering from the Hollow. ***The Hollow Historian*** represents the objective truth of what occurred.

Prologue

689,787 AD Two Years Before the Archway

Evaria sat in the comforting darkness of her quarters, her thirteen-year-old face softened by the glow of her own luminous, amber-hued eyes. They illuminated the shadows as she listened intently for the familiar, heavy footsteps of her father. She was eager for Malachi to finally return home from the deep earth archives; to the rest of their kind, he was the Morlocks' most respected Historian, but to her, he was simply the center of her world. She couldn't wait to show him what she had made.

He's going to be so proud, she thought, her heart racing with a quiet, subterranean thrill. *He'll see that I finally mastered the weave.*

Spread out beside her on the bed lay the culmination of weeks of meticulous threading and immense patience: a flawless, deep purple silk sash. She ran her pale fingers over the smooth, unblemished weave, searching for a flaw that wasn't there, and a proud smile spread across her face. At thirteen, she practically vibrated with cheerful energy in the subterranean gloom—a lively, radiant girl ready to present her father with a masterpiece, and a rare spark of vibrant life in their world of stone.

A few minutes later, the heavy thud of her father's boots signaled his return. Evaria remained in the shadows, listening to the sharp, exhausted edge in Malachi's voice echoing through the dwelling. The endless politics between Morlock and Eloi had drained him yet again. She heard the soft rustle of her mother, Seraphina, moving to calm him.

"They will not listen! They never do," Malachi vented, his voice thick with frustration. "I uncover history in these tunnels—relics from levels sealed for thousands upon thousands of years—and the Eloi simply deny it. They ridicule the truth. They will not even descend from their elegant surface dwellings to view what I have found."

He paused, letting a heavy silence fill the room. "Why, Seraphina? Why do we make everything for them, yet they treat us with such disrespect? What makes us so different? Our eyes? Our skin? Our hair? Our ears?

Granted, theirs are slightly pointed, while ours remain curved and round, but still..." He attempted a hollow, sarcastic laugh as his wife stepped close and wrapped her arms around him.

Seraphina was slightly shorter than him. Her light blue-gray skin, tinged with a subtle green, complemented her dark hair, which was threaded with black and grey highlights. Her eyes glowed with the same bioluminescent gold as their daughter's. She reached up, her hands firmly but gently massaging the tight knots of tension in Malachi's shoulders.

He let his head fall forward, emitting a soft, resonant gurgle from deep in his chest—not a beast's growl, but a uniquely Morlock sound of profound stress leaving the body.

"Malachi," she said softly, "I know your work is hard. But I believe in you. I believe in the historical finds you bring from the dark, and so does our kind. You are respected and loved. You do not need to prove yourself to the Eloi. If they treat you with disrespect, so be it. It is on them, not you. I know you want to bridge our worlds, but the politics of what they believe and how they perceive us never seems to change."

As she spoke, Malachi's fingers turned an older Aeterna stone over and over in his hand. Inside his worn satchel sat at least four others. They were smooth, black, and oval—about three to four inches across—though one bore a jagged chip. They were not mere stones; they were the encoded records of a forgotten age. They held the voices of the past, waiting only for the precise frequency of a special quartz crystal to unlock the history stored inside.

"This one here... it still holds a charge. I need you to see it." He placed his hand over the smooth black stone. Seraphina leaned in as a faint glow pulsed from its center.

A date materialized in the air: 555,879 AD.

Slowly, a violet holographic projection fanned upward from the stone, forming a miniature, five-inch-tall rendering of a young, full-grown Morlock man. Though scaled down by the flickering light, his exhaustion and terror were unmistakably life-sized.

"They are murdering us!" the tiny violet figure cried out, his voice a static-laced whisper. "They wanted more of the chemical—the one that made them forget their problems, the one that produced a fragile peace for over five hundred years. But it's gone. There is no way to synthesize the drug that kept them happy and content with us. Now they are trying to slaughter us as we seal the caves."

The miniature hologram flickered, the man's chest heaving with panic. "It's some kind of withdrawal they are all experiencing. The Eloi have gone insane. Chancellor Zaldova has ordered us to seal the hatches but leave the communication arrays open until this passes. My children are terrified. My wife... she's... dead. They killed her in one of the upper service tunnels. She was a courier, trying to run back below ground when they swarmed her. They wanted the *Calvenine*. The drug that can no longer be made. They killed her when she told them she had nothing left to give them. If this continues—"

The projection abruptly snapped out of existence. The stone went dead.

Seraphina stared at the empty space in absolute horror. She had seen the way the unknown Morlock's eyes dilated in that final fraction of a second. The look of death. Something, or someone, had breached his room and killed him mid-sentence.

"Almost a hundred and thirty-four thousand years ago..." her voice trailed off into a stunned whisper.

Malachi watched the color drain from her face. It was his second time viewing the recording, but the physical sickness in his stomach hadn't lessened.

"Calvenine," Malachi said quietly. "I had never heard the word until I found this today. Imagine it, Seraphina. An entire population controlled, kept happy and docile by a narcotic, and then suddenly the ability to manufacture it is gone. Resources. They are not stable."

He looked at the dead stone in his hand, his jaw setting with grim determination. "We cannot remain trapped in the dark as their caretakers. We must claim our right to the surface. We have to find a way to live side by side with the Eloi in the daylight. And beyond that..." He looked up, as if trying to pierce the miles of rock above them. "We must reach out to the heavens again. The oldest fragments I have translated confirm there are other planets out there. Other spheres of rock and gas that our ancestors once traveled to. I do not know their ancient names, or what was lost to the blackness of space, but I know this: we were meant for the stars, Seraphina. Not just the dirt."

Seraphina knew this argument well. And she knew he was right. If the Morlocks ever failed to produce the luxuries the Eloi demanded above, the fragile, unspoken truce would break. History had proven that the Eloi were capable of slaughter. If the resources ran dry, life below ground would become impossible to bear.

"You are the voice of reason for our kind, Malachi," Seraphina said gently. "The Eloi do not see you that way. But even if they did suddenly decide to listen, it would take time to reintegrate—"

Malachi threw his hands up in heavy frustration, cutting her off. She was right, and the cold truth of it gnawed at him. *To the surface dwellers, my intellect means nothing; I am just a Morlock.* Yet, he still clung to the desperate hope that he could force some spark of peace or reasoning upon them.

"They have to listen," he urged, his tone thick with anxiety. "If they do not listen... we all die. Eloi and Morlock alike."

He caught himself, forcing his voice into a harsh whisper on those final words. Through the walls of their dwelling, he remembered that his pride and joy was waiting for him in the dark of her room. The political anger immediately drained out of his posture, replaced by a fierce, protective warmth. He had to go to her. He had to tuck Evaria in and be the gentle father she adored. *Above the history, above the archives, my family comes first.*

He was a passionate man, but a reasonable one—a delicate balance he had inherited. A sharp pang of grief touched Malachi's chest at the thought. His father had walked this exact path before him, serving as both a Historian and an Ambassador to the Eloi, fighting the same exhausting wall of indifference until the day he passed away.

Malachi took a deep, shaky breath, letting the heavy chain of his father's legacy settle onto his shoulders. *I will not let my family inherit a dying world.*

"You are right again, Seraphina. My own father... they never listened to him." Malachi's voice thickened with an old, unhealed grief. "When I wanted to bury him above the surface, they ridiculed me. They embarrassed me. You were there! You and your best friend, Casia. It was before our own daughter was even born. The Eloi didn't care about him at all. Complete disrespect. We always have to compromise ourselves just to provide for them. They live in complete comfort in the sun, while we have to compartmentalize our very souls in the dark to appease them. It has to end!"

Malachi shook his head, the exhaustion of a lifetime of subservience pulling at his features. This time, Seraphina stepped closer, looking deeply into his glowing eyes with a soft, steadying smile.

"You know I always agree with you," she whispered, her hands resting gently against his chest. "If I could just take this burden away from your heart and soul, I would. But Malachi, you have to ground yourself. Accept the things they will not change, and find peace in knowing you spoke your truth to them. The truth will eventually come out, for good or for ill. But for now... we have today. Not just tomorrow, which will come regardless. We have right now."

The heavy tension finally broke, melting away under her touch. He smiled back at her, a look of profound, quiet devotion, before pulling her into a close embrace and kissing her gently in the shadows of their home.

"Have dinner ready soon," he murmured, giving her one last squeeze. "I must go be with Evaria. Our little pride and immense joy."

Seraphina smiled, turning to prepare the evening meal as Malachi headed for their daughter's room.

Evaria heard his heavy footsteps approaching. The moment he crossed the threshold, she ran to him, launching herself into his arms. Malachi caught her effortlessly, a genuine smile finally breaking through his exhaustion. Her luminescent eyes were glowing brighter than usual in the dim light, practically vibrating with an excited energy he could feel radiating from her small frame.

"Father!" she squealed, pure happiness in her voice.

He chuckled, gently brushing a stray lock of black hair from her face. "Evaria, how are you doing tonight?"

She gave his neck one last tight squeeze before he set her down. Immediately, she darted over to her bed. Lying across the blankets was a long, meticulously woven swath of deep purple silk.

Malachi knew his daughter loved to create clothing for him, and he proudly wore the shirts and trousers she crafted. But this was different. This was unlike anything she had ever made before.

"I made you this," she announced, proudly lifting the purple sash to show him.

Malachi's eyes widened. In Morlock culture, when a daughter presented her father with a sash of this design, it was a formal signal. It meant she was declaring her readiness to take on adult responsibilities—to learn the deeper tasks of the household, like cooking and cleaning alongside her mother. But she was only thirteen. She was highly intelligent, yes, but a sudden, protective ache bloomed in his chest. *She is growing up far too fast.*

"A sash?" Malachi said softly, his joy mingling with the sudden, heavy pressure of time passing. "Do you know what this means?"

"It means—" Evaria began, stepping forward with a bright smile to drape the fabric over him.

But she hesitated. She reached up to place the silk over his shoulder and bring it around his waist to secure the clip, but her hands stopped. Malachi watched her carefully. Her pale fingers, normally so deft and precise with a needle and thread, began to fumble clumsily with the simple clasp.

"It means..." she tried again, her brow furrowing in confusion.

He looked down into her glowing eyes. The bright, intelligent spark flickered. Her hands continued to tremble against his chest, unable to coordinate the basic physical task. Frustrated, she let out a small gurgle—but it was not the resonant, expressive sound of a civilized Morlock. It was harsh, raw, and startlingly feral.

The sound sent a spike of pure ice through Malachi's veins. His thoughts raced, time seeming to stretch into an agonizing thirty seconds as she continued to helplessly twist the beautiful purple silk, her mind entirely blank.

No, his mind screamed. *It is the cognitive shear. She is showing signs of PCR... the "Great Forgetting."*

Then, just as suddenly as the terrifying fog had descended, it lifted. Evaria regained her composure, her pale hands moving deftly once more, and she snapped the clip securely at her father's waist. She looked up and smiled, completely unaware of the agonizing thirty seconds she had just lost.

Malachi swallowed hard, forcing the panic deep down into his chest. He quickly smoothed his own expression, desperate not to alarm her. He had noticed everything, but he could not let her see the raw terror behind his eyes.

"It means I am becoming a female adult, and I can help Mom and learn the ways of being an adult," she said, her smile beaming with innocent pride.

Malachi nodded, pulling her into a tight, grounding hug. When he pulled back, he turned to look at the deep purple sash in the reflection of her mirror. The craftsmanship was truly stunning, a vibrant streak of color in their dark world.

"Evaria," he said, his voice trembling slightly. "You will always be my pride and joy. Always."

She stepped back, her smile faltering as she noticed the wetness gathering in her father's glowing eyes. It alarmed her. She had never seen him cry quite like this before. It was a heavy, complicated tear—a warring mixture of immense pride and profound, agonizing sorrow. Her sharp mind sensed the dark edge of that sorrow, but she wanted so desperately to focus on the joy. Puzzled, she tilted her head.

"Father, why are you crying?" she asked softly. "Did I do something wrong? Am I not ready?" She paused, her voice filling with absolute, unwavering adoration. "You are the 'King of History,' my father."

She climbed into her bed, settling down onto her soft pillow as Malachi took a seat at her bedside. He studied her face in the dim light, taking a deep, ragged breath. He did not want to reject her readiness. And he absolutely refused to shatter her peace by revealing what she had just done, or the terrifying glitch he had witnessed.

"Evaria, let me tell you this... you are my pride and joy," he whispered gently. "But I am not the 'King of History'."

"YES, YOU ARE!" she cut him off, her voice ringing with fierce, childish certainty.

He looked down at his daughter, frantically searching for the right words to say, wanting to preserve this perfect moment. But before he could speak, Evaria let out a soft, heavy yawn. Her eyelids drooped, and she reached over, pulling one of her woven dolls close to her chest.

As he stroked her dark hair, he let her absolute faith wash over him, but his mind raced with the frantic, bargaining work of a desperate parent. *Maybe she is just tired. Maybe her hands simply slipped.* He thought all these things to himself, trying to force the terror back down into the dark, but the cold reality remained. He could not ignore the signs of the "Great Forgetting"—the insidious genetic decay he had studied, the disease the Morlock medical professionals were still so slowly, so helplessly, trying to find a cure for.

He swallowed the heavy lump in his throat. He was not ready to accept it, but as he watched his daughter drift toward sleep, he knew with a sickening certainty that he had to tell his wife.

He leaned in close, his voice dropping to a low, resonant hum. It was an ancient melody he had unearthed from a fractured Aeterna stone—a rhyme from a forgotten age, perhaps familiar to the ancestors, but the original words had been lost to time. Malachi had given it new words. Words for the dark. Words for her.

"You are my messenger, my little one," he sang lowly, the deep, steady vibration of his chest soothing her. "My daughter, when stars are so bright."

Evaria's breathing slowed, her grip on the woven doll relaxing as her eyes finally fluttered shut.

"Your moonlight will never fade, when moonlight shines throughout the night. I love you, my daughter... my messenger, my bundle of love, every night..."

His voice caught slightly on the final line, the crushing weight of the "Great Forgetting" pressing hard against his throat. He forced the last words out in a desperate, whispered plea into the dark.

"...Please, night, do not take my moonlight away."

He sat in the quiet shadows for a few minutes after she fell asleep, listening to the steady rhythm of her breathing. When he was certain she was resting peacefully, Malachi slowly stood up, the heavy burden of what he had to do next pulling at his posture. He turned his back on the moonlight of his life and walked out into the main corridor to face his wife.

Seraphina could clearly see the deep distress radiating from Malachi the moment he sat at the small dining table. He stared blankly at his meal, mechanically picking at a small cluster of peachberries on his plate. She took her seat across from him, the warm domesticity of the room suddenly feeling very cold. Tears pooled in his glowing eyes, and she watched him physically swallow hard to hold them back.

"What is wrong? What happened?" she asked quickly. Then, her eyes drifted downward. "Is that... Evaria made the sash?"

A sudden burst of genuine joy and pride broke through her concern as she studied the flawless purple silk wrapped around his waist. Malachi did not smile. He simply reached for his cup, taking a slow, shaky sip of his drink.

"Malachi? She made that for you? Right?" Seraphina pressed, her smile beginning to falter.

"Yes, she did!" he snapped, a quiet, irritated whisper designed specifically not to wake their sleeping daughter. "We need to take her to a doctor as soon as possible, though."

The bright, proud smile vanished from Seraphina's face in an instant. The silence in the room stretched thin. Malachi's hands clenched into fists on the table. He was immensely proud of Evaria—the flawless purple silk bound around his waist was a testament to her sharp mind—but a furious, helpless annoyance boiled beneath his skin. *How do I protect her from an enemy I cannot see or understand?* The paradox of his joy and his terror was suffocating.

"Why?" she asked, her voice dropping to a terrified murmur.

"She may or may not have it," he choked out, forcing himself to chew and swallow a bite of food he could not taste. He finally looked up, meeting her gaze. The raw pain in his expression was absolute.

"Have what?" Seraphina asked, her concern deepening into dread. Her hands trembled slightly as she reached over to pour him more of his drink, studying the rigid tension in his jaw.

"Seraphina... as Evaria placed the sash over me, she had trouble with her words. She let out a feral gurgle." He paused, unable to hide the shudder that ran through him. "She became completely distant for at least fifteen to thirty seconds. When she finally managed to get the sash connected to my waist..."

He pushed his chair back and stood up, the purple silk hanging perfectly against his frame. It was undeniably beautiful, which only made the horror worse.

"She finally was able to finish what she was saying, and acted as if absolutely nothing had happened." The tears Malachi had been fighting finally broke, welling over his lower lashes.

Seraphina stood up, moving quickly to his side as her own vision blurred with tears. As an educator, she knew exactly what he was describing. She had seen the horrifying reality of this disease creeping into her own classrooms, and heard the whispered warnings from her fellow teachers.

"I did not know this... are you sure?" she pleaded, her heart hammering against her ribs. She knew exactly the progression of the disease. It always started small—forgetting simple words, experiencing blank stares. Then came the terrifying regression. In adults, the feral behavior was reported to escalate into violent psychosis, eventually reducing civilized Morlocks to the point of primal cannibalism. Those extreme cases were still rare, but the threat was real.

"I am sure of what I saw, but I do not know if she actually has it. That, I am not sure of," Malachi insisted, his voice cracking with desperate hope. "This is why we must get her tested immediately."

Seraphina wrapped her arms around him, and he buried his face in her shoulder. In the quiet gloom, they desperately wanted to believe the impossible—that their daughter was safe, and this was not the Great Forgetting—the Progressive Cortical Regression known as PCR.

Chapter I — PCR "The Glitch"

Malachi had called his colleagues the night before, sortly after dinner, to tell them he would not be at the archaeological site where he had secured the old stones for further study. He explained only that he was dealing with a medical issue regarding his daughter. They respected him enough not to press for details, simply giving him the time he needed to take care of his family first.

Malachi looked at his wife as he lay next to her. They had been restless as they tried to sleep, and now that it was morning, it offered them no relief. There was no sunrise to break the shadows, for there is no natural light in the darkness of the underground caverns where all Morlocks are forced to live.

"Seraphina, there are two outcomes. She has it, or she does not. If she has it, maybe there is a treatment? If she does not have it, then we should forget about this present nightmare. You have always told me to try and be positive, and that is what I need to do," Malachi said. His wife yawned softly, her luminous eyes holding his gaze in the dim light.

"If she has the disease, Malachi, you know in your heart there are no known medical cures," Seraphina said, fighting away fresh tears. "I want to suppress the symptoms. I am willing to try whatever the doctors suggest to fight this, but they must assure us it will not leave her in a constant, catatonic state. I will not subject our daughter to heavy chemicals if the cost of suppressing the disease is rendering her an incoherent, vegetative shell. If a medicine exists but only strips away her remaining cognitive abilities, I will not allow her to stay on it. And Malachi... we cannot bear this in complete isolation. If the worst is true, I want to tell Casia. I trust her with my life, and with Evaria's."

She wiped at her eyes, the exhaustion of silently crying through half the night weighing heavily on her features. Watching her, Malachi swallowed hard, forcing his own tears back just as he had done for hours in the dark. *I must be the strong one,* he thought, though his racing mind left him feeling entirely weak. *I certainly do not feel like the 'King of History' she called me last night.*

"I know, and I agree with you. I do not want that life for our daughter," Malachi replied gently. "And you are right about Casia; we will need her support. But first, let us focus on this morning. Perhaps we should take Evaria for her favorite dessert before she goes to the medical facility with us? We do not want her to become anxious that she will not be at school today. You already made your plans known to your educational superiors, that you had a medical emergency and were granted immediate time off for Evaria." Malachi sat up, and she did the same.

Seraphina took a deep, unsteady breath before stepping through the stone threshold of their daughter's bedroom. The heavy, subterranean silence of their dwelling pressed in around her, broken only by the faint, rhythmic hum of the sector's distant air shafts. The darkness of the room was absolute, softly pushed back only by the ambient amber glow of her own eyes. As she stepped closer, that pale light swept across the smooth rock walls, revealing Evaria fast asleep beneath her thick blankets, still tightly clutching one of her favorite woven dolls.

Seraphina slowly reached out, her soft, light blue-gray hand gently shaking her daughter's shoulder. Evaria's eyes fluttered open in the gloom. They brightened with warmth as she smiled, reaching up to give her mother a fierce, loving hug.

But when she pulled back, Evaria's smile faded slightly. "Mother... you look a bit sad?"

Evaria's quick perception—sharp enough to catch the minute tightening of her mother's jaw even in the dim light—instantly made Seraphina uncomfortable. She fought desperately to hold her composure.

"Why do you say that?" Seraphina replied, trying to keep her voice perfectly steady.

But her body betrayed her. A single, heavy tear escaped and fell from her eye right in front of Evaria.

"Because I see you have been crying. Why, Mother?" Evaria asked gently, reaching up to place her soft hand against her mother's wet cheek.

Evaria was incredibly smart for her age. She was considered gifted, and not simply because her mother was a teacher; Evaria had a natural, exceptional aptitude for mechanics and mathematics. She was at the top of her class, an undeniable source of pride for both her parents. That sharp intellect made it impossible to hide things from her easily.

Seraphina covered her daughter's hand with her own, quickly wiping the tear away. "I have just been so proud of you. You are becoming a young adult. Because of that, your father and I want to take you to the medical complex today. We just need to make sure you are doing well. But we are also taking you to your favorite place before we go there."

Evaria studied her mother for a long moment. She wore a serious expression, her sharp mind clearly sensing that something was still wrong, even if she could not put the pieces together just yet. But she chose not to say it. Instead, she smiled, her expression lighting up as she realized they were going to *Olesya's Café.* They baked the absolute best cakes and breads in the enclave subterrain sector.

"Alright, Mother. Thank you," Evaria said.

Evaria hopped out of bed to begin her morning routine. Seraphina left to finish her own, finding Malachi waiting in the main living area. He had already completed his morning tasks; he always moved fast, his rushing a quiet reflection of his anxious mind.

"She senses something is wrong, Malachi," Seraphina whispered. She stepped into his arms, and he held her gently to quiet her concerns. He looked down at her tear-streaked face as another quiet wave of sobs broke through her composure.

"We still do not know, Seraphina," Malachi assured her, keeping his voice low and steady. "It might not be what I observed last night. We have to have courage. Evaria is fine, and this is just a precaution." He tried desperately to make the words sound true.

Seraphina simply nodded, pulling back slightly to point toward the table. Resting there was the deep purple sash their daughter had made for him.

Malachi picked it up. He draped the vibrant silk over his dark tunic, wrapping it carefully around his waist and securing the clasp himself. He looked down, admiring the flawless craftsmanship of his daughter's work. In his mind, he desperately wanted to believe his own reassurances, praying his terrifying instincts from the night before were wrong.

A few minutes passed before Evaria entered the room wearing a dark maroon tunic and loose black trousers. She had tied her long black hair into a bun, her eyes shining as she smiled.

"Let's go to Olesya's, I am so happy!" Evaria's voice carried a distinct blend of childhood innocence and young adulthood. She hugged her father and saw he was wearing her sash, which began to ease her mind that her mother was just telling the truth. Still, a small inner voice nagged at her. *Mother and Father think I might be sick? Why else would they want to take me to the medical complex?* The three of them left their dwelling and stepped onto an automated walkway. The conveyance moved smoothly on its own, designed to prevent nausea or injury should it stop suddenly. It was a highly efficient transportation system utilized by the Morlock population, running seamlessly through the ancient tunnels and the bustling subterranean commercial sectors where they lived.

Ten minutes later, the automated walkway deposited them near the entrance of *Olesya's café.* As the three of them stepped through the doors, Malachi approached the sleek flat-screen display in the lobby, scrolling through vibrant images of the latest menu delights. He ordered his usual: a dense bread baked with sweet subterranean fruit, paired with a chilled fruit beverage crafted specifically to enhance the dessert's rich flavor. Seraphina and Evaria quickly ordered their own favorites as well.

Olesya's was famous throughout the sector for its generous portions, but it was also a place of deep community tradition. Because Malachi and his wife were such highly respected figures, the café's host formally announced their presence to the dining room as they walked to their table. It was a rare sign of immense respect. While other frequent visitors always had the option to decline the public acknowledgment, the community always wanted to honor their Historian and his family.

"Father, they have the new enhanced peachberries! I am so excited to try them! Thank you for taking me here!" Evaria beamed, her amber eyes wide with genuine delight.

Malachi forced a warm smile, reaching beneath the edge of the table to take Seraphina's hand. His wife squeezed his fingers tightly, a silent, desperate tether between them as they waited for their order.

"Evaria, we love you and are so very proud of you," Seraphina told her daughter, leaning in so her voice carried over the ambient noise.

"I know, Mother," Evaria giggled.

Olesya's Café was a vibrant hub of life, offering a stark, comforting contrast to the quiet, heavy stone of their home. Soft, lively acoustic music drifted through the warm air, blending with the cheerful chatter of the morning crowd. All around them, other Morlock families were gathered in the dim light, parents talking while children could be seen smiling, eating, and simply enjoying the safety of the café.

Finally, their server arrived, carefully balancing a large tray loaded with their chilled drinks and thick slices of warm, sweet fruit bread. Set precisely next to Evaria's plate was a small bowl of the newly enhanced peachberries. They were the latest triumph of subterranean horticulture—small, delicate fruits engineered to perfectly marry the soft, juicy bite of a peach with the deep, sweet tartness of an ancient, seeded red berry whose true name had long been forgotten.

Evaria eagerly picked up her first peachberry and popped it into her mouth.

Malachi took a bite of his thick plumberry-bread, chewing it slowly. The bread was a masterpiece of infusion, bursting with the bright, layered flavors of plum and apricot. For a fleeting second, the sweet taste offered a tiny reprieve from his anxiety.

But as Evaria reached to pick up her second peachberry, her hand froze mid-air.

Malachi noticed it instantly. An uncertain, vacant look washed over his daughter's features. Seraphina froze, stunned, and slowly turned her head toward Malachi. The color drained from her face. Something was terribly wrong.

"Evaria?" Malachi said lowly.

He watched her face contort with a sudden, rigid confusion. For a terrifying second, Seraphina thought she might be choking, but her airway was clear. Instead, the entire right side of Evaria's face seemed to seize, the muscles locking involuntarily. She opened her mouth and spat the half-chewed first peachberry onto her plate.

Then came the sound.

A loud, harsh, feral gurgle ripped from her throat. It was so unnatural, so devoid of civilized Morlock restraint, that the occupants of the neighboring tables snapped their heads around, exchanging alarmed expressions.

"Malachi? She's..." Seraphina choked out, her voice paralyzed by raw terror.

Malachi didn't wait for her to finish. He was already out of his seat and sliding into Evaria's side of the booth. He grabbed her shoulders, looking closely into his daughter's face. She wore a dead, blank stare. A thin line of drool formed at the corner of her slack mouth, and her chest heaved as she let out a second, even louder guttural noise.

The cheerful chatter of the surrounding tables died instantly. More patrons began turning in their seats, their eyes searching for the source of the distressing sound as fearful murmurs rippled through the café.

Malachi frantically waved his hand directly in front of Evaria's eyes, but she didn't blink. She was completely disconnected, trapped in some dark, unreachable void inside her own mind.

Come back to me, Evaria, his mind screamed in the silent dark. *Please come back.*

His heart hammering against his ribs, Malachi snatched the cloth napkin from the table. He gently but firmly wiped the drool from her chin and cheek.

The physical touch acted like a switch.

Evaria blinked rapidly, the sharp intelligence immediately flooding back into her eyes. The facial seizure vanished, replaced instantly by her bright, innocent smile. She looked up at him, completely oblivious to the terrified silence of the patrons around them.

"Father, what are you doing over here?" she asked, her voice light and cheerful.

She had absolutely no idea that for almost an entire agonizing minute, she had experienced something profound and terrifying.

Slowly, the surrounding patrons stopped staring, awkwardly returning to their meals with hushed whispers. Evaria's cheerful expression faded, shifting quickly into deep confusion. She looked from her father's trembling hands to her mother's tear-streaked face. Then, she noticed the server standing there, hovering with an expression of guarded pity.

The weight of their collective terror pressed down on her all at once. Her lip began to quiver, and her eyes welled with sudden, hot tears.

"Why are you looking at me like that?" she whispered, her voice breaking. "Father... what did I do? Why is everyone quiet?"

A single sob escaped her as she buried her face into Malachi's deep purple sash. The vibrant silk, which had been a symbol of her pride only an hour ago, was now dampened by her tears of confusion and fear.

The server cautiously approached the table, keeping her voice quiet. "Is everything okay, Malachi? Is the food alright?"

As the server spoke, she glanced toward Evaria. Evaria followed the server's gaze down to her own plate, suddenly noticing the half-chewed peachberry sitting there. She quickly placed one hand over her mouth.

Did I spit this out? What happened? Why is everyone staring, but trying to pretend they aren't? she thought.

Overwhelmed by the sudden, inexplicable shame and the fearful tension radiating from her parents, Evaria began to sob quietly.

Malachi simply motioned for the server to leave the payout terminal on the table. The server nodded and stepped back. Malachi firmly pressed two fingers against the screen to confirm the payment, and they stood to leave abruptly.

They walked away from the half-eaten food—abandoning what was supposed to be a brief, happy celebration of their daughter coming of age and embracing her female adulthood. Malachi looked down at the deep purple sash tied around his waist and winced, the beautiful silk suddenly feeling impossibly heavy as Evaria stepped over to her mother and continued to sob against Seraphina's side.

Just outside the café, Seraphina guided Evaria toward a quiet stone bench along the thoroughfare. While mother and daughter sat down, Malachi remained standing. He frowned, stepping directly in front of Evaria to physically block the view of any passing Morlocks. He was a fiercely loving father, and his immediate instinct was to shield his daughter's dignity from any potential stares or whispers of ridicule.

"Evaria, listen carefully," Seraphina said, keeping her voice incredibly gentle as she held her daughter's hands. "In our family, we do not lie to one another. Inside Olesya's... something happened to you."

But before Seraphina had a chance to fully calm her down or handle the delicate situation, Malachi's desperate anxiety clouded his judgment. He did not mean to be cold or disrespectful to his wife by interrupting, but his suffocating panic simply boiled over. He had to know right now if Evaria was conscious inside that dark void when her body seized, or if her mind had simply paused and un-paused like a skipped moment in time.

"Do you remember what happened in there?" Malachi cut in abruptly, looking down at her, his voice tight with fear.

Evaria sobbed harder. She now knew with absolute certainty that something was indeed wrong, and she was the cause. *What is wrong with me?* She desperately tried to reconstruct the missing seconds of her life, but there was nothing. It was just a terrifying, seamless jump from tasting the fruit to the horrified stares inside Olesya's. Now, shivering on the thoroughfare bench, the grim reality settled over her: this was why they had to travel to the medical subterranean enclave center.

"Father, all I did was place one peachberry in my mouth and begin to chew. Then I reached to take the second one, and suddenly you were wiping my face... yet the first peachberry was sitting half-eaten on my plate? Why? What happened? Father? Mother?"

She stopped sobbing, wiping her eyes as she stared up at both of them. She focused on her mother's words echoing in her mind. *In our family, we do not lie to one another.* Taking a deep, shaky breath, she forced herself to ground her emotions. She desperately wanted to prove she was a brave young adult.

"You spat the peachberry out of your mouth," Seraphina said softly, her voice trembling. "You made loud gurgling noises, and you did not hear our voices."

"I did?" Evaria's eyes widened.

The revelation was terrifying, but her highly analytical mind immediately seized on the facts. She knew exactly what this meant, and it was not good. Several months ago, she had been at school when the sudden lockdown alarms echoed through the corridors. She had been sitting safely in Auntie Casia's classroom, but she remembered the terrifying sounds—a sudden, feral rage and guttural gurgling erupting from Teacher Dephera's room down the hall. Though Casia had quickly secured their door, Evaria and her classmates had heard the violent crash of light-stone chair-desks being overturned. The whispered rumors later confirmed that two teachers had rushed in to physically wrestle a thrashing male student to the ground.

The entire school had never seen or heard from that student again.

"My beloved daughter, you must stay strong. We will find out exactly what has happened. This is why we are taking you to the medical facility," Malachi said, his hand dropping to rest against the deep purple sash at his waist. "We love you, and we stand by you."

"You must trust us that we will help you," Seraphina interjected gently.

"What if it turns out I have this... this disease?" Evaria questioned pointedly. She wiped her eyes and stood taller, looking up at her parents as a sudden, fierce spark ignited in her gaze. *I will fight whatever this is and beat it.* It was the exact same logical, determined mindset Malachi had instilled in her years ago. Back when she was six years old and first learning how to sew, she had grown terribly frustrated because she could not figure out the correct needle to use with a specific silk thread. He had taught her then to push past her panic and solve the problem—a lesson she was summoning now.

"We will figure it out," Seraphina assured her. "There has to be some treatment that can help, but we must remain positive. If we cast our thoughts on negativity, it will do no good for any of us."

A heavy silence lingered between them for a few moments. Finally, the three of them stood up from the stone bench, stepped back onto the automated walkway, and proceeded toward the subterranean medical enclave.

Nothing more was said on the journey. Evaria stood facing forward on the moving belt, while her parents stood just half a step behind her on either side, each of them tightly holding one of her hands in a quiet, fiercely protective wedge. *I will be brave,* Evaria told herself, her eyes fixed straight ahead. *I have to prove it.*

Fifteen minutes later, the automated walkway smoothly decelerated, bringing them to the entrance of the medical facility. The sprawling, brightly lit space was a stark, uncomfortable contrast to the warm, lively dimness of the café. Morlock medical staff moved efficiently through the wide corridors, assisting the elderly and treating those who were unwell. The atmosphere was rigidly sterile, cold, and highly professional.

Malachi looked down at his daughter. He could see the firm set of her jaw. She was trying desperately to maintain her composure, but through her small hand, he could physically feel the deep, vibrating tremor of the fear she harbored.

They bypassed the general healing wards and walked toward a highly secured, heavily reinforced sector. Above the thick, heavy doors, a starkly illuminated sign read: **PROGRESSIVE CORTICAL REGRESSION: TESTING & INTAKE.**

The three of them made their way to a sleek intake cubicle. Malachi placed his hand flat against the glowing biometric console. Instantly, his family's complete medical history materialized on the screen. With a heavy heart, he carefully entered Evaria's information into the system, officially checking his daughter in as the patient.

The three of them took their seats in a quiet, isolated waiting area. Hanging quietly on the smooth stone walls were a few rare, carefully preserved pictures of what appeared to be the surface world and the moon—a beautiful, aching reminder of the sky they were denied.

After five minutes of agonizing waiting in the quiet alcove, a senior physician approached them. She wore deep red robes cinched with a vibrant blue sash—the formal, respected attire of a high-ranking Morlock medical official.

"Malachi? The Honorable Historian?" she asked, her voice carrying a calm, practiced warmth.

Malachi stood up, his lips twitching with a faint, embarrassed smile. He possessed no vanity for the grand titles his kind bestowed upon him; he preferred to remain humble, seeing himself only as a servant to their forgotten past.

Before he could politely deflect the title, Evaria stepped forward, her eyes shining brightly despite the sterile gloom of the clinic. "My father is the King of History!" she announced, a sudden, bright giggle escaping her lips.

For a split second, the heavy, suffocating terror that had been crushing Malachi and Seraphina all morning finally fractured. It didn't vanish entirely—the dread was still waiting in the wings—but the sheer, innocent pride radiating from their daughter forced a genuine, breathless chuckle from Malachi's chest. Seraphina covered her mouth, a teary, overwhelmed smile breaking through her rigid anxiety.

"That's my father," Evaria repeated proudly, pointing up at him. "He is the King of History."

The doctor's professional posture softened. She looked down at Evaria, her eyes crinkling with sincere warmth. "Yes, you are absolutely right. He is," she agreed gently.

She then looked back up to Malachi, the quiet, professional gravity returning slightly to her tone as she assessed the grim reality of the ward they were standing in. "It is a profound honor to meet you both. What brings you to my sector, Malachi? Is this brave young princess my patient?"

"She is indeed," Malachi replied, catching the fragile lifeline his daughter had thrown him. "She is to go with my Queen, her mother, to be tested by you, as you have read in the report I filled out."

Evaria smiled this time. It was not out of fear, but again out of deep love and respect for her father, realizing that he too was playing along with her jest of him being the King of History. Seraphina looked at Malachi and smiled inwardly. *You had to just go along with the game our daughter started. Okay, I am game.*

"I see, Your Majesty. Do you require anything as you wait?" Doctor Klorioa asked, instantly understanding the protective charade.

For a moment, Malachi paused. Beneath his regal performance, his logical mind desperately clung to a single, fragile hope: *We still do not know for certain. She might not have this disease. This is only a test.* But if his worst fears were about to be realized, he needed to understand the exact nature of the enemy.

Then, he spoke boldly. "Your King kindly requests that one of your assistants brief me personally about this entire situation. So that I, the King, will know exactly what I am facing, and may brief my Queen later... my loyal and able physician."

He watched the doctor walk over to a biometric console and place her hand flat against it. A few moments later, another, younger Morlock in medical robes stepped out from the secure ward and greeted Malachi and his family formally.

Having just arrived, she did not know about the new etiquette that had just been playing out. Yet again, Evaria spoke up.

"You are to brief my father, the King of History! With briefings on anything he asks, you must answer."

The young assistant looked at her superior, Doctor Klorioa, in total puzzlement. A quiet, breathless ripple of laughter passed through the group again, a fleeting shield against the dark reality of the ward.

"Just go with it," Doctor Klorioa whispered to her assistant, her voice thick with sympathetic sorrow. She then turned to Seraphina and Evaria, gently gesturing toward the reinforced security doors. "Come, my Queen. Let us take the Princess to the scanning room."

They followed her as the heavy stone doors slid apart with a soft, pneumatic hiss, sealing shut behind them and instantly cutting off the ambient noise of the waiting area. The corridor beyond was silent and seemed vast at first, bathed in a cool, clinical light. They walked in quiet apprehension until the hallway took a sharp right angle, suddenly shifting into a unique, circular design.

The smooth stone walls here thrummed with the low, vibrating hum of heavy power conduits. Doctor Klorioa finally guided them into a specialized chamber. In the center of the room rested a sleek, contoured medical bed. Surrounding it was a dizzying array of advanced medical equipment that looked heavily experimental—a complex web of glowing scanning arrays and modified sensory monitors, pieced together by the finest medical minds desperately trying to understand a disease they did not yet have the genetic tools to cure.

"Well, Your Majesty, how can I assist you?" Doctor Klorioa's assistant asked, offering a polite but visibly nervous smile.

She shifted her weight slightly under his steady gaze. She knew exactly who he was. Every Morlock in the subterranean city knew about Malachi. He was known for making significant historical and archaeological finds regarding Morlock culture, their deep history, and the countless wars and purges the Eloi had inflicted upon their species throughout thousands upon thousands of years. To see him in person was like seeing a renowned icon.

Malachi let out a slow, heavy breath, shaking his head gently at the young assistant. He dropped the theatrical behavior he had displayed for his daughter. Without it, he simply looked profoundly tired and worried.

"You do know she was only jesting, right?" Malachi asked, offering a faint, weary grin to try and put the young Morlock at ease.

"I do," she replied, her voice softening, though the nervous reverence remained. "I am Zeangol, the head medical assistant to Doctor Klorioa."

Malachi nodded, the brief, tired smile fading from his lips as his sharp, logical mind returned to the terrifying problem at hand.

"Zeangol, I need you to show me exactly what we are facing. I do not want theories. I need the factual reality of this disease. And please, tell me... Doctor Klorioa is one of our best neurologists, is she not?"

"She is," Zeangol assured him without hesitation. "She graduated with top honors in her field."

Zeangol's eyes widened slightly, filling with deep concern and genuine empathy. She did not need to imagine the terror he was feeling. She had watched her own family members develop this exact affliction, and she intimately knew the devastating outcomes of Progressive Cortical Regression, or PCR for short.

She took a slow, steadying breath, nodding in understanding. "Follow me," she said quietly.

"I need you to understand that this disease seems to be a mutation stemming from something that happened in our deep past, thousands of years ago," Zeangol explained softly as they walked down a separate corridor, moving further away from the secure area where his wife and daughter remained. "Our top scientists believe something happened to all Morlocks who carry a certain gene. We believe it is a genetic disorder of some sort."

Malachi's logical mind seized the data instantly. "So, if you can identify the gene and what is causing it to mutate, it can be treated or repaired?" he asked, his voice tightening with a focused, eager hope.

Zeangol did not answer immediately. They came to a halt in front of a heavy security door. The metal was forged from a shiny, pitch-black steel, emblazoned with a stark, glowing restricted access warning. She placed her hand flat against the security pad.

"Right now, the goals are for treatment, and to isolate the exact problems causing the mutation," Zeangol reassured him, her voice carefully measured as the heavy black door slowly slid open before them.

Malachi peered inside. Immediately, the distant, unsettling sounds of banging and muffled screams echoed down the long corridor. The walls flanking them were lined with heavy, rounded metal doors, each fitted with observation windows forged from extremely thick, reinforced glass.

"This is a security facility? What is this?" Malachi asked, looking around in deep puzzlement.

Past the heavy entrance, the corridor stretched out, lined with individual rooms. Directly outside each room, stationed in the hallway itself, was a dedicated medical console. At every workstation sat a young assistant, their eyes fixed on the screens that monitored the diagnostic vitals of the patients inside. Glancing through the thick observation windows, Malachi noted that the rooms held either one, two, or three Morlocks.

"This is a secure area where we monitor the progression of the disease," Zeangol explained softly. "In this section—we call it the Green Area—the 'Glitch' has become a noticeable, daily occurrence that happens every few hours. The 'Glitch' is considered one of the first early signs of impairment. It starts with either a slurring of words or a gaunt, vacant gaze that can last for ten seconds or longer. Almost as if the patient becomes frozen."

She paused, her eyes briefly dropping to the floor. "It can also manifest as involuntary drooling, or a feral, growl-like noise. We are currently investigating an experimental medicine that so far seems to work, but only for the very first stage of this disease."

"Stages?" Malachi repeated, a heavy grimness settling into his voice as his logical mind struggled to grasp what this disease was actually doing to his species.

"Malachi, I saw my own father go through this. Trust me, learning the stages of this disease is not going to bring good news. It is cruel, and it leads to the outcome no one wants to hear," she said softly.

Malachi shook his head, the cold, logical realization settling heavily over him. *If Evaria truly has PCR, it is a death sentence.* He forcefully buried that agonizing thought behind a wall of factual necessity. *I must be strong.*

"Tell me more."

They walked further down the corridor. The ambient lighting shifted abruptly; the clinical green light gave way to a stark, warning amber-orange glow. At the medical consoles stationed directly outside these rooms, Malachi noticed that the assistants were slightly older, their postures more rigid and alert.

Zeangol stopped, and the two of them looked through another thick observation window.

"Malachi, it is important for you to understand that they cannot see us through these windows," Zeangol explained gently. "To them, looking in this direction simply looks like starlight. Think of it as looking at a beautiful, glowing painting. This area is considered Stage Two."

She turned to face him, ensuring he understood the grim mechanics of the mutation. "The three stages are a tragic, chained progression. As you saw in the Green Area, Stage One traps the mind in those frozen, catatonic glitches—a locked-in state where the patient has absolutely no awareness of the missing time. But when they cross into Stage Two, the higher cognitive functions shatter. Logic fractures. It is a terrifying bridge where they lose the ability to communicate and begin acting on early primal instinct. If the progression is not stopped here, they fall into Stage Three—the final stage. That is a complete, uncontrollable descent into a feral, ravenous state of madness and cannibalism that our medical science currently deems irreversible."

She gestured to the older staff members in the hall. "The medical assistants at the consoles here are equipped with stunners, to be used only if the automated stun gas in the rooms fails to subdue a patient."

She pointed through the glass at the occupant inside. "Notice how they are now at a point where they no longer realize who or what they are. They are acting entirely on primal instinct. Some of them, like the one you see here, simply talk to themselves in endless, repetitive loops. They cannot understand what they are saying, and they can no longer interact with anyone."

Malachi watched the tragic scene unfold in silence.

"Fascinatingly, their bodies retain muscle memory," Zeangol continued, her voice clinical but laced with deep sorrow. "They still somehow know how to eat. They know the motions of how to use things to cook, or how to shower themselves, but they cannot effectively communicate anymore. Because their primal state makes them unpredictable, they might violently throw themselves against the walls or accidentally cut themselves in their confusion. That is why we do not give them utensils or any sharp objects to use."

She paused her briefing, her voice catching as she suddenly noticed that the Honorable Historian had tears pooling in his eyes.

"How could this happen? Why?" Malachi asked. His voice was calm and cold, yet laced with profound, terrified concern. In the back of his mind, his vast intellect frantically searched the historical archives of his memory. *There must be a record of this origin. A precedent hidden in the deep past.* But he could not quite grasp what he was looking for.

"The disease seems to fundamentally rewrite a patient's DNA and RNA," Zeangol explained, her voice steadying into clinical precision. "Specifically, the genetic anomaly we classify as the 1543 mutation. Our top scientists believe that something synthetic was introduced into our biology thousands of years ago. We simply do not know what the original substance was, or if we possess the ability to cure it."

She paused, taking a breath before delivering the crushing reality of their medical options. "As I mentioned, we have been able to develop an experimental treatment. I must be clear: it is not a cure, and it only works during Stage One. The goal of the drug is to purposefully lock a patient safely within that initial phase, suppressing the mutation just enough to prevent them from fracturing into Stage Two. But there is a cruel trade-off. During a natural 'Glitch,' a patient has absolutely no memory of the fifteen to thirty seconds they lose. On the medication, they remain fully conscious. They hear and see everything around them, helplessly trapped inside a paralyzed body. Because their mind remains awake, a physical nudge from someone else can snap them back to normal, but they will retain the terrifying memory of being frozen. And once the disease inevitably breaks past that first stage and reaches the feral, cannibalistic madness of Stage Three—which I am about to show you—the medicine becomes entirely ineffective."

She lowered her eyes, swallowing hard as she looked away from the window. A horrific, silent memory flashed through her mind. *The primal, unstoppable rage of Stage Three. The way my father violently took Mother's life. If my two older siblings had not been there to physically intervene and pull me to safety, I would have been his next victim.*

She pushed the devastating memory down, forcing herself to look back up at the Honorable Historian.

"You look upset, my friend." Malachi infused his voice with gentle empathy, clearly observing that it was becoming increasingly difficult for the young assistant to suppress her own painful memories.

"My father—" Zeangol choked out the words, and finally, she broke down and wept.

A few of the other medical assistants stationed in the corridor briefly took their eyes off their monitors, glancing down the hall at Malachi and the crying assistant. They did not expect Zeangol to cry, but they understood deeply that this sector was unforgiving. Everyone had to remain razor-sharp in the amber ward. Just as quickly as they had looked over, they rigidly returned to the strict business of monitoring the volatile patients in their rooms.

Malachi immediately stepped forward, wrapping his arms around her in a gentle, reassuring hug as she sobbed.

"My father tried to kill me when he reached Stage Three," she confessed, her voice trembling against his shoulder. "I was washing the dishes. I heard a sudden scream from the dining room. When I ran in, I saw my mother slumped over, and blood was already pooling around the table. I knew instantly that my mother was dead... and then he lunged at me! My two older siblings saw everything, and they had to physically wrestle him to the ground to restrain him. It was a nightmare."

She sobbed harder for a moment, the weight of the memory crushing her.

"I am so sorry," Malachi said quietly, holding her securely.

Zeangol shook against him, then drew in a deep, ragged breath. She physically pushed the grief back down, stepping out of his embrace and meticulously adjusting her robes. She knew that a loss of emotional control compromised her professional standing in this highly dangerous area, and she needed to completely regain her composure before taking him any further.

"I am thankful for your compassion toward me," Zeangol said, her voice finally steadying over the low, sterile hum of the amber ward. She straightened her heavy medical robe and ran a trembling hand over her short, dark red hair. "Even though you are one of the most well-respected Historians of our time, you definitely understand the nature of sorrow and grief."

"You have no idea how often others assume otherwise," Malachi replied softly. "I do not view myself as superior to anyone. I am an ordinary Morlock, exactly like you. But I thank you."

He turned his gaze down the corridor, and the fragile warmth of their shared bond was instantly crushed by the oppressive weight of the hallway ahead.

The architecture itself seemed to brace for violence. The smooth stone walls noticeably thickened, funneling down toward a set of massive, interlocking security doors that looked more like the blast shields of a subterranean military bunker than a medical facility. Beyond that formidable threshold, the ambient lighting shifted one final, terrifying time. The warning amber bled away, swallowed completely by a harsh, suffocating crimson glare that painted the polished stone floors in the color of grey marble.

"And I believe that is the red area ahead," Malachi continued, his voice dropping into a cold, factual register. He carefully noted the rigid, unblinking posture of the heavily armed security guards and the dense concentration of armored medical personnel stationed outside those massive doors. "That is the final stage of what happens with this terrible disease. Is it not?"

"I am sorry to say, yes," Zeangol replied, her voice dropping to a grave whisper. "This is the sector where extreme violence occurs. We used to keep three patients to a room, but now we must restrict it to two. The violence erupts entirely unpredictably. This is the point where a Morlock acts completely primal. They become animalistic, deteriorating to the point of no longer feeding or dressing themselves."

She looked directly at Malachi, the harsh crimson light reflecting in her own eyes. "What you see here, we do not want the general populace to know about. Because you are the Honorable Historian, Doctor Klorioa granted you this restricted access as a profound courtesy. You must not tell anyone what you have learned on this tour. The sheer panic it would cause... and if the Eloi..."

Her voice trailed off, the unspoken threat hanging heavily in the red-lit corridor.

"I know all too well what the Eloi would do if they discovered this vulnerability," Malachi said, his voice turning as cold and hard as the stone walls around them. "This could trigger yet another purge, or a full-scale war. They do not tolerate any perceived deviations in our society, nor do they care about our struggles. We manufacture their luxury goods, we maintain their world, and they treat us as nothing more than bond-servants. It is absolute cruelty."

He paused, forcing his sharp mind to calm the sudden surge of disgust and deep-seated distrust he harbored toward the surface dwellers. His logic, heavily shaped by the hundreds of thousands of years of historical oppression he had unearthed, automatically assumed the worst of them. *If they discovered this weakness, they would use it to orchestrate our final extinction.*

"If our species is to survive into the future, we must eventually reintegrate above ground," Malachi continued, his tone shifting from anger back to the visionary hope that drove his life's work. "We must find mutual understanding and peace with them. But it is so incredibly hard to get that message across."

Zeangol raised her brow in solemn understanding.

"I must also warn you," she said, her voice dropping as they approached the final set of observation windows. "It is entirely possible you might see violence occur. If that happens, we will have to leave just as fast as we came. Because of the ravenous, cannibalistic nature of this final stage, the medical staff and guards here have the authorization to terminate the patients if they begin to attack one another, or attack themselves."

She pointed high above the containment cells. The stone walls of the rooms were polished completely smooth, offering no handholds or leverage. Instead of traditional vents or grates, the high, vaulted ceiling was lined with a seamless panel of pitch-black steel, perforated with thousands of micro-holes.

"Those micro-perforations are designed for our final euthanasia protocol," she explained softly, the clinical detachment failing to mask the sorrow in her voice. "When a patient's violence becomes an absolute threat, a fast-acting, lethal gas is released directly into the chamber. It is the only civilized course of action left to ensure their end is not brutally inflicted upon themselves or others."

She sighed heavily as they stepped up to the thick glass. Malachi braced himself, looking through into the stark, red-lit chamber to see how the terminal patients lived.

The Morlocks inside were no longer clothed. Thick, coarse fur had grown over their bodies, and they were crouched low to the floor, moving as if they were entirely primitive. No longer able to stand upright, they looked completely feral. Some of them paced the perimeter, emitting low, guttural growls. Others were heavily drooling, their jaws slack, while a few simply sat in the corners, staring blankly into the empty space as the Honorable Historian observed the utter devastation of his species.

Malachi placed his hand over his mouth in deep, visceral horror. The cold logic of his mind fractured against the terrifying, factual reality of what his species could become. He desperately clung to a single, fragile hope. *If Evaria truly has this affliction, please let her only be in Stage One. Let the medicine be enough to trap the progression.*

"I am ready to leave this entire area and get back to my wife and daughter," Malachi said, his voice trembling despite his best efforts to control it. He turned away from the thick glass; his gaze fixed on the exit. "Still, tell me more about the medicine. Do you have more knowledge about it?"

They immediately walked away from the nightmare of the Red Area. As they moved toward the massive blast doors, a sudden, guttural scream echoed from within one of the secure cells behind them. The sound was muffled by the thick stone and heavy steel, but it sent a violent chill down the corridor, only adding to Malachi's profound distress.

"The medicine has shown promising results in locking patients within Stage One," Zeangol assured him as they crossed the threshold, leaving the suffocating crimson glare behind and stepping back into the amber-lit sector. "Currently, we have nearly four hundred patients in the active trial. The most vital success rate we are seeing is actually within the twelve-to-fifteen age group. For young adults in that specific demographic, it has completely prevented the onset of Stages Two and Three so far. If your daughter does have this, she falls exactly into our most successful bracket and will be given access to it immediately. Doctor Klorioa will brief you more thoroughly on the specifics. She was actually one of the lead neurologists who helped develop it."

Malachi nodded silently, absorbing the data as he forced his legs to keep moving. They continued their long walk backward through the facility. Behind them, the heavy security doors slid shut, sealing away the horrors of the lower wards with heavy, pneumatic hisses. The warning amber light eventually yielded back to the clinical green glow of the early-stage ward.

Finally, they passed through the last pitch-black steel door and stepped out into the neutral, quiet lighting of the primary medical sector. The oppressive, physical weight of the containment area lifted, only to be instantly replaced by a sharp, agonizing spike of parental anxiety.

Zeangol led him back down the vast corridor, rounding the sharp right angle toward the circular scanning room. As they approached, the heavy doors slid open smoothly.

Malachi looked inside. The experimental machinery had powered down; its complex web of arrays now completely dim. Evaria was sitting quietly on the edge of the sleek, contoured medical bed, looking small but unharmed. Seraphina sat close beside her, her arm wrapped protectively around their daughter. Standing near the primary diagnostic console was Doctor Klorioa, holding an illuminated data pad in her hand. She looked up as Malachi entered, her expression unreadable, waiting to deliver the factual reality of their future.

Zeangol, having returned him safely to the scanning room, offered a deep, respectful bow that made Evaria smile brightly before stepping back into the hall. The heavy doors slid shut, sealing the family inside.

"My King, I have the results." Doctor Klorioa looked down at her data pad.

The doctor's eyes met Malachi's. "I have also tested your Queen. She is negative. But your daughter is positive. It is Stage One, Your Highness. Very early Stage One."

Malachi frowned deeply, and Seraphina's breath hitched in her throat as a matching look of devastation crossed her face. Evaria simply looked puzzled, glancing between the two adults.

Malachi fought with all his formidable intellect to suppress the absolute horror threatening to consume him. *I must stay in control. I have to make her believe I can manage this.*

"Your assistant did well to inform me that there is a highly promising new treatment for what Evaria has," Malachi said. His voice was a masterclass in controlled, regal calm, completely masking the tragic panic screaming in his thoughts. "She will be fine."

"I can assure you that we have a medicine that can help Princess Evaria," Doctor Klorioa said, picking up on his desperate cue to keep the tone manageable for the young Morlock. "It is called Regrestat. As Zeangol likely mentioned, we currently have nearly four hundred patients in the active trial. We have been monitoring those in her specific demographic—the twelve-to-fifteen age group—very closely. So far, they have remained stable, and none of them have shown any progression to the feral break of Stage Two."

The doctor stepped closer, speaking with measured, factual precision. "In the short term, the side effects are manageable, though they can be frightening. She will experience periods of deep tiredness, and she will still experience the 'Glitch.' However, with Regrestat, she will not lose consciousness during those freezes. She will remain awake and aware, trapped momentarily in her own body. Because her mind remains active, a simple physical touch or the sound of your voice will snap her out of it. She will remember the episode, but the medicine prevents the immediate threat of her progressing into the primal stages."

Doctor Klorioa paused, her expression tightening slightly as she looked from Malachi to Seraphina. "However, I must be entirely transparent with you both about a severe, long-term risk. Because this drug acts as such a heavy anchor against Stage Two, a possible side effect over time is complete catatonic syndrome. It could eventually lock her permanently inside a Stage One freeze."

Doctor Klorioa paused, delivering the necessary medical disclaimer with a heavy, sympathetic weight. "Still, this is an experimental treatment. I cannot personally guarantee that she will remain completely stable forever, or that she will never progress to the other stages, Your Highness. If you ever notice her exhibiting Stage Two symptoms, or if you find that you cannot pull her out of a Glitch, you must bring her here immediately."

Seraphina's breath hitched, her hands trembling as she pulled them to her chest. "A Glitch? You speak of it as a temporary lapse, Doctor, but I have seen the others. I will not have my daughter existing as a breathing corpse—a vegetable, staring at walls she cannot see. I cannot consent to a medicine that might simply... lock her away inside herself forever."

I would rather her be gone than trapped in that hollow silence, Seraphina thought, the jagged edge of the idea tearing at her soul.

Klorioa stepped closer, her voice dropping to a calm, factual anchor.

"I understand the terror of the vegetative state, Seraphina, but the molecular structure of this treatment is designed specifically to prevent that 'locking.' This medicine is a key, not a cage. It is formulated to stimulate the neuro-pathways during a lapse, giving her the chemical leverage to snap back to us. While I cannot guarantee the long-term shielding of her mind, I can tell you that without this, the descent into Stage Two is a certainty. With it, we give her a fighting chance to remain whole."

Seraphina looked down at her daughter, the radiant light of Evaria's thirteen-year-old spirit feeling so fragile. She closed her eyes, the weight of the crown feeling heavier than ever.

"Then we proceed," she whispered, her voice thick with a mother's desperate hope. "If it is a key, then let us pray it never turns the wrong way."

Evaria nodded slowly, trying to act brave. She did not have the full, horrifying context of what those later stages truly meant, but her sharp intellect processed the gravity in the room. Seraphina squeezed her husband's hand with a tight grip, tears welling in her eyes, but she nodded in agreement.

Doctor Klorioa knelt slightly, bringing herself to eye level with the young Morlock. "Princess Evaria, while your father was on his tour of the facility, you told me a story about the lockdown alarms at your school. About the male student down the hall in Teacher Dephera's room who became very sick and acted wildly."

Evaria's eyes widened slightly at the memory of the terrifying incident, and she nodded solemnly. Seraphina, who had heard the harrowing story directly from Evaria when it happened, placed a comforting hand on her daughter's shoulder.

"I want you to know that the student did not have this special medicine," the doctor explained gently.

Over his daughter's head, Malachi locked eyes with the doctor. His analytical mind instantly translated the clinical subtext. *That student reached Stage Two right in the middle of a public classroom, completely unmedicated.*

"Because he did not have Regrestat, his illness made him act that way," Doctor Klorioa continued, her focus remaining warmly on Evaria. "But your friends at school do not understand how this works. If you tell your classmates that you have the same illness, or that you are taking this medicine, they might become very frightened. They might treat you differently."

The doctor offered a reassuring smile. "We do not want that to happen. So, because this medicine is experimental, it must remain a strict royal secret. This stays only between the King, the Queen, and your royal physician. Do you understand?"

"I understand," Evaria said softly, sitting up a little straighter to shoulder the responsibility.

"Very well," Malachi said, his voice thick with a mixture of immense pride for his brave daughter and sheer terror for her future. "We will begin this treatment immediately."

Evaria offered a small, brave smile. Seraphina and Malachi immediately returned it, projecting a flawless, united front of love and absolute certainty for their daughter, even as their entire world shattered around them.

"Seraphina, take Evaria and wait for me out in the main lobby," Malachi said, his voice carrying the gentle but firm authority of a father. "The King must briefly discuss a few more administrative details with Doctor Klorioa before we depart."

Seraphina caught his eye. She saw the microscopic tightening of his jaw and understood instantly. "Of course. Come along, Evaria. Let us go wait for your father."

Evaria slid off the medical bed, taking her mother's hand. As the heavy doors slid open and closed behind them with a soft pneumatic hiss, the air in the room seemed to physically shift.

The moment the door sealed, Malachi dropped the regal posture completely. The King vanished, leaving only a deeply terrified father and a highly analytical Historian.

"The student down the hall in Teacher Dephera's classroom," Malachi said, his voice low and urgent, devoid of any royal pretense.

"You and I both know the progression of Stage Two and Stage Three is inherently linked to age. The older a Morlock gets, the higher the genetic probability of the 1543 mutation accelerating. That classmate is, at most, one or two chronological years older than my daughter. How did he jump to Stage Two so rapidly?"

Doctor Klorioa did not immediately answer. Instead, she stepped closer, her professional gaze sharpening as she assessed him.

"Before I answer that, Malachi, I need to examine you for a moment."

He blinked, his brow furrowing. "Examine me? Doctor, my daughter is the one—"

"While you were with my assistant seeing the devastating reality of my life's work, I realized we are missing a critical data point," she interrupted gently but firmly. "I have tested Seraphina, and she is negative. But to fully understand Evaria's genetic inheritance, I must test your baseline for the 1543 genetic disposition. It takes less than two minutes to verify."

Before he could protest further, she retrieved a sleek medical cylinder from the console and pressed it firmly against his arm. A sharp, brief pinch signaled the extraction of a micro-sample of his blood.

Malachi's jaw clenched. A flash of profound irritation spiked in his chest—he wanted answers now—but his rigorous, analytical mind instantly grasped the necessity of her thoroughness. *She is isolating the genetic variables. She is doing her job.* He forced himself to exhale, nodding rigidly in understanding as he watched the cylinder process his genetic sequence.

The agonizing two minutes stretched in heavy silence. Finally, the cylinder chimed softly, and Doctor Klorioa reviewed the data readout.

"Your 1543 sequence is perfectly fine and stable. You do not carry the active mutation," she confirmed, though her clinical gaze remained fixed on him. "However, your biometric markers indicate you are under a massive, dangerous amount of stress. You must take care of yourself, Malachi, if you are to be strong for her."

Malachi simply nodded, dismissing his own well-being entirely. "The student, Doctor. Explain it."

Doctor Klorioa sighed, the heavy weight of her profession settling over her. She turned to the primary console and tapped a sequence on the glass. A highly detailed, illuminated three-dimensional holographic scan of a Morlock brain materialized between them.

"You are correct, Malachi. The mutation feeds on the aging process of the brain," the doctor explained, pointing to the highlighted neural pathways. "But we must separate chronological age from biological age. What you are looking at here is a phenomenon we call accelerated cortical senescence."

She expanded the hologram, highlighting specific, darker areas of the cortex. "While that young Morlock was only slightly older than Evaria in years, his brain was biologically much older. Some brains simply age faster than others due to genetic micro-factors or environmental stress. His neural density and synaptic decay resembled that of a Morlock at least five years his senior. His brain crossed the biological threshold for Stage Two before his body did."

Malachi stared at the scan, his formidable mind rapidly processing the terrifying mathematics of the diagnosis. "So, you are telling me that the mutation does not care how long my daughter has been alive. It only cares how old her brain thinks it is."

"Exactly," Doctor Klorioa said softly. "Which is why Regrestat is so vital. It is designed to artificially stabilize the neural pathways, preventing the brain from biologically aging into the danger zones. As long as we keep her biological brain age suppressed, we can keep the mutation trapped in Stage One."

Malachi absorbed the data. The cold logic of the science provided a roadmap, but his mind instantly caught the terrifying paradox of the doctor's explanation. *Wait. If the drug freezes biological aging... what happens to her intellect?*

"Doctor Klorioa," Malachi said, his voice tightening with a new wave of dread. "Are you telling me my daughter's cognitive development will be stunted? Evaria is exceptional. She reads constantly. If she continues to learn and study as she does, her neural pathways must physically expand to retain that knowledge. If Regrestat suppresses her brain's biological aging, will it also freeze her mind exactly where it is today? Will she never grow up intellectually?"

Doctor Klorioa shook her head, instantly understanding the terrifying paradox Malachi had just deduced.

"No, Malachi. You do not need to fear that," she said gently, but with firm, scientific certainty. "We must separate cellular decay from synaptic plasticity. Regrestat halts the physical degradation—the cellular senescence—that the 1543 mutation feeds upon. It stops the physical wear and tear on the organ itself. It does not, however, stop her brain from forming new neural connections or retaining new information."

The doctor turned off the holographic display, letting the low, sterile ambient light of the room return to normal. "She will still grow intellectually. She will still mature emotionally. She can still become the extraordinary Morlock you and Seraphina are raising. The medicine protects the structure of her brain so her mind can continue to expand."

Malachi let out a slow, trembling breath he did not realize he had been holding. The relief was a physical weight lifting off his chest. *Her mind is safe.* "However," Doctor Klorioa added, maintaining her clinical honesty, "you must remember that intense cognitive strain—such as processing massive amounts of historical data or complex emotions—is exactly what triggers her Glitches. Her intellect will continue to grow, but occasionally, the physical neural pathways will temporarily overload. That is when she will freeze. And that is when she will need you to pull her back."

Malachi nodded, the factual parameters of their new reality firmly locked into his mind. The disease was a shadow they would have to live with forever, but his daughter was still his Evaria. Her sharp intellect was safe.

"Thank you, Doctor," Malachi said softly. He paused, his vast mind already calculating the impossible odds ahead of them. "I will make it a personal goal of mine to find the medical Aeterna stones that could help you. If this could be cured..."

His voice trailed off into the quiet hum of the clinic. The sheer magnitude of what he was proposing struck him. He was effectively declaring an open war on their own biology, committing himself to searching for a literal needle in a massive, subterranean silkworm lair.

He grounded himself, offering her a nod of profound respect. "Thank you. For everything."

Doctor Klorioa stepped closer, her clinical detachment replaced entirely by a fierce, determined empathy. "I will do my absolute best to find a way to cure this, Malachi. The mutation is incredibly complex, but I truly believe it can be cured."

He adjusted his posture, the regal mantle of the King settling back over his shoulders as he prepared to face his family. He turned and walked toward the smooth marble door. As it slid apart, he stepped out into the low, warm ambient light of the main medical lobby.

Seraphina and Evaria were sitting quietly on a bench near the exit. Evaria looked up, her amber, intelligent eyes locking onto his, completely unaware of the devastating biological war her father had just agreed to wage on her behalf.

Malachi offered them a calm, confident smile, projecting the absolute certainty of a King, while carrying the heavy, silent burden of a father. Together, the three of them walked out of the medical sector, stepping back into a world that would never be the same.

Chapter II — Seraphina's Tragedy

The next morning, Seraphina arrived at the educational complex well before her own teaching shift began. She immediately sought out Casia. Not only was Casia Evaria's instructor, but she was also Seraphina's fellow colleague and her closest friend since their university days. Seraphina and Malachi had concluded the night before that Casia, at the very least, needed to know about the PCR diagnosis. The intention was strictly protective: if Evaria experienced any cognitive glitches during the school day, Casia could intervene and mask the symptoms from the other students. Even with the Enclave doctor's strict mandate of secrecy, the factual reality was that a public incident could not be entirely prevented without an ally inside the classroom.

Seraphina found her in the secluded faculty lounge. It was still early morning, and the two of them were the only ones in the room. Casia was huddled over a smooth stone table in the dim, warm ambient lighting, aggressively tapping at a stack of illuminated data pads.

Casia looked up, her emerald eyes flashing with mild exhaustion. "If you are here to tell me the commissary is already out of those newly enhanced peachberries before first meal, I am officially going on strike," she muttered dryly. "I practically need them to survive grading these data pads."

Seraphina forced a weak, fractured smile, the terrifying weight of her secret instantly crushing the brief moment of colleague humor. "I wish it were only that, Casia. It is Evaria."

Casia's sarcastic demeanor vanished instantly. She set the data pad down, her sharp gaze scanning Seraphina's pale, exhausted face.

"Evaria? What is wrong with her?" Casia asked, her voice tightening with sudden dread.

As Seraphina quietly explained the diagnosis, Casia's horror grew.

"Are you telling me she has the same disease that has consumed the media for the past few months? That she could become violent?" Casia asked. Her voice was an urgent, hushed whisper, instinctively keeping the volume low just in case another instructor walked through the heavy doors.

"You remember that student in Dephera's class—the young Morlock who jumped on the tables and started growling until he had to be physically restrained? Now you are asking me to harbor this secret? This is a massive risk to take on, Seraphina. For both of our careers."

In the warm shadows of the lounge, Casia's eyes held the exact same piercing intensity as any other Morlock, but rather than the typical bright amber, hers radiated a sharp emerald that matched the subtle green highlights woven into her light blonde bun.

"You were always the one at university who reminded me to gather the facts first," Seraphina countered gently, keeping her tone measured to prevent panic. "Malachi and I did exactly that. You need to understand the mechanics of this disease. It is not an immediate descent into what happened in Dephera's class. There are progressive stages, and Evaria is only in Stage One. We have her on an experimental medication to halt the regression."

Seraphina stepped closer, appealing directly to her friend's logic and empathy. "I know that look in your eyes, Casia. You are calculating the risk and searching for a reason to say no. But I am asking you to look at the facts and hear me out. Please."

The low, quiet hum of the subterranean ventilation system filled the tense silence between them. Casia closed her eyes for a brief second, shaking her head. She had always felt that Seraphina was like a sister to her. The logical part of her brain was screaming to walk away, but she had no desire to abandon her best friend.

Casia let out a long, defeated exhale, offering a faint, strained smirk. "You know this is absolute madness, right? If the educational superiors find out, they will strip my teaching credentials right alongside yours." She paused, her expression softening with genuine affection. "But... it is Evaria. If I ever enter into a formed Rite of Union and start a family of my own, I would want a daughter exactly like her. She is just like us, only much smarter. So, against all my better judgment, I will hear you out."

The heavy silence of the subterranean lounge settled back over them, broken only by the distant, rhythmic cycling of the lower air shafts. Having made her deeply emotional concession, Casia physically shifted gears. She pushed her stack of data pads aside and leaned forward, resting her arms on the smooth stone table. When she looked back up at Seraphina, the protective, analytical sharpness of an educator had fully returned to her gaze.

"However, what you are asking is incredibly risky if this ever gets out," Casia continued, her voice dropping into a focused, clinical register. "Tell me the facts, please—what are the exact stages? And why the extreme secrecy if there is an experimental treatment?"

Seraphina kept her voice steady, leaning into the scientific reality of the diagnosis. "Stage One is strictly cognitive, Casia. It manifests as temporary neural overloads. The doctor warned us she will still experience 'glitches'—moments where she might freeze in place for ten to thirty seconds. But because she is on the experimental medication, she will not lose consciousness. She will be entirely awake, trapped inside her own paralyzed body, and unable to speak. That is where Evaria is right now, and the Regrestat is designed to lock her safely in this stage. If she freezes in your classroom, all you have to do is physically touch her shoulder or call her name, and it will instantly snap her out of it before the other students notice. But if the medicine fails, Stage Two brings the physical and neurological breakdown. The loss of language. The hyper-aggression and the feral state. That is what actually happened to the student in Dephera's class. He was in Stage Two. I know you did not witness the attack yourself because you were focused on keeping Evaria and your own students safe, but that is exactly why you saw the security guards dragging him away down the hall."

Seraphina paused, letting the clinical cruelty of the disease hang in the air.

"The medical Enclave professionals are demanding absolute secrecy. If the general public learns that the daughter of the Honorable Historian can contract PCR, our social order will fracture. And if the Eloi find out... you know their arrogance and their loathing for us. They would use this as an excuse to start a purge."

Casia absorbed the facts, the sharp emerald of her eyes dimming slightly with the weight of the tragedy. She looked at Seraphina not just as a colleague, but as a sister.

"It is devastating," Casia whispered, the reality of Evaria's diagnosis finally settling in. "I will help you, Seraphina. I will watch her closely and mask any glitches that occur in my classroom."

Casia reached out, resting a hand on her friend's arm, her tone shifting to a stark, factual warning. "But you must understand the immediate gravity of this. If the educational superiors discover we are bypassing the monitoring mandates, our careers will end immediately. They will terminate us to keep their own records clean. Because if a public incident happens, and the surface-dwellers hear even a whisper that we Morlocks are turning feral..."

"You do not think I realize the risk?" Seraphina's voice spiked with sudden, desperate emotion, echoing slightly in the empty lounge. She instantly caught herself, casting a fearful glance toward the heavy doors, and forced her volume back down to a harsh whisper. "Malachi's position would be heavily scrutinized, and you could be stripped of your credentials, too. But the other educators are getting ready to arrive soon. Look at the clock, Casia. Malachi is dropping Evaria off before first meal. The danger is already upon us."

"And what is the final stage?" Casia asked, trying to anchor the conversation back to the medical facts.

Seraphina grimaced at her. Sometimes Casia played ignorant just to force the factual reality of the grim news reports out into the open.

"Come on. You act like you do not know," Seraphina scolded her gently.

"Complete, ravenous madness that leads to death," Casia whispered, acknowledging the terminal reality of Stage Three. The silence of the empty educators' lounge seemed to press in around them, broken only by the distant, rhythmic thrum of the geothermal vents deep below. Fear bled into her voice as the factual reality settled over her: Seraphina was absolutely right to take these drastic risks.

"Exactly." Seraphina nodded, her posture rigid.

Casia leaned forward, her sharp eyes searching Seraphina's face for a lifeline. "This medicine is experimental, you said? This indicates that the doctors are indeed working on a solution to cure the disease. So, there is hope?"

"The doctors desperately want to cure this. But if the true scope of this disease gets out, you know exactly what the Eloi will do." Seraphina's eyes narrowed into sharp, unyielding slits in the dim light. It was a precise, dangerous look—the kind of narrowing that told Casia instantly to stop playing naive. The political reality was just as lethal as the biological one.

The psychological weight of the surface world seemed to bear down on the stone ceiling above them.

"They will view the afflicted as a contagious threat to their luxury," Casia breathed, the realization fully extinguishing her earlier optimism.

"They would initiate a massive purge just to protect themselves. The doctors are right to demand strict secrecy. This is a matter of survival."

With the terrifying parameters of their pact firmly established, the two educators settled back into their heavy stone chairs. Resting their data pads on the polished, black obsidian surface of the table, they drank cold fruit nectar in the quiet of the lounge, pulling up their educational files to review exactly what they needed to teach their students for the day.

"Evaria is going to be okay," Casia promised softly, breaking the heavy silence. "I will do my absolute best to protect her. She is one of my brightest students. Polite, respectful, and she always makes the others laugh."

Casia chuckled softly, the memory bringing a warm, genuine light back to her emerald eyes. "Just a few days ago, she had the whole class laughing about silkworms. She told them that to get a specific shade of purple, the silkworms have to hold their breath until they turn the right color, and if you startle them, you end up with pink. I even laughed myself."

Seraphina let out a genuine, ringing laugh that finally broke the lingering tension in the room. She wiped a slight tear of mirth from her eye and nodded. "Yep. That is my daughter."

Casia smiled, tracing the rim of her nectar glass against the cold obsidian table. Her eyes suddenly widened slightly as the pieces clicked together. "Purple... Wait, is that what she was working on? Did she finally finish the sash for Malachi?"

Seraphina nodded, a proud, wistful smile touching her lips. "She gave it to him just over twenty-four hours ago."

"So that is what she was working on," Casia said, a fond realization dawning on her face. "It makes me think of the day I prepared for my own Rite of Adulthood. I spent weeks weaving a green sash for my father to show him I was ready to take my place in our society."

Seraphina looked pleasantly surprised, the heavy dread in her chest lifting for just a moment as she learned this new piece of her friend's past. "I never knew that about you, Casia. Green is a beautiful choice for the Rite." She leaned back, the warmth of their shared cultural traditions settling comfortably between them as a quiet anchor against Evaria's new PCR illness. "Mine was orange."

A few minutes passed in comfortable silence as they returned to their lesson plans. The large mechanical clock on the stone wall ticked steadily as more educators finally began to filter into the lounge, bringing with them the quiet hum of morning routines—eating breakfast and pouring glasses of fresh fruit nectar.

One of the arriving teachers activated the wall-mounted telescreen, tuning it to the morning broadcast. The anchor's voice filled the room, first detailing a recent triumph by the Honorable Historian, Malachi. He had just overseen the discovery of five Aeterna stones at a construction site slated to become a new factory reclamation center. The broadcast specifically noted that while one of the recovered stones bore a deep fracture along its casing, it remained fully functional—a testament to the enduring architecture of their deep past.

Then, the broadcast's tone shifted heavily to a report on PCR.

Seraphina and Casia looked up sharply as the screen displayed the face of Doctor Klorioa, the exact Enclave neurologist Seraphina had consulted the morning before. The broadcast confirmed everything Seraphina had just explained in private: the disease was being actively targeted, and the public was now being informed that the experimental medication, Regrestat, was being utilized with the hope of halting the regression, provided it was caught in Stage One.

The Enclave was clearly trying to manage the narrative and prevent a panic. A profound wave of relief washed over Seraphina. Casia caught her eye across the obsidian table and offered a subtle, reassuring nod. She now had public proof of the facts, and her promise to protect Evaria's secret remained ironclad.

"So, there is an experimental treatment now?" Dephera asked, stepping closer to the screen.

As she spoke, her hand instinctively drifted up to brush against her cheek, tracing the jagged, pale scar that permanently disfigured her otherwise smooth features. It was the physical aftermath of the student who had gone feral in her classroom months ago. Her voice was hollow, stripped of its usual morning energy, carrying a heavy mix of lingering bitterness and a weary, profound relief that the medical community was finally acknowledging the nightmare.

"I wish it had come sooner," she muttered to herself, the traumatic memory of the violent incident clearly flashing in her haunted gaze.

A few more minutes passed in the lounge until a gentle, melodic chime resonated through the stone corridors, announcing the start of the first hour. The educators filed out of the room, their quiet murmurs blending into the steady rhythm of the school day beginning.

As Seraphina walked toward her designated teaching sector, she passed along the grand gallery walls, which were softly bathed in a warm, ambient illumination, highlighting the ancient, proud history of the Morlock civilization. Breathtaking murals and holographic displays depicted their ancestors building the first subterranean cities under the peaceful light of the stars and the moon. Emblems of academic pride—interlocking gears, polished Aeterna stones, and celestial maps—decorated the archways, reminding the faculty and students alike of their highly civilized heritage.

Reaching her classroom, Seraphina took a deliberate, steadying breath, leaving the heavy dread of the morning out in the hall. She stepped through the doorway, paused, and let a warm, genuine smile cross her face. She walked to the head of the room, sat down at her polished stone table, and looked over the fifteen young, eager Morlock faces looking back at her. Despite the quiet terror threatening her own family, in this room, she was simply their teacher—caring, fully present, and entirely devoted to their futures.

Seraphina stood up as her students took their seats at their obsidian stone desks and quieted. She then activated the primary holographic display.

"Today, my students, I want to talk to you about Chancellor Bealight," Seraphina began slowly, bringing up a projection on her holographic pad that displayed a female Morlock of striking elegance.

The historical figure wore a flowing robe of deep orange, matching the straight, vibrant orange hair that cascaded down her sides. Her face appeared youthful yet carried the profound wisdom of a leader, and her complexion held the same subterranean, green-grey skin tone that all Morlocks shared. Beneath the rotating projection, the historical date of 689,352 shimmered into view.

"Chancellor Bealight was the first Morlock to reintegrate dialogue between the Eloi and our sector dwellings. It had been over a thousand years since we had communicated with the Eloi. Four hundred and thirty-five years ago, she broke through to the surface in the hopes of reunifying our two great species... that Eloi and Morlocks should be one and united," Seraphina explained to her students.

Malachi would say these exact words, she thought to herself. She, too, desperately wanted to believe that reunification was the only way forward—a path for reaching out from the darkness and learning, all over again, to adapt to the natural light of the Earth and its above-ground grandeur.

"It is important for you all to understand that we, as Morlocks, should strive to rise above the current political divisions you may be hearing about from your families, your neighbors, and the daily broadcasts," Seraphina continued, her voice echoing gently but firmly across the stone classroom.

"Chancellor Bealight was just like you and me. She was a common worker who rose to a position of leadership, and she treated everyone she encountered with absolute dignity and respect. It did not matter what your profession or station was; she was a caring, daring politician who actively fought for peace."

The fifteen students sat in rapt attention, their eyes fixed entirely on her and the rotating, orange-hued hologram at the front of the room, listening carefully to every word of the lesson.

"She was also the one who inspired the subterranean horticulture of Peachberries," Seraphina said, a warm smile breaking through her academic tone. "Even my own daughter loves them."

Stepping away from the rotating hologram, Seraphina retrieved a small, woven satchel from her desk. She walked up and down the stone aisles, pausing to give each of her fifteen students one of the small delights. The Peachberries were vibrant violet spheres, dense and heavy for their small size, with a smooth, glossy skin that caught the dim, warm ambient light of the classroom.

Walking back to her desk, Seraphina sat down and simply watched. A quiet joy filled the room as her students smiled, their eyes widening in delight as they bit into the sweet, delicious fruit—a tangible piece of the peaceful legacy Chancellor Bealight had left behind.

The classroom settled into a comfortable, quiet rhythm as the students enjoyed the sweet violet fruit. Toward the middle of the stone rows sat Omri, a male student with short, black wavy hair neatly parted to the side, and eyes that were typically a vivid, inquisitive orange. He was slightly older than the rest of the cohort, having been held back a year due to what previous instructors had formally documented as severe memory lapses and an inability to focus.

As Seraphina settled behind her desk, she watched Omri's arm slowly extend upward into the air. It was not the fluid, eager motion of a student wanting to participate in the lesson. The movement was rigid and entirely mechanical. His fingers remained slightly curled, and the smooth violet peachberry slipped from his relaxed grip, rolling across his stone desk and dropping to the floor.

"Omri, do you have a question?" Seraphina asked, keeping her voice incredibly steady, though the unnatural angle of his arm sent a cold spike of alarm through her.

Omri did not react. He did not blink. His vivid orange eyes were locked straight ahead in a vacant, deadened stare, and his face suddenly took on a stark, gaunt composure. A cold stab of realization hit Seraphina—his documented "academic struggles" over the past year had not been a learning deficiency. They were the untreated, progressive symptoms of Stage One.

"Omri? Can you hear me?"

A thick line of drool pooled at the corner of his lips and slowly dripped down his chin. The factual reality crystallized in Seraphina's mind instantly: Omri was not just experiencing a cognitive glitch. He was actively crossing the threshold into Stage Two of Progressive Cortical Regression right in front of her.

She shifted her gaze to the rest of the room, masking her rising dread. "Students, I need you to listen to me carefully. Get out of the classroom slowly. Go directly to the guidance sector and bring Vandar here immediately."

The class obeyed without question, rising from their stone desks in a quiet, synchronized panic and filing out into the corridor. Everyone moved except for Omri, and the young female student seated directly in front of him. Maliva was completely paralyzed. She had not turned around, but she could hear the heavy, wet sound of Omri's erratic breathing just inches behind her. Her wide eyes were locked straight ahead on Seraphina, fixed with absolute terror, her small body trembling against the stone desk as she remained trapped in her seat.

"Maliva, come over here, please," Seraphina instructed softly. She never took her eyes off Omri, raising her hand and motioning slowly for the terrified student to step away from the desk and come to the front of the room. The classroom was now entirely empty save for the three of them.

"Teacher," Maliva began to cry softly, the tears spilling down her cheeks. "I—I can't."

Behind her, Omri's erratic breathing suddenly stopped. For those agonizing three to five seconds of absolute silence, Seraphina's mind rapidly calculated two desperate hopes. *Please let Vandar burst through those corridor doors immediately. Let this merely be a prolonged Stage One glitch.* She prayed Omri's cognitive function would somehow reboot, returning him to his senses.

"Come, Maliva. It is okay. I promise," Seraphina urged softly. She forced a warm, reassuring smile to her lips, desperately trying to anchor the terrified young Morlock.

But Maliva just shook her head, entirely paralyzed by primal fear, unable to command her legs to move.

And that was when the silence broke. Omri began to make an unnatural, wet gurgling sound deep in his throat. It started as a mere whisper.

"Maaaa—livaaaa," Omri choked out. His voice was completely disjointed, straining and growling her name in a quiet, unnatural distortion.

Maliva's paralysis left Seraphina with only one logical choice. If the young student could not command her legs to move, Seraphina had to go to her.

Seraphina took a slow, deliberate step out from behind her stone desk. She kept her hands visible and her movements incredibly smooth, inching down the narrow aisle. The wet gurgling deep in Omri's throat grew louder, vibrating with a rapid, unnatural clicking sound.

"I am right here, Maliva," Seraphina whispered, reaching her hand out.

Just as her fingertips brushed the fabric of the terrified student's shoulder, the disease completely severed the final thread of Omri's conscious mind. He launched himself forward with terrifying, feral speed.

Seraphina reacted on pure instinct, shoving Maliva hard out of the way just as Omri collided with her. The explosive violence instantly shattered Maliva's frozen state. The young female Morlock scrambled forward, away from the stone desks, let out a piercing scream, and bolted frantically for the open doorway.

Seraphina took the full kinetic impact of the student's lunge. She instantly brought her knees up, kicking out fiercely to push him away and break his hold. But the sheer, unnatural strength of Stage Two was overwhelming. Omri absorbed her defensive strikes without flinching, thrashing wildly as his hands struck out like claws. His nails raked brutally across the side of Seraphina's face, tearing deep, severe lacerations into her cheek and brow.

Seraphina threw her arms up to protect her neck, but Omri's feral momentum drove them both backward. Seraphina's skull slammed violently against the unyielding stone floor with a sickening crack.

The pain flared white-hot for a fraction of a second, and then the world instantly went black.

Just outside the doorway, Maliva bolted into the corridor and accidentally ran headlong into a massive, unyielding form. It was Vandar, the security administrator. Heavyset and thickly muscled, Vandar possessed an imposing physical presence that commanded immediate respect. His spikey white hair, streaked with sharp patches of black, stood out starkly against the stone walls, and his eyes radiated a fierce, protective orange in the dim light. He was widely known to the students as a profoundly kind guard, but his sheer size and stern posture carried a permanent, unmistakable warning not to test him.

Vandar instinctively caught the trembling student to keep her from falling, pushed her safely down the hall, and stepped into the classroom.

He assessed the threat in a split second. Rushing down the aisle, Vandar wrapped his massive arms around Omri's torso. With sheer, overwhelming physical power, he hauled the feral attacker off Seraphina's unconscious body, pinning the thrashing student firmly against the cold stone floor.

While holding the thrashing student down with one massive arm, Vandar immediately reached to his belt and unclipped a device that resembled a thin metallic rod. It was a high-voltage stun device. He pressed the tip firmly against Omri's shoulder and triggered the charge.

However, fueled by the terrifying adrenaline and sheer neurological override of the Stage Two regression, Omri completely resisted the initial shock. For a split second, a flash of genuine amazement crossed Vandar's imposing face. The student's continued feral growls and wet grunts deeply offended the security administrator's strict sense of order, an ugly and unnatural disruption to the peace he was sworn to protect.

Calculating the factual reality of the student's unnatural strength, Vandar quickly toggled the rod to a much higher output—a setting strictly reserved for subduing fully grown adults. He pressed the rod against Omri once more. This time, the heavy electrical surge took hold. The feral noises abruptly ceased as Omri instantly slumped backward, falling entirely limp and unconscious in Vandar's heavy arms.

Moving with practiced, mechanical efficiency, Vandar gently laid the unconscious student on the floor. He stood up, his fierce orange eyes sweeping the empty classroom, and slammed his heavy hand against the wall-mounted emergency panel.

Within seconds, he broadcast an urgent call for the medical sector and triggered the automated protocols, placing the entire educational center on a full, immediate lockdown.

Vandar immediately pulled a set of restraining cuffs from his belt. Woven from a high-tensile, silk-like cord, he tightened them securely around the unconscious Omri's wrists. He used a second heavy string to bind the student's ankles, ensuring that if he woke, he would be entirely immobilized and unable to escape.

With the threat secured, Vandar turned his fierce orange eyes toward Seraphina. When he saw the horrifying extent of the damage, a sharp, ragged gasp escaped his massive chest, the sheer shock breaking instantly through his hardened exterior.

His massive frame dropped heavily to the stone floor beside her battered body. He assessed her with a trained eye, though his large hands were now visibly trembling. She was breathing, but completely unresponsive. Deep, bloody lacerations marred her green-grey cheek, and he noted with a heavy heart that the feral impact had knocked out a few of her teeth. Her right arm lay at a twisted, unnatural angle, clearly fractured.

The sight of her brutally torn face violently pulled him back to the horrific memory of Dephera's disfigurement months ago. The heavy, crushing burden of his duty crashed down on him all at once.

"No—Not again," Vandar whispered, tears welling in his eyes as he gently supported Seraphina's head to stabilize her neck. *I was too late. Again.*

For five agonizing minutes, the usually stoic security administrator wept quietly over the respected teacher. He was shaken to his absolute core by the profound guilt of failing to protect another innocent colleague, keeping her stabilized until two medics finally stormed through the doorway.

Dephera, having seen the terrified students flee past her own classroom just before the lockdown protocols engaged, appeared briefly in the doorway. She stared in absolute horror at Vandar kneeling over Seraphina's broken body.

Then, she shifted her gaze to Omri. The effects of the high-voltage stun were beginning to wear off. The student groaned, his heavy eyelids fluttering open. For a fraction of a second, the cognitive shear paused. He looked around the room, his voice cracking in raw, conscious confusion as he screamed, "WHAT HAPPENED!"

But the clarity violently snapped. His body twitched, his vivid orange eyes deadened once more, and he instantly reverted to feral growling, thick foam gathering at the corners of his mouth. He thrashed against the silk bindings, entirely consumed by the disease, as if his mind were caught in a horrifying loop between two completely separate realities.

Two additional security guards, responding to Vandar's lockdown alert, rushed into the room. Acknowledging the factual reality of the student's unnatural strength, they bypassed standard juvenile protocols, locking heavy adult restraints over Vandar's silk bindings. Together, they hoisted Omri's thrashing, growling form and carried him swiftly out of the classroom and down the corridor.

With the threat removed, the medics immediately dropped to the stone floor beside Vandar. Their hands moved frantically, working to stabilize Seraphina's violently fractured arm and stem the heavy bleeding from the deep lacerations across her face before they could safely move her.

Unable to watch any longer, Dephera stepped back from the doorway and retreated to her own classroom. She keyed her instructor's override into the wall panel, allowing the heavy lockdown doors to slide open just long enough for her to step through before sealing her and her pupils safely inside.

She stood at the front of the room and looked out over her students. They were huddled tightly at their obsidian desks, staring back at her with wide, terrified eyes. The heavy silence of the lockdown was broken only by the sound of their quiet, muffled sobbing.

Hot, unbidden tears welled in Dephera's eyes, blurring her vision of their frightened faces. Her trembling hand moved instinctively to her cheek, her fingertips tracing the jagged, uneven ridge of the scar—the permanent memory of the student who had turned wild under the fever of the disease so many months ago. It wasn't the sickness itself that had marked her, but the desperate, frantic attack of a boy who no longer knew his own name.

Her students remained perfectly still. The room was cloaked in absolute, suffocating silence. The students did not ask questions; they simply watched her, the heavy, unspoken reality settling over them all. Even through the thick stone walls, they knew with terrifying certainty that something horrible had just shattered the safety of their school.

Three classrooms down the wide stone corridor, the heavy doors of Casia's room slid shut with a definitive, mechanical thud. A sweeping, low-frequency siren resonated through the stone walls, accompanied by the pulsing amber warning lights of the automated lockdown protocols engaging instantly across the entire complex.

Moving with practiced authority, Casia immediately ushered her class into the designated secure alcove at the back of the room. She stood firmly between her students and the locked doors, projecting a calm, unyielding aura of safety. Her sharp gaze found Evaria, who was huddled quietly among her classmates. Evaria knew the lockdown drill protocols perfectly, but she remained completely unaware of the actual, devastating nightmare unfolding just down the hall.

A small, urgent light pulsed on Casia's stone desk terminal just a few steps away. It was a secure, internal message from Dephera. Dephera was a close friend to both of them, and knowing that Casia and Seraphina were absolute best friends, it was only natural she would bypass standard administrative channels to warn Casia directly. Casia stepped over and tapped the screen, her face remaining a mask of absolute calm. The text was brief and completely devastating: *Omri regressed to Stage Two. Seraphina was attacked. She is unconscious and severely battered. Medics are with her.*

Casia's breath caught in her chest. The factual reality of the words struck her like a physical blow, her mind instantly racing with terrifying calculations regarding her best friend's survival. But as Evaria looked up at her from the secure alcove with innocent, intelligent eyes, Casia forced her own terror deep down into a tightly sealed compartment. She had promised to protect Evaria as if she were her own daughter, and she would not fail.

Moving with quiet, deliberate precision, Casia opened an external communication channel. She typed a high-priority emergency override directly to Malachi's personal device: *Malachi. The school is on full lockdown. Seraphina was attacked by a feral student and is severely injured. Medics are stabilizing her now. Evaria is completely safe in my locked classroom. I am watching her. Come immediately.*

Miles away from the educational sector, deep within the cavernous site of the new factory reclamation center, the air was thick with the hum of excavation equipment. Malachi stood in the center of the site, carefully brushing centuries of compacted dirt away from a newly discovered sixth Aeterna stone.

His personal device emitted a sharp, piercing chime—the distinct, undeniable tone of an emergency override. Malachi set his delicate brush down and retrieved the device from his belt. As his vivid yellow eyes scanned Casia's message, the blood ran completely cold in his veins.

There was no outward display of panic, only the absolute, chilling logic of a father and husband realizing his family was in immediate peril. He placed the ancient stone gently into its protective transport casing, closed the lid, and turned to his excavation crew.

"Cease operations," Malachi commanded, his deep voice carrying heavy authority over the noise of the machinery. "The educational complex has just been placed on full lockdown due to a violent incident. I must leave immediately. Any of you who have young Morlocks in that sector, drop your tools and go get them now. That is a direct order."

Malachi strode out of the excavation site, followed closely by several concerned colleagues rushing to retrieve their own children. He stepped onto the primary subterranean transport walkway, his hand gripping the cold metal rail as the walkway accelerated.

His mind raced with terrifying questions. *What happened? Is my wife alive? This disease has to be stopped.* But he forcefully reined in his rising panic. *I do not have the facts,* he reminded himself, gripping the handrail tighter. *I cannot act on speculation. I must know exactly what happened before I react.*

Pulling out his personal device—a sleek, circular metallic wafer—he raised it to his mouth. Preferring the speed of a voice transmission, he spoke with quiet, tightly controlled precision. "Casia. What happened? Do you have the specific medical facts of her condition? Also, thank you for securing Evaria. I trust my wife informed you of our daughter's diagnosis before this incident occurred? Tell me where I should be routing."

Casia did not use the voice-to-text prompt, acutely aware of the sharp, intelligent Morlock sitting just a few feet away. Instead, she typed her reply immediately:

Seraphina was severely injured in the attack. Medics have stabilized her and are transporting her to the Medical Enclave now. And yes, she told me about Evaria's diagnosis. I understand fully the gravity of her condition, and I know how sharp Evaria is. Because of that, I am not bringing her anywhere near the Medical Enclave or the main transit hubs.

Malachi watched the text scroll across his circular wafer, profoundly grateful for Casia's tactical foresight. A second message immediately followed:

The news crews are already swarming the educational sector's main gates. If she sees them, or hears the murmurs, she will piece it together instantly. We bypassed the main corridors and used a secondary staff exit. I told Evaria the facility drill resulted in an early dismissal, and I am treating her to a visit to the Subterranean Horticulture Gardens to see where the peachberries are grown. Meet us at the Garden Atrium first. It is bad, Malachi, I will not lie. See Evaria so you know she is safe, then go to the Medical Enclave. I will watch over her at the Gardens while you find out what has happened.

Reading the factual update, a heavy physical ache settled in his chest. His immediate instinct was to rush directly to Seraphina's side, but the clear logic of Casia's message anchored his panic. He desperately needed to lay his eyes on his daughter and ensure she was completely oblivious and unharmed before he could face the absolute devastation waiting for him at the medical ward. *I must see Evaria first,* he thought. *I have to know she is safe before I go to Seraphina.*

Malachi tapped the console on the handrail. He bypassed the medical route entirely and transferred seamlessly onto the high-speed line heading deep into the agricultural sector.

As the walkway accelerated, a heavy tide of emotion threatened to override his disciplined focus. He forced himself to compartmentalize the fear, tethering his thoughts instead to the factual reality of his wife's character. Seraphina was not merely his partner; they had been childhood friends long before they became soulmates, growing up together in the subterranean sectors. She was his mirror in every aspect of life. As his mind cycled through decades of shared memories, he grounded himself in her undeniable resilience. Lacking the medical data of her condition, he refused to speculate on the worst. He locked his mind instead to her profound internal strength, desperately needing to believe she would fight through whatever physical trauma she had just sustained.

He knew that if Seraphina were conscious, her absolute first command to him would be to secure Evaria. The physiological stress of the school attack was exactly the kind of intense cognitive strain the doctors had warned them about. He would protect their daughter first, honoring his wife's ultimate priority, and then he would face whatever nightmare waited for him at the Medical Enclave.

At that exact moment, Casia and Evaria stepped into the sprawling Garden Atrium. The air here was cool and fragrant, a sharp contrast to the sterile stone corridors of the transit hubs. The very first thing Evaria noticed was an illuminated holographic display erected in the center of the new botanical Enclave: *Birthplace of the Peachberry*. Evaria beamed in delight. She absolutely loved the sweet, peach-like taste of the violet fruit, and seeing where they were grown felt like a special treat. But despite the pleasant distraction, her highly active mind was already processing the sudden break in their daily routine.

"Where is my mother, Auntie Casia?" Evaria asked, her bright amber eyes looking up with innocent curiosity.

Seeing that pure, happy smile sent a sharp, physical ache through Casia's chest. Having just finalized the tactical rendezvous with Malachi on her personal device, Casia now faced her most difficult task yet. She had to maintain absolute composure and weave a flawless, logical distraction to protect her best friend's daughter from the devastating reality of the blood and violence left behind at the educational complex.

"Your father will be here shortly," Casia said, forcing her voice to remain warm and steady. "He asked me to bring you here first so that you could see the latest advancements in your favorite fruit."

The lie tasted like ash in Casia's mouth, and she absolutely hated it. Her moral compass was strictly governed by compassion and truth, and she deeply despised falsehoods. However, the factual reality remained: telling Evaria her mother was currently bleeding in the Medical Enclave was the worst possible course of action. To protect the young Morlock's fragile cognitive state, Casia squeezed Evaria's small hand gently, projecting a calm assurance that everything was perfectly fine as they stepped further into the atrium.

A female Morlock approached them, her uniform featuring a tailored jacket the exact vibrant violet hue of a peachberry. She introduced herself warmly as Relania.

Relania escorted them to a sleek staging area and handed them what looked like lightweight protective clothing. Evaria recognized the garments immediately; they were the exact type of sterile environmental suits her father often wore when conducting highly sensitive historical digs.

"As your tour guide, I will be happy to answer all your questions about Peachberries, as well as the other fruits we are currently hybrid-engineering," Relania said warmly. Reaching into a small pouch at her waist, she produced what appeared to be the fossilized remains of a real peach pit.

Evaria held the rigid, deeply grooved seed in her small palm with amazement and wonder. "How did you take something with a center this big and make the fruit so small? Yet so tasty?"

"You are a very smart one," Relania noted with an impressed nod. "Over a century ago, our botanical division discovered a sealed, pre-cataclysm seed vault buried deep within the northern bedrock. From those dormant husks, we were able to extract the original RNA and DNA sequences and completely regrow this."

Relania reached into a temperature-controlled display case and pulled out a real, ancient peach—the exact kind that grew naturally on the surface over thousands of years ago. Evaria stared at it. It was massive, roughly the size of her own clenched fist.

"Please, take a bite," Relania encouraged, handing a whole peach to both the young Morlock and Casia.

As Evaria took her first bite, the juice ran down her chin. She giggled and beamed with delight, thoroughly enjoying the complex, sweet-tart flavor as she chewed and swallowed.

Casia took a cautious bite of her own. She chewed the strange, fibrous pulp slowly. The fuzzy skin felt completely unnatural against her teeth, and the raw, acidic tang made her jaw instinctively clench. She forced her mouth into a wide, completely unconvincing smile of approval for Evaria's sake, swallowing the bite through sheer, stubborn willpower. She had to keep Evaria perfectly happy and distracted, no matter how much the ancient fruit tasted like acidic loam.

"Well, that is certainly... historical," Casia managed to say, her tone dripping with forced enthusiasm.

While Evaria was happily distracted by her own messy, juicy bites, Casia casually, yet swiftly, dropped the remainder of her massive peach into a nearby compost bin. She wiped her hands quickly on her environmental suit and pivoted straight back to the science to cover her tracks.

"It has a completely different taste and texture than the Peachberry," Casia observed, looking at Relania with genuine curiosity. "What exactly did you do to it?"

Relania chuckled lightly. "Well, to make it thrive underground without natural sunlight, we had to perform a little botanical genetic splicing. We took the baseline genome of this large peach, stripped out the specific alleles responsible for the fuzzy skin and the massive pit, and sequenced it with the compact cellular structure of our native subterranean violet-berries. Essentially, we told the peach's DNA to stop growing outward and start packing all that raw sugar inward! It condenses the flavor, removes the fuzz, and shrinks it down to the perfect, bite-sized sphere."

Evaria's eyes widened with complete understanding as she took another happy bite of the ancient fruit.

"Violet-berries do not have that distinct Peachberry taste. You have to be kidding me," Casia said, realizing the wild botanical science was entirely accurate.

Evaria paused mid-bite, her sharp mind immediately connecting the botanical dots. She looked up at Relania, juice still on her chin, realizing her aunt had a very valid point.

"You are absolutely right," Relania conceded with a conspiratorial grin.

She placed her palm against a biometric stone slab on the wall. A hidden, refrigerated compartment hissed open, releasing a wisp of chilled, fragrant air. Inside sat a small, climate-controlled tray holding something entirely foreign to their subterranean world. Relania carefully lifted a 21st-century strawberry. It was a vibrant, glossy ruby-red, tapering to a delicate point, its surface studded with tiny golden seeds and crowned with a crisp, green leafy collar.

Sitting right next to the strawberries on the chilled tray, Evaria noticed a separate, sealed container holding a cluster of small, perfectly round, deep-blue berries. A crimson warning tag hovered just above their container: *Experimental Botanical Splice. Do Not Distribute to Public. Projected Mass Production: In two years.*

Evaria's gaze lingered on the strange blue spheres for only a second before her attention was completely captivated by the vibrant red fruit Relania was offering her.

"Usually, I do not have the luxury of sharing this particular botanical secret," Relania whispered, handing one of the small red strawberries to Evaria and another to Casia. "Eating raw 21st-century fruit requires strict biological protocols. That is why I had you put on the white environmental suits. They prevent our contemporary subterranean microbes from cross-contaminating the ancient root systems. But since we are only sampling the extracted fruiting bodies in this staging area, you do not need to engage the enclosed hoods."

Evaria took a cautious bite. Her bright amber eyes went wide as the sharp, juicy sweetness hit her tongue. She let out a delighted, sugary laugh, chewing happily.

Casia popped her strawberry into her mouth and bit down. The flavor was an absolute revelation—a sudden, vibrant shock of sun-drenched sweetness and tart acidity that she had never experienced in her life. Her eyes fluttered shut, and a deep, involuntary hum of pure satisfaction vibrated in her throat.

"I do not even care what the botanical science is," Casia pleaded, her eyes still blissfully shut as her professional composure completely vanished. "Please. I am begging you. Just hand over the rest of the tray."

She reached her hand out blindly, wiggling her fingers and expecting Relania to immediately place another 21st-century strawberry into her palm. Instead, the heavy sound of footsteps approached the staging area and stopped directly in front of her.

Expecting fruit, Casia's eyes snapped open.

Standing just a few feet away, fully clad in his own white environmental protective suit with the hood pulled down, was Malachi. He was being escorted by another agricultural worker. His vivid yellow eyes were fixed squarely on Casia, blinking in mild, silent bewilderment at her completely unguarded, desperate pleading over a piece of fruit.

Casia froze. Her outstretched hand dropped slowly to her side. Her green-grey cheeks flushed with profound embarrassment, a stray drop of red juice still lingering comically on her lower lip. In an instant, the lingering sweetness vanished, replaced by the crushing, factual reality of exactly why Malachi had come.

"Father!" Evaria dropped her half-eaten strawberry and quickly ran over, throwing her arms around him.

Malachi crouched down, ignoring the stiffness of his white environmental suit, and picked her up with both hands. He looked deeply into her bright eyes, silently scanning her for any signs of physical or psychological stress. Seeing only pure, happy innocence, a genuine smile broke across his face.

"Evaria, my princess," Malachi said, his deep voice radiating warmth. He shifted his gaze to the educator. "And Casia, how are you doing? I am so glad you brought my daughter here for the rest of the tour while the school finishes its facility drill."

"We are having a wonderful time," Casia replied smoothly, perfectly matching his calm tone despite the violent twisting in her stomach. "We were just sampling the ancient surface fruits."

"I can see that," Malachi noted, a subtle, knowing warmth in his eyes. He gently wiped a smudge of red strawberry juice from Evaria's chin, then set his daughter safely back down on the stone floor. He glanced back at Casia and subtly tapped his own lower lip, innocently signaling to the embarrassed educator that she still had juice on her face.

"Listen to me, Evaria. I only have a brief moment," Malachi continued, seamlessly shifting gears. "I just came from the excavation site to make sure you were enjoying your surprise trip. But now, I have to go join your mother."

Evaria tilted her head. "Where is Mother?"

"She is just three minutes away at the Medical Enclave," Malachi answered, maintaining absolute, factual composure. "Since the facility drill caused an early dismissal, your mother decided to use the sudden free time to finalize the administrative paperwork from your medical scan yesterday. She knew the press would be swarming the main gates to report on the drill, which is exactly why she asked Auntie Casia to take you out through the secondary staff exit. Medical Biometric signatures are very boring adult work, so we both agreed you would have much more fun here."

Evaria's sharp mind quickly processed the logic. The explanation connected perfectly to her visit to the doctor the day before. She nodded, completely satisfied with the facts. "Okay. Will you and Mother come back to get me when the paperwork is done?"

The question hit Casia like a physical blow, forcing her to look away toward the refrigeration units so Evaria would not see the tears suddenly pooling in her emerald eyes.

"Yes," Malachi promised, entirely unaware of the tragic reality waiting for him at the medical enclave. "Auntie Casia is going to finish this tour with you, and then your mother and I will come collect you. Be good for her."

He stood up to his full height and glanced toward the agricultural worker, noting the violet name tag pinned to her jacket.

Relania's eyes widened as she finally connected his imposing figure to the name Casia and Evaria had just spoken. She let out a soft, genuine gasp of awe. "You are... Malachi. The Honorable Historian."

Malachi offered her a polite, grounding nod, gently deflecting the grand title he had never been comfortable claiming. "Just Malachi, please. But thank you, Relania, for sharing your time and your knowledge with my daughter today."

He gave Evaria one last, gentle squeeze on the shoulder. He gave Casia a single, solemn nod of profound gratitude, turned around, and walked away from the staging area, heading straight for the Medical Enclave.

Five minutes later, Malachi stepped off the high-speed walkway just outside the main gates of the Medical Enclave. He had used the final two minutes of his transit to strip off the sterile white environmental suit, depositing it in a transit receptacle. He now stood in his standard attire: a heavy, flowing black historian's robe, cinched firmly at the waist by the vibrant purple sash Evaria had made for him.

The entrance was a chaotic swarm of overlapping voices and dense crowds. The moment he approached the glass barricades, a young male Morlock reporter spotted his towering figure.

"Malachi! How is your wife?" The reporter shoved an illuminated recording device and a hovering camera lens directly into Malachi's face.

Before Malachi could process the intrusion, a dozen more reporters surged forward, surrounding him in a tight, physical perimeter of shouted questions and aggressive mechanical shutters.

"Is it true your wife was attacked at the educational complex?" a young female reporter demanded, thrusting her own recording device forward.

Hearing the word *attacked* shouted so casually registered in Malachi's mind with cold, factual dread. Casia's emergency text had informed him of the violent altercation in private, but hearing the press actively reporting it confirmed that the school's strict containment protocols had completely failed.

"ENOUGH!" Malachi's deep voice boomed with absolute, commanding authority, easily cutting through the noise of the press mob. "I have no facts regarding what has happened. Give me my space!"

The sheer force of his presence, combined with the sudden realization that the Honorable Historian truly did not know the status of his own wife, caused the majority of the press pool to immediately step back. They lowered their cameras, offering a rare moment of respect.

However, one reporter refused to retreat. A sleek, aggressive Morlock pushed his way to the front, stepping unapologetically into Malachi's personal space. He held his recording device inches from Malachi's chest. "But the public needs the facts, Malachi! Was it a Stage Two Morlock? Did a feral student do this to her?"

Malachi's vivid yellow eyes narrowed, his rigid self-control tested by the blatant, invasive disrespect.

Before Malachi was forced to physically move the man himself, a massive Medical Enclave security guard stepped directly between them. The guard forcefully shoved the aggressive reporter backward by his shoulders. "Step back! He said he needs space. Move behind the barricade right now!"

As the first guard maintained a physical wall against the sleazy reporter, a second security officer quickly flanked Malachi.

"Right this way, sir," the second guard said respectfully, opening a secure side door to bypass the main lobby. "The medical administrators are waiting for you inside."

The heavy doors sealed behind Malachi, instantly cutting off the chaotic roar of the press. He found himself standing in a private, deeply hushed medical consultation room. As his sharp yellow eyes scanned the space, the cold dread in his chest crystallized into absolute certainty.

He looked at the faces of the medical staff waiting for him. Several of them immediately lowered their eyes to the floor, unable to meet his gaze. Malachi's analytical mind rapidly processed this behavioral data. The aggressive reporter's shouted questions echoed loudly in his thoughts: *Attacked. Feral student. Stage Two PCR.* If Seraphina had merely suffered a severe but survivable injury, these professionals would be engaging him directly to discuss recovery protocols. Instead, their averted eyes and heavy silence communicated a devastating truth before a single word was spoken.

A distinguished Morlock stepped forward from the group. His posture radiated both high-level medical authority and profound, quiet empathy.

"Malachi," the man said, his voice gentle but steady. "I am Dr. Zachari. I am the Chief Medical Administrator, and I am personally overseeing Seraphina's care."

Dr. Zachari gestured toward the center of the private room. Resting on the floor was a beautifully crafted, circular stone table. Its completely smooth surface was heavily embedded with polished veins of deep red ruby and clear quartz crystals, catching the dim ambient light of the room.

"Please, sit with us," Dr. Zachari offered softly, pulling out a chair.

The other doctors moved to take their seats around the crystalline table, their movements slow and deeply respectful. Malachi stepped forward and lowered his physically fit frame into the chair opposite Dr. Zachari.

As he sat, he recognized the familiar faces of Dr. Klorioa and her assistant, Zeangol—the exact same medical team who had diagnosed Evaria just the morning before. It was Zeangol who had directly explained the grim, progressive stages of PCR to Malachi. Now, acutely understanding the compounding trauma this family was enduring, Dr. Klorioa and Zeangol moved quietly to flank Malachi. They took the seats on either side of him to offer a silent, tragic symmetry of support.

Malachi placed his hands flat against the smooth quartz and ruby surface, actively bracing himself for the clinical data.

Dr. Zachari folded his hands on the table, looking directly into Malachi's eyes with deep, professional compassion. A soft hum vibrated from the stone table as a holographic display materialized above the quartz crystals. It projected a sterile, clinical rendering of Seraphina's battered body, brutally detailing her violently fractured arm and the severe lacerations tearing across her face.

Malachi gasped, his vivid yellow eyes rapidly welling with tears as Dr. Zachari detailed the horrific extent of the physical trauma his wife had endured.

"No," Malachi choked out, his voice thick with rising grief. "I cannot believe it."

Recognizing the immediate psychological toll the images were taking on him, Dr. Zachari tapped the table, instantly shutting off the holographic display. The room plunged back into heavy silence. For two agonizing minutes, no one spoke, allowing Malachi a brief, respectful moment to process the visual shock.

Then, Dr. Zachari leaned forward. "Malachi, I will be completely direct with you to ensure you understand the absolute severity of what has happened to Seraphina," Dr. Zachari began, his voice heavy with an unnatural tremor. "Right now, we have her physically stabilized and she is not in pain, but—"

Malachi violently shook his head. A sharp, involuntary gasp escaped his chest, loud in the hushed room.

"But what?" Malachi interrupted. Despite his highly disciplined mind fracturing under the cold reality of the data, his heart desperately clung to the hope that his wife could somehow survive this. He needed to believe she would live.

"She is dying," Dr. Zachari stated, his eyes downcast with profound empathy.

The absolute finality of those words severed his last thread of hope. As the crushing realization set in, Malachi began to sob, physically trembling under the grief. Flanking him, Dr. Klorioa and Zeangol placed gentle hands on his shaking shoulders.

The Chief Medical Administrator kept his gaze fixed on the crystalline table, his professional composure breaking under the weight of his medical failure. "There was massive blood loss. Cortical scans confirm the blunt force trauma induced rapid, severe brain swelling. We reduced the pressure, but the internal damage is irreversible."

Dr. Zachari's voice cracked, and tears began to fall freely down his face.

Around the table, the collective grief was palpable. Dr. Klorioa covered her mouth, her shoulders shaking, while Zeangol and the other specialists wiped silently at their own eyes. Medical professionals were rigorously trained to maintain a sterile, clinical distance when delivering terminal news, but the sheer, unprecedented brutality of a Stage Two attack inside a school had completely shattered their professional shields. They were not just doctors looking at a chart; they were members of a peaceful society profoundly traumatized by what they could not fix.

Malachi sat bowed under the weight of his shattered reality, surrounded by the quiet, shared weeping of the medical staff. There was no logic left to apply, only the profound, agonizing truth that he was losing the other half of his soul.

A heavy, suffocating silence filled the room as several minutes passed. Dr. Zachari and the rest of the medical staff struggled to regain their composure, quietly wiping their faces. Across from them, Malachi had collapsed forward. His forehead rested against the cold quartz and ruby surface of the table, his broad shoulders trembling with quiet, broken sobs.

"No... no... not Seraphina," Malachi whispered blindly to the stone. The sheer, compounding volume of tragedy was entirely overloading his ability to process reality. "She is my everything. First Evaria with the PCR diagnosis... and now this. No. No."

Because Dr. Klorioa and Zeangol were already seated directly beside him, they did not hesitate to breach standard professional protocols. Dr. Klorioa leaned in close, offering her voice as a compassionate, grounding presence in the middle of his shattered world.

"You will not do this alone, Malachi," Dr. Klorioa promised softly. "We will help you."

Beside him, Zeangol gently reached out and closed her own hands over Malachi's trembling fist resting on the table.

Malachi slowly lifted his head from the stone. Heavy strands of his long hair fell forward, clinging to his tear-streaked face as he turned to look at them. His vivid yellow eyes were completely broken, utterly devoid of their usual commanding, analytical focus. He was the picture of absolute, distraught ruin, holding onto the physical reality of Zeangol's grip as the only thing keeping him tethered to the room.

But as his highly disciplined mind desperately tried to piece together the next logical step, a fresh wave of grief violently gutted him. The crushing realization of who was waiting for him in the botanical gardens struck him like a physical blow.

He squeezed his eyes shut. His deep voice caught in his throat, reducing his final words to a ragged, fragmented whisper.

"Evaria..." Malachi choked out, the sound barely carrying across the table. "How do I... how do I possibly tell my daughter?"

Chapter III — Only Time

Malachi looked at Zeangol, his vivid yellow eyes pausing to study her face for a few heavy seconds through a blur of tears. She offered a subtle, resolute nod, reaffirming her silent promise to help him. He turned his gaze to Dr. Klorioa, his chest heaving as he began to speak, his deep voice choked with an emotion that entirely defied his usual logic.

"I... I have never had to face death like this," Malachi whispered, his voice trembling. "As some of you may know, my father passed away long before my daughter was even born. Even though he was one of the most revered historians in the subterranean sectors, the Eloi refused to grant me the rite of an above-ground burial for him."

A sudden, bitter anger flared through his grief, a repressed memory violently surfacing. "They will not honor the surface rite for my wife, either, even though they know exactly who I am!" He let out a ragged breath, the sheer injustice of their political reality compounding his absolute devastation.

He looked back down at the crystalline table, shaking his head. "You are telling me there is nothing that can be done for my beloved wife. I am expected to handle this with respect and dignity, but I find myself completely broken. I have to go look my daughter in the eyes and face the nightmare of telling her that her mother is dying. If the Regrestat fails, I... I lose her, too."

Malachi squeezed his eyes shut, desperately fighting back the tears and struggling to forcefully organize his fractured thoughts.

Dr. Klorioa's eyes widened slightly at the raw, unfiltered desperation in Malachi's voice. As one of the founding architects of the Regrestat formula, she was rigorously trained to maintain a sterile, clinical distance from her patients.

But seeing the great historian completely shattered, terrified of the very disease she had dedicated her entire existence to fighting, broke through her final professional barrier. She realized that clinical distance was no longer what this father needed. He needed an unyielding, grounded foundation.

She shifted her chair closer to him, her voice dropping into a low, steady cadence that instantly commanded absolute silence around the crystalline table.

"Malachi, look at me," Dr. Klorioa commanded gently. "I am not sharing this to burden you with my own history, nor to take a single ounce of focus away from the absolute tragedy of what you are enduring right now. But I need you to know exactly who is treating your daughter. PCR violently took my own family when I was young. That is the sole reason I became a doctor, and it is the entire reason I helped synthesize Regrestat."

A stunned stillness fell over the room. Even the head of the Medical Enclave, Dr. Zachari, and Klorioa's own assistant, Zeangol, turned to look at her in profound shock. Klorioa was notoriously private; her peers knew her only as a brilliant researcher, completely unaware of the personal fire driving her intellect.

Dr. Klorioa pressed her hands flat against the cold quartz and ruby table, leaning in to ensure Malachi heard every single word.

"I know exactly what you are terrified of," she continued, her tone deeply sincere and heavily grounded in the science they had discussed the day before. "You and I both know the biological reality: as Evaria grows, her brain will naturally mature and expand, which will constantly test the boundaries of the medication. But I want you to understand that Regrestat is not a permanent cage. It is a guardrail. It is a preventative measure designed strictly to stall the cognitive shear and buy us time."

She paused, her eyes narrowing with absolute, fierce resolve.

"Most of the Enclave believes that containing this disease is the best our society can achieve. I do not. I study PCR every single waking cycle because my ultimate goal is to cure it. Not to manage it, but to end it entirely. I am fighting to break this disease before it has the chance to break Evaria."

Dr. Klorioa's voice dropped to a tender but incredibly firm whisper.

"I know you are losing your soulmate today, Malachi. There is absolutely no medical data or comforting word that can soften the cruelty of that reality. But Evaria still needs you. She needs her father to rise above this nightmare and stand. And I swear to you, by my own life's work... when you do, you will not be fighting for your daughter's mind alone."

Around the table, Dr. Zachari and the other specialists looked at Dr. Klorioa, offering quiet, solemn nods of solidarity. Her unyielding vow had visibly shifted the heavy gravity in the room, forming a protective shield around the grieving father.

Malachi absorbed her words, taking a slow, ragged breath to forcefully steady his heaving chest. He looked around the crystalline table at the medical team, his profound humility grounding his shattered composure.

"I study time," Malachi began slowly, his voice a raw, broken whisper. "I spend my entire life excavating the past. But today... my present is completely shattered. Yet, amidst all this horrific chaos, you are offering me the one objective piece of hope I need to survive it."

He closed his eyes, the memory of his childhood sweetheart washing over him.

"I know I have a duty to Evaria, and a responsibility to our society to ensure our lost history is not forgotten," he continued, struggling to keep his voice from breaking. "But it was never just my work. I only dug up the past. Seraphina was the one who actually taught it. She brought those ancient stones to life for the next generation."

The doctors could see his vivid yellow eyes, fresh tears spilling over his lashes as he looked back down at the smooth ruby and quartz surface.

"Seraphina and I were just Morlocks in the lower sectors when we realized we shared that exact same devotion," Malachi whispered, his heartbreak absolute. "I found the fragments, and she gave them meaning. That shared purpose... that is why I fell in love with her. She was my mirror." Malachi swallowed hard, fighting back a heavy sob. "And now I have to figure out how to navigate time without her."

He paused again, the crushing reality of the immediate future pulling him forcefully back from his memories. He looked around at the medical team, his eyes searching theirs for an answer no science could provide.

"How do I tell my little princess that my Queen... that her mother is dying?" Malachi asked, his deep voice finally breaking.

Dr. Zachari stood up slowly from the crystalline table, his posture projecting quiet, steady support.

"You do not have to carry that burden alone, and you do not have to tell Evaria this very second," the Chief Medical Administrator answered gently. "We will help you find the words for your daughter when the time comes. But in this immediate moment, your place is beside your wife. Her time is incredibly short. Let us take you to her."

Malachi nodded slowly. He pressed his hands against the crystalline table and forced himself to stand. Around him, the rest of the medical team rose in solemn unison.

As Malachi reached his full height, the sheer, crushing weight of reality finally hit his physical body. His legs buckled beneath him, suddenly too heavy to support his own frame. Because Dr. Klorioa and Zeangol were already flanking him, they reacted instantly. The doctor and her assistant each grabbed one of his arms, bracing his weight and holding him firmly upright for a few agonizing seconds while the physical vertigo passed.

Malachi took a deep, shuddering breath and slowly steadied himself, offering a silent nod of profound gratitude to the two women holding him together.

With Dr. Zachari taking the lead, Dr. Klorioa and Zeangol gently released his arms but remained closely at his sides. Together, they escorted the broken historian out of the private consultation room and down a quiet, highly secure medical corridor.

The medical corridor was illuminated with a soft, bioluminescent blend of green and teal. The stone walls were adorned with vibrant murals of the surface world—sweeping fields of ancient mallows and deep, tulip-like flowers blooming beneath a canopy of painted stars. It was intentionally designed to be warm and comforting, a stark contrast to the cold, sterile environments of the upper-level Eloi structures.

When they finally reached the trauma room, Dr. Zachari, Dr. Klorioa, and Zeangol respectfully held back. They remained in the open doorway, offering Malachi the silent grace of stepping inside alone.

He moved slowly toward the bedside. Seraphina lay completely motionless, dressed in a pristine white surgical gown. Her beautiful face was heavily bandaged, and her long hair had been carefully gathered into a gentle ponytail resting against the pillow. The only sign of life was the steady, mechanical rise and fall of her chest.

Malachi reached out, his trembling fingers wrapping around her cold hand. He grasped it firmly, bowing his head as he silently shook it. *No.* The absolute agony of seeing his beloved Queen, his wife, and the mother of his daughter reduced to this state was a visceral, suffocating pain unlike anything he had ever endured.

As he stared at her bandaged face, his father's dying words suddenly echoed through his mind. His father had been a profoundly respected historian and the official Ambassador to the surface, a visionary who understood the absolute biological truth that the Eloi constantly discarded: the Morlocks and the Eloi were not two distinct species.

"Never surrender yourself to the Eloi when you uncover our past," his father had whispered on his deathbed. *"It is our right to be at peace with them. We are a part of them, and they are still a part of us. Although we live in the subterranean dark and they live in the light above, we are the exact same. Do not let them rob you of your dignity, Malachi. We are one."*

At the time, those words had felt like the overly optimistic dream of a dying man. But sitting here now, holding his dying wife's hand, they burned into Malachi's soul with absolute clarity.

Dignity, he thought bitterly. He remembered how the Eloi had instantly rejected his father's message of reunification. Despite his father being one of the most revered historians in the subterranean sectors and having served as their dedicated Ambassador, the Eloi had denied him the simple dignity of a surface burial. They had completely disrespected a lifetime of brilliant diplomatic work. They robbed him.

Malachi choked back a heavy sob, his grip tightening gently on Seraphina's hand. When his father died, that profound disrespect had nearly consumed Malachi with anger. It was Seraphina who had pulled him back. She was the one who always reminded him to look for the good in others, gently warning him never to let the coldness or indifference of the Eloi corrupt his intellect or cloud his judgment.

His father had hoped for a unified spark, but as Malachi looked at his broken Queen, the stark reality was suffocating: the only thing the Eloi ever continued to offer the subterranean world was oppression. And now, the one person who kept him from hating them for it was slipping away.

"How do I tell Evaria?" he asked gently, his voice a ragged whisper directed at his motionless wife. From the open doorway, Dr. Klorioa and Zeangol watched in a silent, heavy vigil. Doctor Zachari nodded at the two doctors and excused himself to his office, keeping his communication wafer active to listen in through his earpiece.

"You always kept me grounded," Malachi pleaded softly, his tears soaking into the white fabric of her surgical gown. "You always knew exactly what to say when my interactions with the Eloi turned bitter and cold. What do I do now?"

He lowered his head, resting his brow gently against her arm, as if his sheer willpower could force her to open her eyes just one last time. She was completely comatose. She was not tethered to heavy life-support machinery—her physical body was still stubbornly taking steady, rhythmic breaths on its own. The medical staff had successfully reduced the severe swelling in her brain, but the massive internal hemorrhaging and irreversible structural trauma left her entirely unresponsive.

A few agonizing minutes passed in the quiet hum of the trauma room. Malachi sobbed softly against her arm. There was no miraculous awakening. The brutal science of her injuries offered no sudden reprieve.

Standing in the doorway, fresh tears welled in Dr. Klorioa and Zeangol's eyes. They were not just weeping for the dying educator; they wept because they understood exactly what Malachi meant. It was a shared, unspoken trauma among their people. Both the doctor and her assistant had family members who were forced to interact with the surface dwellers, and they, too, had always been met with that exact same systemic, cold indifference. In that quiet room, Malachi's grief was not just his own; it was the collective sorrow of an entire oppressed society.

Malachi slowly pulled back from her side. His large hands were visibly shaking as he reached to his belt and withdrew his circular metallic wafer.

He rapidly typed a secure override message directly to Casia: *Bring Evaria to the intensive care ward immediately. Time is of the essence. Conceal Evaria's face completely with a hood. The media is swarming the main gates.*

Three minutes away, standing beneath the illuminated canopy of the Garden Atrium, Casia stared at the secure text appearing on her personal device. Her stomach plummeted. The specific instruction to route to the intensive care ward, combined with the urgent mandate to conceal Evaria's face, told Casia everything she needed to know. She did not have the exact medical data, but the stark reality was undeniably clear: Seraphina was not just injured. She was slipping away.

Casia quickly typed her response back to Malachi: *We are on our way.*

Back in the trauma room, Malachi felt the immediate vibration of Casia's reply. The last thing in the world he wanted was to expose his highly intelligent, emotionally fragile daughter to the ruthless chaos of the press mob now that they were actively moving. He lowered the device and motioned for Dr. Klorioa and Zeangol, who were still standing respectfully in the doorway, to come inside.

As they approached the bedside, Malachi tapped the surface of his wafer, projecting a crisp holographic image.

"This is my daughter, Evaria, and our closest friend, Casia," Malachi said, his voice returning to its deep, commanding cadence despite the tears staining his face. "They are currently enroute from the Subterranean Horticulture Gardens, which is only three minutes away from this enclave. Can you get a priority message out to your security team to intercept them? I told Casia to use a hood to cover my daughter's face, but you know exactly how aggressive the media can be. I will not have my daughter rushed or recognized by that mob."

Recognizing the tactical reality of the threat, Dr. Klorioa did not hesitate. "I will handle it right now," she promised.

She immediately tapped her own medical comms-link, broadcasting an urgent alert directly to the Medical Enclave's Head of Security to deploy an extraction escort to the main gates.

Meanwhile, Casia slipped the device back into her pocket and took a deep, steadying breath. She despised lying. Her entire moral framework as an educator was built on absolute truth. But looking down at Evaria's pure, innocent face, Casia knew she had to construct a flawless, logical illusion. If Evaria's sharp mind detected even a fraction of the horrific truth before they reached the safety of Malachi's arms, the psychological shock could trigger another PCR shear.

Casia quickly typed her response back to Malachi: *We are on our way.*

She slipped the device back into her pocket and took a deep, steadying breath. She despised lying. Her entire moral framework as an educator was built on absolute truth. But looking down at Evaria's pure, innocent face, Casia knew she had to construct a flawless, logical illusion. If Evaria's sharp mind detected even a fraction of the horrific truth before they reached the safety of Malachi's arms, the psychological shock could trigger another PCR shear.

"Evaria, sweetie," Casia said, keeping her voice incredibly warm and gentle as she knelt to the Morlock's eye level. "Your father just messaged me. Do you remember that boring medical paperwork he and your mother are finishing up?"

Evaria nodded, her bright amber eyes widening with understanding. "Yes. Father said they would come back for me when it is done."

"Exactly," Casia smiled, gently pulling the soft hood of Evaria's violet tunic up over her dark, wavy hair. "Well, it turns out the medical administrators need you to be present for one final biometric signature before they can officially close the file. So, since we are only three minutes away, we are going to take a quick walk over there, get it signed, and bring your parents back here to finish our tour."

Evaria tilted her head, accepting the logic perfectly. "Why do I have to wear my hood up?"

The second lie tasted like poison in Casia's mouth, but she grounded it in a factual event to ensure it held together. "Because your father is a very famous historian. This morning, before he dropped you off at school, your mother and I were in the educators' lounge, and it was broadcasted that your dad found another Aeterna stone. The news media is crowding the medical gates right now trying to ask him questions about his discovery."

Casia smoothed the soft violet fabric around the young Morlock's face. "He does not want all those loud reporters and hovering recording drones bothering you. So, a nice security guard is going to meet us at the gate. We are going to keep our heads down, ignore the reporters, and walk right past them. Can you do that for me?"

Evaria smiled proudly, pulling the edges of the hood a little closer to her face. "I can do that, Auntie Casia. Like a secret mission."

"Just like a secret mission," Casia whispered, her heart breaking entirely. She stood up, taking Evaria's small hand in her own. "Let's go find your father."

Casia and Evaria left the Garden Atrium immediately, though Relania kindly insisted on pressing a small, woven bag of Peachberries and 21st-century strawberries into Evaria's hands just before they stepped onto the high-speed walkway.

The transit was a blur for Casia, her mind racing with terrifying calculations, but Evaria happily held her bag of fruit, entirely oblivious beneath her violet hood. Almost the exact moment they disembarked at the Medical Enclave's transit hub, a massive, imposing Morlock with a thick, coarse beard rushed through the crowd to intercept them. It was the Head of Security.

"Are you part of the secret mission?" Evaria asked, looking up at him through the folds of her hood.

The tall, heavily muscled guard stopped in his tracks, blinking his vivid yellow eyes in sheer confusion. "Mission?" he echoed softly. He looked over Evaria's hooded head to the educator, lowering his deep voice to a polite, cautious whisper. "You are Casia, and this is Evaria, daughter of Malachi?"

Casia looked the formidable guard directly in the eye. Despite the crushing weight of the tragedy sitting in her chest, a fleeting, desperate urge to laugh at his utter bewilderment bubbled in her throat. She masked it instantly, offering him a firm, commanding look.

"Just go with it," Casia whispered back.

The Head of Security blinked once, his rigid professional training instantly adapting to the strange tactical request. He looked back down at the young Morlock and gave her a very serious, solemn nod.

"Yes. I am part of the mission," he said, his deep voice carrying absolute authority. He tried to play along. "Keep your hood up, Evaria. No witnesses."

Evaria giggled, and Casia followed with a soft laugh.

"Follow me," the guard instructed gently, turning his massive frame to lead them securely through the transit hub.

Casia made sure Evaria's violet hood remained drawn far forward, completely concealing her face. To keep the youth entirely shielded from the chaotic press mob at the outer gates, Casia had simply scooped the thirteen-year-old up into her arms. While carrying a youth of that age for nearly five minutes would have been physically impossible for a frail, surface-dwelling Eloi, Morlock biology was vastly different. Their dense musculature and natural subterranean strength allowed Casia to carry Evaria effortlessly as they bypassed the reporters and passed through the secure, heavy doors of the intensive care wing.

Casia popped one of the 21st-century strawberries from Relania's woven bag into her mouth just as the massive guard stepped closer to them.

"So, operative Evaria," the Head of Security said playfully, keeping his deep voice to a smooth, rumbling whisper as they walked. "The mission is simply to get you safely to your father. It will not take long. If there are any problems along the way, I will protect you."

Evaria had always loved immersing herself in a good fantasy role-playing game. Much like when her parents playfully treated her like royalty, slipping into this pretend mission made her feel completely safe and secure. She peeked out from Casia's shoulder, looking up at the heavily muscled man. "I think you can protect us. You are very tall."

The unexpected, deadpan delivery of the compliment caught Casia entirely off guard. She barked out a sudden, rich laugh, quickly slapping a hand over her mouth to stop from almost spitting out the strawberry.

"Yes, he is very tall, Evaria," Casia agreed, her chest shaking with a mix of genuine amusement and underlying dread. She shot the guard an appreciative look. In those short five minutes, the formidable security chief's gentle willingness to protect a young Morlock's innocence had earned Casia's profound respect and quiet friendship.

They turned the final corner into the green and teal-lit corridor. At the far end of the hall, Casia immediately spotted Malachi standing outside the trauma room. Even from a distance, she could see the absolute devastation emanating from him. The playful illusion Casia had built instantly evaporated in her mind, replaced by the crushing reality of what was waiting inside.

The guard slowed his pace, recognizing the heavy shift in the atmosphere. He looked down at Evaria in Casia's arms and offered a crisp, formal nod.

"Mission is completed," the security chief announced gently. "But your final objective is that you must follow Casia's directions until you reach your father. Understood?"

Evaria nodded seriously beneath her hood. "Understood."

Casia gently lowered Evaria to her feet, keeping a protective hand on her small shoulder. "That's right," Casia added softly, her voice carrying a maternal warmth despite her breaking heart. "And your first direction is to keep your face completely covered by your hood at all times, right up until I am finished speaking with your father."

Always a gentle, kind, and deeply observant young Morlock, Evaria simply smiled beneath the violet fabric. "Okay, Auntie Casia," she whispered obediently.

Before Casia could take another step toward the devastated historian, Dr. Klorioa stepped out from the trauma room doorway and approached them.

Because Klorioa had initiated the emergency extraction, she had logically left the encrypted two-way frequency open with the Head of Security to monitor their progress through the hospital. Listening to the live audio feed, the brilliant doctor had already pieced together the parameters of the "secret operative" game Casia, Evaria, and the guard had developed. She knew exactly how to step into the illusion.

Klorioa knelt slightly to address the hooded youth, her voice a gentle, reassuring whisper.

"Operative Evaria," the doctor began, perfectly mirroring the security chief's tone. "I want you to go with my assistant, Zeangol. Keep your head fully covered. This will take just a few more minutes, but I promise you that your father is almost finished signing the biometric paperwork from your examination yesterday."

Trusting the doctor who had treated her, Evaria immediately agreed with a small nod beneath her violet fabric.

Zeangol stepped forward and gently scooped the young Morlock up into her arms. At exactly four foot five inches, Evaria was small, and carrying her was absolutely no problem for Zeangol's natural subterranean strength.

Without a word, Zeangol carried her a few yards down the corridor to a secure waiting lounge. The room was sealed by a thick, transparent enclosure, specifically engineered to be entirely soundproof. It was a clinical necessity in the intensive care ward, designed to ensure that waiting families were completely shielded from any traumatic conversations or medical emergencies occurring in the hallway.

As the heavy, soundproof door closed securely behind Zeangol and Evaria, Casia was finally left alone in the corridor with Malachi.

Malachi stood just a few paces away in the quiet, teal-lit hallway. He looked at Casia, his shoulders slowly beginning to tremble, and he just shook his head no.

Casia's breath caught in her throat. She knew that exact look on his face. It was the identical, hollow stare of absolute devastation he had worn years ago when his revered father was dying. Back then, it had been Casia and Seraphina standing by his side, the two of them working together to help him navigate the agonizing reality of that loss.

Because his father had passed away long before Evaria was even born, the youth had grown up without ever knowing her grandfather. She only knew him through the holographic projections stored within their private Aeterna stone family recordings. But Casia remembered the grim reality of those dark days. She remembered how, for months, the sheer grief had completely shattered Malachi.

Seeing that exact same, broken look return to his eyes now, Casia knew the unyielding medical truth before she even had to ask. Seraphina was not going to survive.

Casia closed the short distance between them, wrapping her arms tightly around Malachi's trembling frame. He accepted the embrace for only a fractured second before pulling away gently, his expression completely hollow as he motioned for her to follow him inside.

Stepping through the doorway of the green and teal-lit trauma room, Casia let out a sharp, devastated gasp. Her best friend—the woman who had always been a sister to her—lay completely motionless and heavily bandaged on the bed. Numb with grief, Casia slowly sank into the chair Malachi had just vacated beside the mattress.

A few feet away, Dr. Klorioa glanced down at the neurological diagnostic monitors. The brain wave readings, which had been nearly flatlining since the swelling was reduced, suddenly registered a brief, sharp burst of electrical activity. Klorioa's eyes narrowed slightly, but she remained entirely silent. Clinically, she could not be certain if this sudden, erratic spike was a miraculous sign of neurological recovery, or the well-documented physiological surge that so often immediately preceded a comatose patient's terminal demise.

Unaware of the shifting data on the screens, Casia leaned closer to the bed. Her eyes brimmed with tears. "Seraphina, I am here if you can hear me," Casia whispered, her voice trembling but resolute. "You have always treated me like a sister. I agreed to help you with Evaria and her PCR diagnosis, and I promise you, I will be here for them."

Standing near the monitors, Dr. Klorioa's eyes widened in brief surprise, pulling her attention away from the brain scans. Just yesterday, she had personally warned Malachi and Seraphina to keep Evaria's PCR diagnosis an absolute secret to protect the young Morlock from societal stigma.

But as Casia paused to catch her breath, Klorioa's rigid clinical protocols softened into deep understanding. Listening to the raw grief in the room, Klorioa realized Casia was not simply an educator; she was the foundational bedrock of this family.

"I will always put your daughter and Malachi first," Casia continued, sobbing softly as she gently placed her hand near Seraphina's. "You have my absolute word. I will protect your family's secrets because you were always there for me when I needed a sister and a best friend."

Malachi nodded heavily, his own tears falling freely.

Watching them, Dr. Klorioa exhaled a quiet, respectful breath. There was no malice in this breach of medical secrecy. Given the horrific reality of the day, Klorioa firmly believed that Malachi and his wife had made the logically correct and deeply compassionate choice to trust their closest friend with the truth.

"How do I tell Evaria? How?" Malachi whispered, his voice shattering. He glanced up at Casia, who was trembling beside the bed, knowing she had to find the exact right words to help manage the situation.

"You tell her the absolute truth," Casia whispered back, wiping her own tears and forcing her voice to steady. "Her intellect is too sharp, Malachi. If we construct another illusion now, the betrayal could trigger a severe PCR shear."

Dr. Klorioa stepped closer, her voice a calm, clinical murmur over the hum of the monitors. "Casia is correct. I am the physician, and I can tell you this is not an ordinary set of tragic circumstances. Evaria's neurological response could go either way. Grounding her in the truth is the safest medical path."

Malachi nodded heavily. He keyed his comms-wafer, signaling Zeangol to bring Evaria back from the soundproof lounge.

When the heavy doors opened and the young Morlock stepped inside, Malachi dropped to his knees. He did not hide his tears. Looking directly into his daughter's bright amber eyes, he gently and clinically explained the irreversible trauma her mother's brain had sustained.

Evaria froze. Her breathing hitched, and her wide eyes instantly darted away from her weeping father to Casia. Her sharp mind rapidly calculated the timeline.

"There was no biometric signature," Evaria stated, her young voice shaking violently as her intellect deconstructed the variables. "The secret mission... you lied to keep my heart rate down. You lied to prevent a PCR spike when we were at the Horticulture area."

The absolute betrayal of the lie threatened to crush her, but as she looked at her motionless mother on the bed, Evaria's intellect engaged exactly as Seraphina had always taught her. She knew her mother would demand dignity, not a neurological collapse. Evaria gripped her father's tunic, her small frame heaving with sobs, but she physically forced herself to breathe, fighting the sensory overload to maintain her control.

Seeing the immense, painful effort Evaria was exerting to hold the line, Casia stepped forward. She placed both hands firmly on the young Morlock's shaking shoulders to ground her.

"We will channel this," Casia announced to the room, her voice carrying absolute, unwavering resolve. "I formally declare the Ritual of the Deep Earth, and the Rite of Guardianship."

The moment the words left Casia's lips, the neurological monitors beside the bed erupted into a rapid, sustained trill. Dr. Klorioa instantly stepped forward, pulling a sleek, metallic medical scan wand from her coat and passing it directly over Seraphina's bandaged head.

On the bed, Seraphina's vivid eyes slowly fluttered open.

The terminal lucidity had taken hold. But she did not awaken to a peaceful acceptance. Her fractured mind was still violently tethered to the chaotic violence of the school lockdown.

"What is going on?" Seraphina gasped weakly, her breathing ragged as her eyes darted around the trauma room in a sudden, disoriented panic. "Omri... Maliva... where is Maliva? Did I protect her?"

Malachi instantly leaned over the bed, his massive, trembling hands gently hovering over her bandaged face. "Omri attacked you!" he blurted out, the sheer thought of what he had heard from the news reporters fueling a sudden, raw anger that tore the words from his throat. But seeing the terror in his wife's eyes, he immediately caught himself, lowering his deep voice to a desperate, soothing whisper. "Maliva is safe at the school. She was saved. And so are you. You are going to be safe."

Beside them, Dr. Klorioa watched the data streaming across her scan wand. She noticed a severe, absolute drop in the neurological baseline. She knew, with absolute medical certainty, that this was not going to be a happy ending. But she remained entirely silent, refusing to agitate Seraphina while frantically running every rapid medical protocol she knew on the console, desperate to engineer a miracle she knew biology would not allow.

Despite Malachi's desperate denial, the profound, tragic clarity of the situation settled into Seraphina's mind. She felt the absolute numbness of her own body and heard the rapid, clinical warning of the failing monitors.

"I accept this Rite," Seraphina breathed, her voice faint but carrying a profoundly beautiful resonance. She turned her eyes to Casia.

"Casia... by all the moonlight and stars that are forbidden to all Morlocks, you will guard Evaria as if she is your own daughter now."

Seraphina gasped, her strength flickering as she fought for a final, absolute command. "You will be Malachi's mate... and his bedrock."

"No... no..." Malachi sobbed hysterically, his massive frame shaking as he clung to the edge of the bed. The brilliant historian was completely unraveling, abandoning all logic in the face of his devastating loss. "Stay! Fight! No... My only night and moonlight and stars are with you!"

Seraphina managed a microscopic, heartbreaking smile, looking at her weeping husband. She reached out, her cold fingers brushing his hand with a sudden, desperate strength.

"Malachi... listen to me," she whispered, her gaze pinning him with absolute urgency. "Do not let the Eloi hollow your mind with their constant arrogance. You are the keeper of the truth... the Historian of this moment in time. We must rise above them, like the stars and the moonlight we are forbidden to see. Stay whole for Casia and Evaria!"

Casia's breath hitched. She remembered the hollowed-out shell Malachi had become after his father's death, and she realized Seraphina was giving him a final, celestial tether to prevent his heart from turning to stone and to keep him bound to the two women who now shared his life.

Seraphina then turned her gaze to her daughter standing at the bedside. Evaria stepped forward, her small hands trembling as she pulled back her hood. Despite the tears streaming down her face, the thirteen-year-old's expression was one of fierce, sharp-minded resolve. She saw her father's collapse and realized, in that moment, she had to be the stabilizing force.

"Mother," Evaria whispered, her young voice steadying through the grief. "I am here. I will look after Father. I promise I will not let him become Hollow."

Seraphina's eyes filled with a final, overwhelming pride. She reached out, her fingers grazing Evaria's cheek. "My miracle... my beautiful daughter. You were the gift I was told the earth would never give me. Your father excavates the past, but without me, he is going to be very lost in the dark. You must hold his hand and remind him to keep walking forward. Be brave. Your mind is your starlight and moonlight."

She turned her gaze back to Casia, her breathing growing incredibly shallow. "Though Casia, we are not of the same mother, we truly are sisters throughout—"

Suddenly, Seraphina's eyes went wide. Her sentence fractured. She stared straight upward, completely past the medical lighting of the ceiling, as if she were suddenly witnessing something incomprehensibly vast and absolute from just beyond the veil of existence.

"TIME..." Seraphina gasped, the single word carrying a strange, haunting weight.

Her chest stopped moving. The rapid trill of the monitors instantly flatlined into a long, continuous, and deafening tone. She was gone.

Chapter IV — The Vow

The deafening, continuous tone of the flatline monitor pierced the heavy air of the trauma room. Dr. Klorioa moved with swift, clinical precision. She reached across the console and deactivated the audio alarm, plunging the room into a suffocating, absolute silence.

Instantly detecting the terminal shift in the medical baseline, the room's automated protocols engaged. The heavy doors locked shut, and the transparent walls polarized into a deep, opaque teal. The chamber sealed itself completely so the other Morlocks in the intensive care ward would not be disturbed by the immense, agonizing grief that was about to shatter the family inside.

The wailing broke through the silence.

Malachi squeezed his vivid yellow eyes shut, trembling coldly as he just kept shaking his head. *No!* The brilliant historian, a man who spent his entire life excavating thousands of years of the past, was completely paralyzed by the horrific reality of the present. He could not accept that this was actually happening. He could not fathom that his wife had used her final, fleeting seconds of terminal lucidity to legally and spiritually confirm the Rite of Guardianship. He was completely unprepared for the devastation of this noon cycle.

Beside the bed, Evaria stared down at her mother's lifeless body. Her breathing hitched, the tears spilling over her bright amber eyes as her sharp mind finally lost its battle against the crushing weight of the visual trauma.

"Mother..." Evaria whispered, her small, trembling hands reaching out to clutch the white fabric of the surgical gown. The profound logic that usually governed her mind completely fractured. She understood the absolute reality of death, but her shattered heart simply refused to accept it. She dropped to her knees, her voice deteriorating into a raw, agonizing sob. "Mother, please! You cannot stop breathing! You told me I was your starlight, but I do not know how to be brave in the dark without you! Please, Mother, please wake up!"

Seeing the young Morlock's intellectual control completely shatter into the raw, devastating grief of a youth losing her mother, Casia immediately stepped into the vow she had just taken. She reached down and effortlessly scooped Evaria up into her arms, cradling the weeping thirteen-year-old against her chest. Casia held her tightly, burying her own tears in Evaria's dark hair, desperate to be the bedrock Seraphina had demanded for both the weeping daughter and her shattered father.

Standing near the diagnostic monitors, Dr. Klorioa wiped a tear from her own cheek before turning back to her medical interface. With a heavy heart, she rapidly typed the factual, permanent record into the subterranean archives: Seraphina had passed a little over two hours past the noon cycle.

Without pausing, Klorioa initiated a secondary, highly secure protocol. She officially logged Seraphina's final verbal command, cementing it into the hospital's mainframe as a legally binding biometric authorization for Casia's Guardianship. The torch had officially been passed.

A few agonizing minutes passed in the sealed room. To protect Seraphina's physical form, Dr. Klorioa had activated a preservation stasis field over the bed. The advanced energy barrier was completely invisible, save for a faint, bioluminescent teal hue that settled softly across Seraphina's body, giving her the peaceful appearance of sleeping beneath a gentle, subterranean shroud.

Dr. Klorioa stepped away from the console and sat down near them. Her usual, rigid clinical distance was entirely gone.

"Malachi... I am sorry," the doctor whispered, her voice tight with genuine anguish. She looked up at the hooded youth still being held in Casia's arms. "Evaria, I am so very sorry. I tried. I really tried."

Malachi, looking utterly dejected, simply offered a slow, heavy nod. Even through his blinding grief, his intellect had registered the absolute truth: he had seen the doctor frantically running every possible medical protocol on the console when Seraphina had briefly awakened, fighting biology until the very last second.

But Evaria's mind reacted differently. Though the thirteen-year-old was deeply mourning, her brain—hyper-active and constantly testing the boundaries of her PCR diagnosis—suddenly and violently rejected the paralyzing despair of cold, logical death. To protect her from a catastrophic cognitive shear, her intellect forcibly pivoted, searching for an immediate, stabilizing action.

Evaria wiped her tear-filled eyes and shifted gently until Casia lowered her to the floor. The young Morlock reached into the small woven bag Relania had pressed into her hands before they left the Horticulture Gardens. She pulled out a perfectly ripe Peachberry.

Stepping toward the devastated physician, Evaria held the fruit out, a sudden, pure spark of innocent delight cutting cleanly through the heavy tension of the room.

"I saw," Evaria said softly. "You were pressing the console buttons so fast I thought your fingers were going to fly right off. You looked like you were trying to play a hundred crystal chimes all at the exact same time."

Dr. Klorioa blinked, entirely caught off guard by the sharp, humorous observation from a grieving youth.

Evaria gently pressed the Peachberry into the doctor's trembling hand. "Mother always said you cannot fix the world on an empty stomach. You should eat this."

"Wisdom... pure wisdom," Dr. Klorioa whispered, her voice thick with emotion. Deeply touched, and recognizing the medical necessity of indulging the thirteen-year-old's coping mechanism, the doctor took a slow bite of the fruit and swallowed.

Casia watched them, briefly stunned by the youth's sudden shift from profound mourning to this attempt at forced, logical joy. But Casia's background as an educator quickly identified the psychological reality. Evaria had always possessed this resilient, positive outlook, instinctively trying to make her parents smile since the day she was born. Now, her sharp mind was weaponizing that exact trait as a biological shield against the trauma.

Malachi watched his daughter, profoundly moved by her desperate attempt to be brave and inject a sliver of warmth into their absolute darkest moment. He managed a weak, tear-filled smile—a shattered reflection of his usual commanding honor—and looked up at his wife's best friend, the woman Seraphina had just named as his mate and bedrock.

"Casia, thank you," Malachi said, his deep voice ragged. "Thank you for everything. Can you please take Evaria back out to the waiting lounge? I need to speak with the doctor privately about a few things. I promise you I will not be too long."

"Of course," Casia whispered, offering him a solemn nod. She gently took Evaria's small hand.

As they approached the exit, the trauma room's automated sensors registered their movement. The opaque teal polarization faded from the glass, and the heavy doors unsealed with a soft hiss, allowing Casia and Evaria to step out into the quiet corridor. Once they were through, the doors immediately sealed shut behind them, plunging the room back into absolute privacy.

Malachi watched the heavy doors close, securing his daughter's safety for the moment. He then slowly turned his vivid yellow eyes back down to Seraphina's stasis-preserved form before looking at Dr. Klorioa.

"I am not at all prepared for any of this," Malachi confessed, his deep voice dropping into a ragged, hollow whisper. "I know you tried hard to save her. All of you did. From the exact moment I arrived at the gates and was swamped by the media..."

He shook his head in absolute disdain, his hands briefly clenching into fists. A surge of protective anger flared in his chest as he remembered the ruthless reporter he had wanted to physically shove out of his way when the horrific allegations of the school attack were first shouted at him.

He forced his hands to uncurl, his brilliant intellect desperately reaching for the rigid structure of history to ground his chaotic grief.

"The Rite of Guardianship," Malachi began, his tone shifting into the factual cadence of a scholar. "It is the ancient mandate to become the secondary mother, father, or relative to a fractured family. It has been a sacred law since the era of Chancellor Olesya, in the year 500,000 AD. She was the absolute last of our kind to be granted the dignity of a surface burial because she brought peace after a catastrophic event—an event that I am still trying to piece together in the archives, exactly one hundred eighty-nine thousand, seven hundred and eighty-seven years later."

He let out a heavy, shuddering breath, the historian fading back into the devastated husband.

"Casia is a profoundly good woman," Malachi continued softly. "But she simply does not know what she is getting into. This is a fractured family dynamic now, and with Evaria's diagnosis, I am not certain Casia can handle the sheer weight of it. I loved Seraphina implicitly."

He paused, searching for the right words. Malachi was not a man of rigid dogma, preferring the tangible evidence of history over blind faith, but he deeply respected the unseen currents of their existence. "I have always believed in the unseen connections that bind all life beneath the surface. The absolute reality that my wife managed to break through an irreversible coma just to formally bind Casia to us... it had to be that energy, or something far beyond our understanding of science, that commanded her to say yes."

He stopped, his deep voice failing him, and looked down again at Seraphina's stasis-preserved form.

"We have support services specifically designed to help families navigate this exact dynamic," Dr. Klorioa replied gently, her eyes filled with profound empathy. "Many choose to utilize them, and many do not. But I want you to understand that there is absolutely no stigma attached to fracturing under the weight of this kind of loss. None. Grief deconstructs all of us differently, even a mind as brilliantly sharp as your daughter's."

Dr. Klorioa looked down at the vibrant fruit Evaria had just pressed into her hand, a sad, reverent smile touching her lips.

"She is one tough little Peachberry. In fact, Malachi... I do not know if you had the chance to watch the news feeds this morning before the chaos at the school."

Malachi shook his head slightly, his brow furrowing in confusion.

"I broke my own clinical secrecy regarding PCR," Dr. Klorioa confessed, her voice steadying with unyielding resolve. "After examining Evaria yesterday, seeing the sheer sharpness of her intellect and the absolute devotion of Seraphina... it shattered my armor of professional detachment. I authorized the immediate mass production and public release of Regrestat. The little moments in life sometimes pierce right through our protocols. The media is not just swarming the gates because of the school tragedy. They are swarming because the entire subterranean world now knows there is a treatment."

She paused, her gaze locking onto his to convey the absolute gravity of her next words. "And as for the Guardianship Rite... it is indeed a massive responsibility for all parties. I know this objectively, because I myself was raised under it."

Malachi stared at her. His formidable intellect, usually so adept at categorizing historical facts, was deeply struggling to process the immediate, legal reality of what had just occurred in this room. Casia had just bound herself to him as his mate. He was not thinking about the mechanics of romance, intimacy, or the logistical obligations of a new spouse. His shattered heart could not even fathom those concepts. Instead, he was simply shocked.

As a historian, he knew the ancient customs implicitly, but he had never suspected Casia would actually invoke the Rite. He had always viewed her as Seraphina's dearest friend—a fiercely loyal, non-biological sister to his wife. He knew Casia was a decent, caring, unmarried Morlock who had grounded him when his father died, but he had been completely oblivious to the possibility that she harbored such deep feelings for him. He had never once imagined she would willingly step into the overwhelming role of a mother to Evaria.

The sheer weight of Casia's unexpected vow cut through the fog of his grief, forcing two immediate, paralyzing crises to the forefront of his exhausted mind.

"How do I handle Casia and Evaria?" Malachi asked, his deep voice thick with a desperate, protective instinct. "I know Casia is aware of the PCR diagnosis, but this... this is vastly more than what Seraphina and I discussed just last night about confiding in her. The tragedy of losing my wife, combined with Casia suddenly stepping in as a mother to my daughter—it is entirely overwhelming to me. And tactically... how do I handle the media right now? I am the premier historian of this region. Our people look up to me. But I absolutely will not allow them to pick apart my daughter, or Casia, or my wife's memory. I need them to back off. What do I say to them?"

He frowned, the prospect of facing the recording drones adding another heavy layer of exhaustion to his grief. He despised speaking to the media unless it was strictly regarding his historical excavations. He was a deeply private man who had cherished the quiet, secure sanctity of his family life.

Dr. Klorioa listened to his plea, a fleeting look of genuine surprise crossing her features. In a subterranean society where prominence often bred arrogance, Malachi's absolute lack of ego was profoundly refreshing. He was arguably the most respected mind in their region, yet he sought no stardom from his position, prioritizing only the safety and dignity of his family.

"You tell the absolute truth to all of them," Dr. Klorioa advised, her voice firm but entirely compassionate. "Be blunt. Be exactly who you are. With the media, tell them that, yes, an attack occurred today that took Seraphina's life. Tell them you demand the immediate privacy, honor, and dignity that they themselves would expect if they were facing the sudden death of their own loved ones. Do not back away from the podium. Be the historian they respect. If you feel the tactical need to answer questions after your statement, take only one or two. Then, tell them to honor your request for privacy, and walk away."

She stepped closer, offering him a look of absolute, unyielding solidarity. "And apply that exact same truth to Casia. Do not attempt to soften the reality of your shock or your grief. Be firm, but communicate exactly what you are feeling. Casia just made a monumental vow to your family. She does not expect you to have all the logistical answers today; she only expects you to be honest with her."

Her voice was firm, yet undeniably compassionate. He desperately needed to hear those exact words. The cold, tactical structure of her advice gave his mind a rigid framework to cling to, pulling him back from the edge of absolute collapse.

Malachi offered a slow, heavy nod, pulling his shoulders back as he accepted the burden of what he had to do.

"Is there a secure way you can get my daughter and Casia out of the facility?" Malachi asked, his focus shifting entirely to Evaria's safety. "Can you use the same internal transport corridors you used to bring them here to me, or do I need to officially arrange an escort myself?"

Dr. Klorioa nodded, already reaching for the circular interface pad mounted on her wrist. She tapped the glass, initiating a priority link to the Hospital Administrator, Dr. Zachari.

"I received the notification. I am so deeply sorry, Malachi," a voice resonated from the device. Instantly, a small, shimmering holographic image of the Doctor flickered into existence above the pad.

"Malachi needs a secure extraction," Dr. Klorioa said to the hologram, her voice professional but urgent. She then glanced up. "Malachi, would you like to continue this conversation in private, or is my presence acceptable?"

Malachi offered a brief, weary nod. He trusted Klorioa; she had earned her place in this circle.

"Malachi, listen to me," Zachari's holographic image said, his expression grave. "We normally do not authorize private escorts for non-medical departures. However, given the severe, public nature of this tragedy, I am personally going to arrange for the same security detail that brought them in to see them safely home. I am paying for the deployment out of my own discretionary fund, not the hospital's."

The administrator paused, his holographic eyes narrowing as he thought of his superiors. "If the medical oversight board gives me any bureaucratic nonsense about 'misuse of resources or budget allocations,' I will handle them. That is my burden, not yours. I am, again, truly sorry for your loss."

Malachi winced at the mention of bureaucracy. Even within their own enclaves, the constant battle of red tape and budget oversight made every moment of compassion feel like a hard-won victory. The fact that Zachari was willing to bypass the board's strict expense protocols just to protect Evaria was a debt Malachi would not forget.

"Thank you, Dr. Zachari," Malachi said, his deep voice thick with the first sign of relief he had felt all day. "Please... just get them out of the medical center enclave and safely to my home. I will handle the rest."

"Consider it done," Zachari replied, and the hologram vanished with a soft static pop.

Dr. Klorioa looked at Malachi, her expression steadying as she prepared him for what came next. "The transport is being positioned in the lower secure bays now. You should go to the lounge and say your goodbyes for now. Then, I will lead you to the front atrium. The media is waiting, Malachi. It is time to give them your truth."

Malachi walked down the quiet corridor and found Casia and Evaria in the soundproof lounge. He noticed Casia was eating one of the violet Peachberries from the woven bag, a small, grounding act of consumption that seemed to offer her some physical strength, though her emerald eyes were still heavy and puffed from mourning Seraphina.

"Father?" Evaria asked, her young voice small as she looked up. "Are we going home? I do not want to be here anymore. I just want to go home."

Casia stood, her gaze meeting Malachi's as he approached. Without a word, he reached into his tunic, pulled out a small, soft cloth, and gently wiped the fresh tears from Evaria's face.

"Listen carefully," Malachi said, his voice dropping into a tone of absolute, unyielding honesty. "I am not lying to you, Evaria. No illusions. No games. You know my position as the Premier Historian. Because of that, I must address the media about what has happened today. I promise you it will not take long. I will come home, and we will all be together."

His voice hitched slightly on the last word. *Together.* He felt the sting of it—the logical fallacy of the word now that Seraphina was gone.

Evaria straightened her shoulders, her bright amber eyes reflecting a sudden, sharp maturity. "Father, I agree. No games."

At that moment, the massive Head of Security arrived at the lounge doorway. He stood tall, his heavily muscled frame rigid, his expression somber; he had already been briefed on the passing of Malachi's wife.

"Malachi, I am so deeply sorry," the security chief said, his rumbling voice low and respectful. He gestured toward the secure exit. "I will get them home safely. That is my only mission."

Evaria turned to the formidable guard, her small hand gripping the strap of her Horticulture bag. "No games, Chief," she said, her voice trembling but resolute. "I know the truth now. I have to be brave for my father."

She paused, reaching into her woven bag to pull out two more of the violet Peachberries. She held them out to the massive security chief and the second guard flanking him.

"Mother always taught me to share our strength with those who protect us," Evaria whispered, her sharp mind clinging desperately to the logic of her mother's kindness. "You have a heavy duty today. You should have these."

The towering Head of Security looked down at the small fruit resting in his massive palm. He blinked, his rigid posture softening completely as he abandoned the earlier pretense of their secret mission. He looked at the grieving youth, seeing not just a child, but the proud daughter of their most revered historian, displaying immense grace in her absolute darkest hour.

"Thank you, Evaria," the chief rumbled gently, his deep voice thick with genuine respect. Treating the simple offering with the utmost reverence, he carefully tucked the fruit into a secure pouch on his tactical belt. "Your mother raised a truly remarkable daughter. We are honored to see you safely home."

As Casia and Evaria walked toward the transport pod, the bravado the thirteen-year-old had summoned began to fray. As the heavy door of the pod slid open, a small, muffled sob escaped her. She did not look back—not because she did not want to, but because she was sticking to the pact. *No games.*

Malachi watched until the pod hissed shut and disappeared into the transit tunnel, leaving him alone in the quiet of the corridor.

A few moments later, the soft hum of an adjacent lift announced Dr. Zachari's physical arrival from the administrative wing. He stepped out to join Dr. Klorioa and Malachi. Malachi nodded at them, pulling his shoulders back into the formal, unyielding posture of a historian preparing for a public defense.

"This is the tactical plan," Zachari spoke first, his tone shifting into the authoritative cadence of an administrator. "We will stand with you. We will field the medical questions if you choose to disclose exactly what happened to Seraphina."

"Please, you do not have to do this for me. I can handle all of this on my own," Malachi assured the doctors, his pride and sense of duty momentarily flaring.

"Malachi, the media is going to be ruthless and insistent on the details," Klorioa implored, stepping closer to ensure he heard the logic in her voice. "Let us field the medical facts."

Malachi paused and then nodded slowly in agreement. He realized she was entirely correct; the absolute last thing he wanted to do was step up to a podium and fracture under the raw, volatile emotions currently churning inside him. Having the doctors there as a scientific shield was the smartest tactical move.

The heavy doors of the medical enclave hissed open, instantly shattering the quiet sanctuary of the hospital. A cavernous roar of shouting reporters and the chaotic swarm of hovering recording drones flooded the entryway. Outside, the subterranean air was thick, heated by the sheer mass of the crowd pressing against the front of the facility. A small, naturally cut rock podium had been hastily positioned just beyond the enclave's quartz arches. A strict perimeter of hospital security and local authorities stood shoulder-to-shoulder, using their physical bulk to hold back the surging throng of journalists who were shouting questions into the noise.

Malachi moved toward the podium with heavy, measured steps, his sharp yellow eyes fixed straight ahead. Dr. Zachari and Dr. Klorioa flanked him tightly on either side, establishing a secure physical barrier. As the swarm of drones pressed closer, capturing the grim reality of Malachi's hollowed expression, Zachari exchanged a sharp, annoyed look with Klorioa. They had both witnessed this cold spectacle before; they knew exactly how ruthless the press became when a high-profile tragedy struck their community.

As Malachi finally placed his hands on the cold stone of the podium, the authorities forcefully pushed a persistent reporter back behind the barricade, ensuring the grieving historian and his medical team remained safely insulated.

"I am going to be brief and direct with you all," Malachi began, his deep, resonant voice instantly cutting through the chaotic roar of the crowd. A sudden, tense hush fell over the atrium.

"First, I must publicly thank Dr. Zachari and Dr. Klorioa for their relentless efforts today," Malachi stated, his voice ringing with absolute clarity. "However, despite doing everything within their medical power, they were unable to save my beloved Seraphina. It is with profound sorrow that I confirm she has passed away due to the catastrophic injuries she sustained during the attack at the educational enclave this morning."

He stopped, his tall frame tightening as the crushing reality of his own words threatened to shatter his composure. He gripped the edges of the rock podium, grounding his sharp intellect to the cold, solid stone beneath his hands.

"I have never asked anything of the media," Malachi continued, forcing the words past the tightness in his throat. "I know you have a multitude of questions regarding the attack. But I only know this absolute truth: life is precious, and once it is extinguished, it cannot be undone. Therefore, I am asking you to give my family the personal space and dignity required for us to mourn."

He stared out at the mass of expectant journalists, bracing himself for the inevitable onslaught of shouted inquiries.

Instead, a slow ripple of movement washed over the crowd. One by one, the hardened reporters lowered their recording devices. In a profound, silent display of communal reverence, the entire assembly of journalists bowed their heads.

Beside him, Dr. Klorioa and Dr. Zachari exchanged a look of genuine, absolute astonishment. They had spent their entire careers watching the media dissect tragedy, and yet here, faced with the sheer dignity of their premier historian, the press had completely surrendered their aggression.

Almost.

"Is it true one of her students—a boy named Omri who was held back a year for slow learning—did this to her? Does he have PCR?"

The harsh, sudden question shattered the reverence. Malachi looked down at the source—a small, bald Morlock with greyish-blue-green skin, aggressively holding up a recording device. Malachi shook his head in absolute disgust; his anger directed not at the absent boy whose mind had been ravaged by the disease, but at the sheer cruelty of the reporter's ambition.

"Listen carefully," Malachi warned, steadying his deep voice. Against the cold stone of the podium, his hand began to physically tremble. Dr. Zachari immediately noticed the subtle tremor and shifted his weight, preparing to step in and intervene.

"I was not there. I do not know the exact details of what happened in that classroom," Malachi stated, his tone rising with an unshakable, commanding authority. "But I will tell you this: do not blame the boy. PCR is a genetic disease. It is a biological shear that has only been surfacing over the past fifty to one hundred years. You yourself could possess the markers. Do not assume Omri is an isolated anomaly. Any of us could have it."

He let the heavy, terrifying logic of that truth settle over the crowd before delivering his final strike.

"This stark reality is exactly why Dr. Klorioa authorized the mass release of Regrestat this morning. She is the hero of this cycle. Do not use my wife's death to incite a panic that will spread through the global subterranean caverns we all live in. Panic will only invite the Eloi to tighten their grip on us."

With that flawless, tactical pivot, Malachi stepped back from the podium and extended his hand, motioning for Dr. Klorioa to take his place. It was a brilliantly calculated move. By responding with pure, logical compassion for the boy, Malachi had entirely disarmed the aggressive reporter and seamlessly shifted the spotlight onto the science of the cure.

"PCR is fundamentally a genetic degradation," Dr. Klorioa stated, her voice projecting with absolute clinical authority. "Specifically, it is an epigenetic mutation manifesting along chromosomal sequence 1543. We have been mapping its degenerative pathways for decades. Panic is a useless biological response. We will isolate this genomic abnormality and reverse the sequencing errors."

She swept her piercing eyes across the gathered crowd, ensuring every hovering recording drone captured the absolute gravity of her next statement.

"Every single Morlock carries the dormant markers for this condition. It is woven directly into the foundational strands of our DNA and RNA. This is not a new contagion. My clinical data strongly suggests this mutation is a dormant genomic echo from our ancient past—dating back at least one hundred and thirty-nine millennia. It is an evolutionary remnant."

She leaned slightly toward the audio receptors, her tone shifting seamlessly from the purely scientific into a fierce, unyielding pride.

"As I stated this morning when we authorized the Regrestat treatments, we cannot afford medical complacency. When this gene actively shears, it aggressively degrades the higher cognitive functions, forcefully devolving the host into a primal, savage state. But we will not succumb to our biology. We are highly intelligent. We are scientifically capable. We are Morlocks."

With that absolute, scientifically irrefutable, and culturally rousing declaration, the press conference effectively ended. She had given them exactly what they needed: the cold, hard science of the disease and the unwavering strength of their people. No one dared to shout another question. One by one, the reporters shut down their drones, turned, and respectfully dispersed, leaving the rock podium in complete silence.

Malachi and the two doctors turned away from the silent stone concourse, walking back through the heavy quartz arches and into the secure, climate-controlled quiet of the medical enclave.

"I have never seen the press back down like that," Zachari said, his voice echoing slightly in the corridor as he shook his head in disbelief. "When tragedy strikes someone of your standing, they are usually merciless. They want to tear apart every single detail. Instead, you completely disarmed them."

Dr. Klorioa nodded in agreement, her eyes reflecting a deep respect as Malachi looked at them.

"You were right, Dr. Klorioa," Malachi said, his deep voice exhausted but steady. "The absolute truth is the only mechanism that can halt the spread of further tragedy. Seraphina would have agreed with your approach. I appreciate the counsel you gave me. I honestly did not expect them to be merciful."

"You commanded their respect by simply demanding it," Klorioa replied softly.

They reached the junction that led down to the private subterranean transport bays. Zachari stopped and placed a firm, reassuring hand on Malachi's shoulder.

"Go home to your daughter," Zachari instructed gently. "I give you my absolute word as the Administrator: Seraphina will remain perfectly preserved in the stasis field within the secure ward. We will hold her safely and respectfully until you are ready to formally decide on the funeral arrangements."

"Thank you. Both of you. For everything," Malachi said, offering them one final, deeply solemn nod before he turned and descended into the transport bay.

The high-speed pod ride back to his residential sector was a blur of dark tunnels and luminescent transit lights. When the doors hissed open at his private platform, Malachi stepped out and walked the short distance to his front door. The biometric scanner registered his presence, and the heavy door unsealed with a familiar, quiet click.

He stepped inside.

Logically, his brilliant mind knew the house was occupied. He could see Casia's travel cloak draped over a chair, and he could hear the faint, comforting hum of the environmental recyclers. He knew his daughter and his wife's best friend were resting somewhere deep within the rooms.

But as the heavy door sealed shut behind him, the historian was struck by a devastating, physical weight. The house was entirely empty. The vibrant, stabilizing energy that Seraphina had always brought into these rooms was simply gone, leaving behind a cold, suffocating void. He stood in the entryway of his own home, surrounded by his ancient artifacts and historical texts, feeling more isolated than he had ever been in his entire life.

He walked deeper into the quiet home. On the central table, he noticed Casia's woven bag, the remaining violet Peachberries and the unusual new redberries still resting inside.

He moved silently down the hall and paused at the threshold of Evaria's room. Casia had not left the young Morlock's side. Exhausted by the sheer emotional trauma of the cycle, Casia had fallen deeply asleep in the large, cushioned stone chair where Malachi normally sat to settle Evaria for her rest cycle. She was already physically and emotionally fulfilling the heavy mandate of the Rite of Guardianship.

Watching them, Malachi winced, a devastating surge of yearning for Seraphina tightening his chest. Seeing Casia instantly step in to protect his daughter was a profound relief, but it also forced his exhausted intellect to confront a paralyzing dilemma. Malachi was a fiercely devoted man. Seraphina had been his only companion since their early educational cycles; he had never even considered courting another female. He had absolutely no emotional framework for how to navigate a sudden, legally bound relationship. Looking at Casia—a woman who loved his wife like a sister and who had grounded him through the dark days of his father's passing—he felt a deep, overwhelming wave of respect. She was sacrificing her own autonomy out of pure loyalty to his family. He silently vowed that he would proceed with absolute honor, determined never to take advantage of her grief or their shared tragedy as they tried to figure out this new reality.

Malachi let out a slow, silent breath. As a lifelong scholar of their past, he possessed an encyclopedic knowledge of his people. He deeply respected the complex customs the Morlocks had embraced and preserved over hundreds of thousands of years of lost and found history. But academically documenting those ancient traditions was entirely different from rigorously practicing them.

He had never been a strictly traditional man in his personal life. Having this specific, ancient rite suddenly thrust upon his household—dictating the very structure of his family—felt both alien and overwhelming.

He walked into his own bedroom, quietly sliding the heavy door shut, though he left it open just a fraction of an inch to listen for his daughter. He stepped into the dim quiet of his closet and knelt, reaching for a smooth, pure white stone resting on a secure shelf. Etched elegantly across its surface was a single name: Seraphina.

It was the Mourning Aeterna stone.

He stared at it, his entirely average frame bracing against the devastating reality of actually holding it. In their subterranean culture, the stone served as a formal holographic Last Will and Testament—a deeply personal recording created by every Morlock to impart their final legal directives and emotional goodbyes to the loved ones they eventually left behind. Though it was a standard, logical part of their life cycle, it was the one historical artifact he had prayed he would not have to activate for many more decades.

His hands, which he had fought so hard to keep steady against the cold stone of the podium, now trembled completely out of his control. Malachi pressed his thumb against the activation surface. With a soft, humming chime, the white stone flared to life, projecting the gentle, vivid holographic image of Seraphina into the quiet shadows of the room.

"Malachi, my beloved soulmate," the holographic projection spoke. "If I have left you to go beyond the veil of our world, know it was not your fault."

He shook his head, a visceral wince tightening his features. Her voice was light and completely full of warmth—exactly like the day she first told him she loved him. The acoustic fidelity of the stone was mercilessly perfect.

Sitting on the floor just outside the dim closet, he glanced inward. His eyes caught the smooth surface of his own Mourning Aeterna stone resting on the shelf, sitting completely alone next to the small, empty space where hers had always been kept. *It should have been me,* he thought quietly. For a terrifying second, he felt the edges of his mind beginning to turn *Hollow* under the crushing weight of his survivor's guilt. But he forced himself to shake it off, gripping the edge of the shelf as he turned his full attention back to her voice.

"You have a responsibility only to our daughter now. No one else." She smiled gently, adjusting the bundle in her arms to reveal Evaria as a tiny infant. Malachi's breath hitched; his sharp mind instantly calculated the timeline. This recording was made thirteen years ago, just after Evaria was born.

"I watched you graduate with top honors from our academies," Seraphina continued, her warm eyes looking directly into the lens, transcending time. "I was there when your father watched us take our vows, and I held your hand when he passed. I never thought I would be able to have a child, Malachi. The healers told me it was impossible. But I did. Now, I am holding our daughter, and she is our absolute bundle of starlight."

Her expression grew serious, yet remained infinitely tender. "Malachi, you are brave, strong, fearless, and humble. You are devoted. But I need you to remember not to let the accomplishments you have achieved, or the ones you will achieve in the future, cloud your judgment. I know how you get when you dive deeply into your historical excavations. I know how the Eloi constantly reprimand your findings and try to diminish your work."

She paused, leaning slightly forward as if to imprint the next words directly onto his soul. "*Do not let them Hollow you out.* You know what that word means in our culture. It is a state to be avoided at all costs—to be rendered 'without significance.' You are significant, Malachi."

Tears finally broke past his rigid control, tracking silently down his face.

"I may be with the ancients now, in the great beyond the veil of life," she whispered. "But you... you are the shining moonlight that all Morlocks need right here, right now, in a timeline that so often feels distorted."

A heavy, ragged sob tore from Malachi's chest.

"This is not goodbye. This is only a temporary time of waiting for you. Do good, my beloved." She held baby Evaria up to the faint illumination of the projection, offering one last, profoundly warm smile. Then, her solemn expression broke into a soft, playful grin as she looked slightly off-camera.

"Okay, Casia, turn the stone off. No, the rune on the left... you have to press it, not swipe it. Oh, by the ancients, just give it here—"

The holographic projection abruptly cut out, softly fading into the ether and leaving the white stone dark and silent.

In the sudden, heavy quiet of the closet, Malachi heard a faint intake of breath. He looked up and noticed Casia standing in the narrow crack of the partially opened doorway. She was weeping silently, her hand covering her mouth. Malachi had no idea how long she had been standing there, but he immediately recognized the profound depth of her mourning—it mirrored the exact, shattering sorrow she had shared with him when his own father had passed.

But now, another layer of understanding washed over him. He realized that Casia had been there, thirteen years ago, helping his wife record her most intimate, final testament. She had been a true, faithful friend to Seraphina even in the quietest, most solemn moments of their lives. A profound, newfound respect for her settled deep into his grieving heart. He finally understood why Seraphina had trusted Casia with the Guardianship Rite.

The ancient Rite of Guardianship had firmly bound them together. Wiping his face, Malachi gently placed the white stone back on the shelf. He stood and walked over to where Casia was standing in the narrow crack of the doorway. He desperately needed to be there for her, just as she was already there for his daughter. He guided her out of the dim shadows of the closet, leading her to the small, cushioned bench resting at the foot of his bed. Exhausted and shattered, they sat down side by side.

Beneath her profound mourning lay a stark, unmistakable apprehension. Her posture was rigid under the crushing, immediate weight of her new reality. Her tear-filled eyes reflected a desperate, silent fear—not merely of failing to protect them, but of the overwhelming, absolute intimacy the ancient mandate required. In their culture, the Rite was a profound, spiritual bonding of souls. It demanded that she step naturally and completely into the sacred, all-encompassing role of a mother to Evaria, and ultimately, a devoted wife and soulmate to him.

"Malachi, I am frightened," Casia whispered, her voice breaking as she looked down at her hands. "I remember making that recording. I remember how much she laughed when I pressed the wrong rune on the stone. And just this morning... we were sitting in the educator's lounge, talking about how fast Evaria is growing up. It feels like a completely different lifetime."

She paused, her tear-filled emerald eyes lifting to meet his with profound vulnerability. "I spent my life as her sister in spirit. And I have always loved you, Malachi, but as a mentor. As a trusted guide. I was there through the dark cycles of your depression when your father passed, and I have stood beside you both to celebrate your greatest joys. I respect you immensely."

She looked back down, her shoulders trembling under the heavy burden. "But I do not know the intimate ins and outs of who you are behind closed doors. Not like this. Not in the way this ancient law demands. I know this is what Seraphina wanted. She trusted me, and I absolutely cannot fail her, or you, or Evaria."

She hesitated, her breathing shallow as she struggled to voice her immediate terror. She had no idea what he expected of her in this exact moment. If he demanded they consummate the Rite tonight to finalize the bond, she did not know if she could, and she feared refusing him would cause irreparable problems before their fractured family even began to heal.

"Please... do not be upset with me for declaring the vow so quickly at the hospital," Casia continued, her voice trembling. "I just... I do not know how you want to proceed with... us."

Malachi let out a slow, exhausted breath. He turned to look at her, his expression entirely gentle and free of any rigid expectation.

"Casia, listen to me," Malachi said softly, his deep voice thick with his own unresolved grief. "I hold an immense amount of respect for you. I hope you do not feel rejected by what I am about to say, but I am absolutely not ready to jump into the physical or spiritual logistics of these ancient customs. I want to honor my wife's wishes and make this family work, but I am terrified, too."

He managed a weak, self-deprecating smile. "I know I am the Premier Historian. I know the rest of Morlock society believes I rigidly observe every ancient tradition our ancestors ever documented. But the honest truth? I only study them. Actually, practicing them is exhausting."

Casia blinked, the crushing tension instantly evaporating from her shoulders. A startled, genuine half-smile broke through her tears.

"Seraphina always told me you were not one hundred percent on board with the ancient customs," Casia whispered, letting out a wet, breathless laugh. "I always thought she was just joking about you. By the ancients... she was not."

"Not even slightly," Malachi agreed, a small measure of warmth returning to his chest at the mention of his wife's sharp humor. "We will take everything exactly at the pace we need. You are here, and right now, that is enough. Over the next few cycles, we can gradually move your belongings here, and we will respectfully pack away Seraphina's things together to make room." He offered a gentle, tired smile. "Though, I must ask you to go slowly—my historical texts and artifacts are already severely running out of shelf space."

Casia looked at him and nodded gently, a soft laugh escaping her as the profound relief settled into her emerald eyes.

At that exact moment, Evaria ran into the bedroom, tears already welling in her eyes. She had woken up from a sudden nightmare, though her mind had already discarded the fragmented details. But as she stopped in the doorway and saw Casia sitting with Malachi, the stark reality set in. The undeniable truth that her mother was no longer alive in this room, or anywhere else, finalized itself in her sharp mind.

With a quiet, heartbroken sob, the thirteen-year-old rushed forward, burying her face into Malachi's side.

He knelt immediately, slipping off the edge of the bench and wrapping his arms securely around his daughter, while Casia reached out and rested a comforting hand on Evaria's back.

"I am here, Evaria. We are both here," Malachi said, his deep voice dropping into a steady, factual cadence to provide her the stability she desperately needed. "I know this reality is agonizing. But listen to me. Tomorrow morning, I will transmit a message to my colleagues at the historical archives to take a brief leave of absence. Then, I will begin the formal preparations for your mother's funeral. Once I have secured the proper arrangements with the administration, I will share the details with everyone. But for tonight, there are no more tasks. Tonight, we simply stay together."

The morning cycle began not with the warmth of the sun, but with the sterile, automated brightening of the subterranean luminescent panels. Malachi sat at the central table, his frame hunched slightly over a sleek, crystalline data-pad. He was meticulously drafting the formal digital petition for Seraphina's burial.

Casia stood near the thermal unit, preparing a small meal of synthesized oats, violet Peachberries, and the strange, sweet red fruit. The heavy, suffocating sorrow of the previous day still lingered in the quiet corners of the house, but the absolute necessity of survival had forced them into motion.

Soft footsteps echoed in the corridor. Evaria walked into the main room, her dark hair neatly brushed. Despite the immense trauma her young mind was processing, she carried herself with a quiet, deliberate control—a direct reflection of both her father's logic and her mother's grace.

She walked over to Malachi and peered down at the glowing ancient Morlock script he was carefully sequencing across the screen.

"You are requesting the Rite of the Ancients," Evaria observed, her amber eyes scanning the digital text. "The surface ocean."

"I am," Malachi replied softly, deactivating his light-stylus and setting it down. He looked up at his daughter. "Your mother loved the historical texts about the night sky. I intend to take her to the surface elevators. We will place her on a ceremonial vessel and let the fire carry her out into the water, under the stars, just as the Kings of Old did."

Casia stopped stirring the oats. She set the spoon down with a soft, definitive click and turned to face him.

"Malachi," Casia said, her tone laced with a dry, protective skepticism. "You know I want that for her just as much as you do. But you are dealing with the Eloi. They view the surface as their pristine Garden, and they view us strictly as the Root. You know exactly what the Administrator told you when you asked for this same honor for your father."

Malachi's jaw tightened at the memory. "My father before me was once the Premier Historian of this region before he became an Ambassador. I have the cultural leverage and the historical precedent to force them to grant an exception."

"They do not care about our history, Malachi," Casia countered bluntly, walking over to the table. She wasn't trying to be cruel; she was trying to shield him from another devastating blow. "They denied your father the surface because they consider our dead to be organic waste that must be processed in the subterranean incinerators. What logical reason do you have to believe they will look at you, or Seraphina, any differently?"

Before Malachi could answer, Evaria reached out and gently placed her small hand over his.

"Because Mother was a hero," Evaria said, her voice completely steady, exhibiting a profound emotional intelligence that momentarily stunned them both. "And because the Eloi know better than to argue with the man who holds all of their ancient secrets. You should go, Father. Make them let her see the stars."

Malachi looked down at his daughter's hand, drawing an immense, grounding strength from her bravery. He gave her a single, resolute nod.

"I will secure the appointment at the Neutral Hub this morning," Malachi stated, sealing the data-file with a swift gesture. "I will not let them deny her this."

"Evaria, I completely support this," Casia said, her tone softening as she looked at the thirteen-year-old. "I am simply saying we need a secondary contingency if the Eloi resort to their rigid, arrogant extremes. That is all I am trying to warn you both about. Please do not view my caution as taking their side. I am only voicing a practical concern."

Across the table, Malachi quietly drew his own bowl closer. He looked up, his deep voice carrying nothing but profound gratitude. "We know exactly whose side you are on, Casia," he assured her softly.

Evaria picked up her spoon, offering a small, sharp smirk to break the lingering tension. "It is entirely obvious. If you were secretly working for the Eloi, Casia, you would have made Father fill out five digital requisition forms and four more just to sit at the table."

Casia blinked, caught entirely off guard, before a short, breathy laugh escaped her. The heavy, protective walls she had put up instantly dissolved.

Malachi let out a quiet exhale of genuine amusement. "Yes, precisely nine forms," he agreed, his deep voice carrying a rare, dry sarcasm. He looked at Evaria, a small, tired smile actually reaching his sharp yellow eyes. "You consistently say things that make me wonder exactly how sharp your intellect truly is. Thank you for making me laugh, Evaria."

He took a slow bite of his meal, pausing as the unique, vibrant sweetness of the strange red fruit registered on his palate. It was a sharp, pure contrast to the heavy sorrow filling the room. "This is... remarkable," he admitted, looking down at his bowl.

Evaria took a bite of hers and nodded, a faint, genuine smile touching her lips for the first time since she had woken. "It is delicious."

Casia relaxed her rigid posture slightly, picking up her own spoon to eat. "Relania told me the agricultural sector is already preparing for mass cultivation. This ancient red fruit will be on the distribution shelves for all Morlocks very soon."

Evaria scooped up another vibrant red piece. "Yep," she said, her tone carrying a quiet pride in remembering the lesson from the gardens yesterday. "Just like Relania showed us. This is the secret as to why our Peachberries are so good. They finally brought the ancestor fruit back."

Malachi found a small, necessary measure of comfort in the shared food, the quiet solidarity of their newly formed family, and the brief, sharp clarity of his daughter's intact memory. It was exactly the grounding he needed before he sealed his digital petition and departed for the Neutral Hub.

Malachi had been sitting in the neutral lounge for two agonizing hours, waiting for the doors to Minister Fena's chamber to finally open. The ground-level view outside the massive window was undeniably magnificent, though the sheer perfection of it felt like a quiet, deliberate insult to his grief.

The glass was laced with a highly advanced chromatic filter. Inside his waiting area, the harsh, burning daylight was completely neutralized, rendering the room's atmosphere into a soothing, Morlock-friendly palette of deep greys and obsidian blacks. Yet, through the specialized tint, the vibrant colors of the Eloi's surface world bled through with flawless clarity.

He looked out at the pristine, genetically manicured "Garden." He could see the brilliant, burning aura of the sun illuminating the sky, though his brilliant mind knew far better than to stare directly at the star, even with the window's protection. High above the horizon, a pale, partially illuminated moon hung quietly in the daylight, a ghostly, ancient sentinel in the vast expanse of blue.

Beneath it all, slender trees with smooth, dark wooden bark swayed in a perfectly regulated breeze, their silver-blue leaves shimmering like liquid metal. Clusters of prismatic flowers bloomed across the impossibly green grass, and flocks of iridescent birds darted gracefully between the flawless, pearlescent spires of the Eloi architecture.

Then, a low, acoustic rumble vibrated deep through the floorboards.

Malachi frowned. His formidable mind, encyclopedic in its grasp of Earth's ancient atmospheric history, identified the sound immediately: thunder.

As he watched, the perfect blue sky began to fracture. Heavy, bruised clouds aggressively moved in, swallowing the sunlight. The regulated breeze swiftly escalated into a turbulent wind. The smooth-barked trees began to sway wildly, shedding clusters of their silver-blue leaves, which whipped frantically through the darkening air. The flocks of iridescent birds abruptly scattered, diving for cover against the pearlescent buildings.

Malachi stood perfectly still, captivated by the chaos. He had read countless historical texts about atmospheric shifts, but actually witnessing the terrifying, chaotic majesty of the weather changing for the very first time in his life left him momentarily breathless.

Before he could fully process the storm, the heavy doors to the inner chamber finally hissed open.

Minister Fena walked in. She was draped in flowing, iridescent fabrics, her posture radiating the effortless, absolute privilege of the Eloi. She took her seat on the brightly lit side of the neutral hub, looking across the invisible optical barrier into Malachi's dimmed section.

"Minister Fena," Malachi began, sitting forward as his deep voice carried the undeniable weight of his grief. "I am here because my wife, Seraphina, passed away yesterday cycle due to a sudden, catastrophic shear of—"

CRACK.

A jagged, brilliant fork of lightning shattered the darkened sky. The advanced chromatic filter of the window, designed to slowly regulate the steady, predictable arc of the sun, was entirely incapable of suppressing the microsecond burst of pure atmospheric electricity. The flash breached the glass like an unshielded energy flare detonating in a pitch-black room.

Malachi flinched, entirely caught off guard. His highly sensitive yellow eyes seared from the sudden, intense light, forcing him to squeeze them shut. He gripped the edges of the table as a sharp spike of physical pain shot through his skull.

Across the invisible barrier, Minister Fena paused. A deeply puzzled expression crossed her flawless features. To an Eloi, a thunderstorm was simply a mundane, natural event. She did not comprehend that the historian had just witnessed lightning for the very first time. For a fleeting second, her gaze hardened, looking at him as though he were some unpredictable, subterranean monster.

Then, smoothing her features into a mask of calculated diplomacy, she leaned forward.

"Oh, Malachi," Fena cooed, her voice dripping with a soft, perfectly manufactured sympathy. "I heard the news about the subterranean school. It is an absolute tragedy. You have my deepest, most sincere condolences for your terrible loss. I cannot imagine the pain you are feeling right now."

Malachi blinked the burning afterimage from his eyes, forcing his composure to return. He drew on his rigid discipline to push past the physical pain, grounding himself in history.

"Thank you, Minister," Malachi said, keeping his tone carefully steady. "Because of her immense sacrifice, I am formally requesting an exemption to the stratum processing laws. I want to give my wife a proper burial on the surface ocean. The Rite of the Ancients. Exactly as Chancellor Olesya received sometime after the year 500,020 AD, though the exact date has been lost to the vast expansion of time."

Outside, the storm finally broke. Heavy sheets of rain began to relentlessly lash against the massive glass.

Minister Fena stared at him through the invisible barrier. For a long, agonizing moment, the room was filled only with the drumming sound of the torrential rain.

And then, Minister Fena began to laugh.

It wasn't a booming laugh, but a light, airy, utterly dismissive chuckle that was infinitely crueler. Her sympathetic facade vanished in an instant, replaced by the cold, absolute arrogance of the Garden.

"The surface ocean?" Fena asked, wiping a tear of genuine amusement from her eye. She leaned back, the pristine lighting of her chamber casting sterile, uncaring shadows across her face. "Malachi, do you actually hear yourself? Chancellor Olesya was a historical anomaly who served the Eloi. Your wife was a casualty of your own diseased, subterranean biology."

She gestured dismissively toward the floor, her tone dropping into a flat, bureaucratic absolute that seemed to freeze the very air between them. "The law is unequivocal. The Garden is for the living. Organic waste remains in the Root. Request denied."

Malachi looked at her in absolute shock. For a fleeting second, the sheer, unapologetic cruelty of her dismissal was eclipsed by her staggering historical ignorance. He leaned forward, his formidable intellect instantly weaponizing the absolute truth against her arrogance.

"Minister," Malachi began, his deep voice dropping into a low, commanding rumble. "Chancellor Olesya was a Morlock. You do not even know your own history."

He pressed his hands flat against the table, his sharp yellow eyes locking onto hers through the invisible barrier. "She brokered a fragile peace with your people after a catastrophic disaster nearly eradicated your entire species. How can you possibly sit there and claim she served the Eloi, when she is the very reason you survived?"

He studied her intently. The absolute conviction in his deep voice seemed to physically rattle her. For a fraction of a second, the Eloi Minister looked genuinely nervous, her flawless, arrogant composure slipping into visible shock.

But Fena recovered quickly, her momentary fear hardening into defensive rage.

"Let me make myself clear," Fena snapped, her voice rising sharply, stripping away any illusion of diplomatic grace. "There is zero historical evidence that Chancellor Olesya was a Morlock! In fact, her physical form was completely destroyed shortly after this so-called 'catastrophic disaster' that you have been claiming happened for almost two decades!"

She leaned closer to the optical barrier, her face flushed with anger. "How dare you! How dare you come to the Neutral Hub knowing your species is actively mutating from a genetic disease! You do not even know if it is contagious to us! Why do you think I made you sit in that room for two hours? Why?"

"Because you are arrogant," Malachi shot back, his deep, resonant voice easily overpowering hers as the tension in the chamber boiled over. "And because your complete lack of scientific understanding dictated an irrational fear of contagion."

Fena's flushed face suddenly went entirely still. The heated, defensive rage drained away, replaced by a mask of absolute, icy disgust. When she spoke again, she didn't shout. She lowered her voice to a venomous, slicing whisper that carried the full, crushing weight of Eloi supremacy.

"I have never been spoken down to by a feral, subterranean savage," Fena hissed, her eyes narrowing with pure contempt. "You are a dying breed, Malachi. Never forget that your place is permanently confined to the subterranean dirt beneath our feet."

A crushing surge of fury spiked in Malachi's chest. His hands curled into tight fists against the table, his intellect fiercely clashing with the primal, biological urge to shatter the invisible barrier between them. He opened his mouth to unleash his absolute wrath—

But he never spoke the words.

Outside the massive window, the torrential rain abruptly stopped. The chaotic storm simply broke, moving past the Garden as swiftly as it had arrived. The bruising clouds parted, allowing a single, brilliant shaft of sunlight to pierce through the gloom and strike the glass.

Drifting lazily through that beam of light was a butterfly.

Malachi's breath hitched. His encyclopedic mind instantly identified it: a Holly Blue. Yet, after hundreds of thousands of years of survival and evolution, its delicate, azure wings now emitted a faint, breathtaking bioluminescence. It fluttered gracefully against the wet glass, completely untouched by the pure hatred inside the chamber he was in, before ascending back toward the endless blue sky.

The quiet beauty of those radiant wings struck Malachi with the force of a physical blow.

Do not let them Hollow you out.

Seraphina's gentle, echoing voice from the Mourning Aeterna stone flooded his mind. She had explicitly warned him about this exact moment. She knew the Eloi would constantly try to diminish his work and his spirit. She had begged him not to let them drag him down into a suffocating abyss of hatred where he would lose his own significance.

If he allowed Fena's vile, prejudiced poison to strip away his intellect—if he let himself scream and rage like the feral savage she desperately wanted him to be—he would be betraying his wife's final, sacred mandate.

Malachi slowly uncurled his fists. He pressed his palms flat against the table and pushed himself up, drawing his frame to its full height. The feral anger completely vanished from his piercing yellow eyes, replaced by a cold, unshakable dignity that no Eloi could ever strip away from him.

Malachi looked at her. Through the invisible barrier, he could see a sudden, fleeting flicker of genuine fear in her eyes. He thought about her vile words. *You are a dying breed, Malachi.* He slowly straightened his shoulders, adjusting the dark, heavy fabric of his black robe and the formal purple sash of his station. He gave her a single, measured nod, his deep voice dropping to a low, chilling calm.

"If we Morlocks truly are the dying savages you claim," Malachi stated, letting the crushing weight of his truth settle over her, "then who will clothe you? Who will manufacture the pristine comforts you take for granted while you casually curse us into extinction?"

He watched the stark reality of his words strike her.

"You reside here in the light... but we are the foundation that keeps you from falling into the dark," he continued softly. "I responded to your cruelty with dignity. Ask yourself which one of us is truly feral. I am sorry for troubling you, Minister Fena."

He turned his back on her, fully intending to walk out of the chamber, when something completely unexpected happened.

"Premier Historian Malachi... wait."

Malachi paused, his hand hovering over the door seal. A soft, electronic hum vibrated through the chamber as the invisible optical barrier abruptly powered down. The stark division between the brightly lit Garden and his dimmed waiting area vanished.

When he slowly turned back around, the crushing emotional toll of the cycle finally fractured his iron control, and a single, silent tear slipped down his face. He was entirely unprepared for what he saw. The Eloi Minister was no longer glaring at him from the safety of her pristine enclave. She was walking directly toward him, stepping effortlessly into the dim, Morlock-friendly shadows of his side of the room. She was completely unafraid, her flawless features tightened by a profound, unmistakable shame.

She stopped just a few feet away from him, close enough that he could see the slight, nervous tremor in her hands.

"I... I am sorry," Fena whispered, the admission visibly costing her. She looked up, meeting his sharp yellow eyes directly, with no barrier to protect her. In that quiet, unprecedented proximity, Malachi realized that the ancient spark of their shared ancestry had not been completely extinguished. Beneath the cold, manufactured arrogance of the Garden, a genuine empathy still survived.

"I allowed the deeply ingrained prejudices of my superiors to overpower my own conscience," Fena confessed, her voice thick with regret. "There are, indeed, classified records—archives that are strictly sealed from the public—which support the fact that Chancellor Olesya was a Morlock. She showed immense compassion to the surface, and in return, brokered the peace after whatever catastrophe occurred... a catastrophe that remains a mystery to us even now."

Malachi stood in stunned silence, his formidable intellect rapidly processing the sheer magnitude of an Eloi Minister openly crossing the room to admit to suppressed history.

"What I said to you just now was cruel," Fena continued, her voice steadying with sudden resolve. "I will permit the burial for your wife, Seraphina. But you must understand the perilous political reality of this. It will have to take place at the Southern Sea, and it must be done strictly at night. Keep it incredibly small. You will be watched by my security perimeter, but we will not interfere with you or the Rite of the Ancients."

She offered him a look of solemn respect, reaching her hand out slightly before letting it fall back to her side.

"You cannot expect everyone else on the surface to suddenly change, Malachi, or even want to change," she said softly. "But thank you for reminding me that, although we are separate species, we still bleed red."

With that, Minister Fena turned and quietly exited the inner chamber, leaving Malachi alone in the dim light.

A soft chime resonated from his pocket. Malachi slowly pulled out his crystalline data-pad. The official, digitally sealed approval from the Eloi Administration was already illuminated on the screen. His thumb swiped across the glass, expanding the heavily encrypted fine print attached to the bottom of the permit:

Only your daughter and one other may accompany you. The rite must occur under the full moon. Please specify your exact coordinates. I will personally ensure no one disturbs you. The coastal area will be sealed off, and you will be escorted directly to the water. Seraphina's remains will be treated with absolute respect and secured upon the ceremonial barge prior to your arrival. Be fast, and make absolutely certain you understand this is a one-time exemption.

Malachi read the words twice, the crushing, defensive tension finally leaving his exhausted frame. He had done it. He had secured Seraphina the stars. And he would return her to them on a full, moonlit night, a beautiful, devastating realization of the final message she had spoken to him through the Aeterna stone. For he was her shining moonlight, and she would forever be his starlight.

He raised his hand and wiped the lingering moisture from his sharp yellow eyes. He looked back toward the massive window just in time to see the radiant Holly Blue butterfly flutter upward, leaving the glass and ascending freely into the endless blue sky.

Securing his data-pad within his black robes, the Premier Historian turned and proceeded back toward the transit elevators, descending into the subterranean dark to bring the victorious news to his family.

They waited in quiet, agonizing solidarity for the lunar phase to peak.

When the night of the full moon finally arrived, the solemn journey to the surface elevators began. For all thirty-eight miles, the transit tunnels were lined with tens of thousands of Morlocks. The media was present, but there was no shouting, no aggressive swarming, and no intrusive hovering of recording drones. The journalists stood among the crowds in absolute, crushing silence. They were still in profound shock from his press conference earlier in the week, deeply moved by the way Malachi had projected such a humble, unshakable strength even while his own grief was so visibly raw. Workers, scholars, agriculturalists, and engineers stood shoulder-to-shoulder with them on the tiered walkways, bowing their heads in deep, quiet respect as the Premier Historian and his shattered family passed by.

The cavernous transit arteries were normally illuminated by a utilitarian spectrum of shifting colors, but tonight, the entire thirty-eight-mile stretch had been manually overridden. The tunnels were bathed in a deep, resonant purple.

It was the exact shade of the formal sash Malachi had worn across his black robes every single cycle since he first addressed the media. The massive crowds had no way of knowing that the sash was a private, deeply personal gift from Evaria to her father; to the Morlock people, the color had simply become the living symbol of his unyielding defense of their species. By shifting the subterranean power grid to that specific light, the engineers and citizens were honoring him with the absolute reverence of ancient royalty. Yet, they all inherently understood the absolute truth: Malachi was not a king, nor did he desire any such absolute power over them. He was simply a Morlock who had held the line.

Against that endless, solemn sea of purple light, the only other illumination came from tens of thousands of brilliant yellow and orange eyes, watching the procession with quiet gratitude.

When the ceremonial transport finally reached the heavy, reinforced blast doors of the Southern Sea surface elevator, the massive crowd stopped at the boundary. They inherently understood the political reality of the Eloi's strict mandate. The Morlocks remained in the dark, holding their silent vigil, as the heavy blast doors hissed shut, sealing Malachi, Casia, and Evaria inside the lift.

The ascent was long and quiet.

When the elevator doors finally parted, the heavy, sterile air of the subterranean world was instantly replaced by the cool, salty breeze of the surface ocean.

It was midnight. The sky was a vast, terrifyingly beautiful expanse of moonlit darkness. Hanging low over the churning, dark waters of the Southern Sea was a massive, brilliant full moon, casting a flawless, shimmering path of silver moonlight directly across the water's surface.

Waiting for them at the edge of the ancient, weathered dock was a small, sleek ceremonial barge, crafted from the same dark, subterranean wood as

Seraphina's bier. A perimeter of Eloi security drones hovered silently in the distant sky, enforcing Minister Fena's promise of isolation, but they kept their respectful distance. Just as the Minister had promised, Seraphina's bier rested securely in the center of the wooden vessel.

Evaria stepped forward, her dark hair blowing gently in the ocean breeze. She reached into her pocket and carefully placed a single, perfectly ripe Peachberry near her mother's resting hands—a final, bright offering of their shared starlight.

Malachi stood at the edge of the dock, resting his hands on the stern of the barge. He looked down at his wife one last time, his sharp yellow eyes locking onto her serene face.

He reached out and manually deactivated the teal stasis field.

The energy barrier dissolved into the cool night air. Malachi stepped back, raising his head to the massive, glowing moon above them. He drew a slow, shuddering breath, filling his lungs with the alien air of the surface, and let the heavy, poetic cadence of his ancestors fill the quiet night.

"From the deep enclave of the Root, Seraphina is returning to the shining stars," Malachi spoke, his deep, resonant voice carrying over the crashing waves. He recited the ancient, sacred words of the Rite, untouched for hundreds of thousands of years. "To the water, where it is recorded that life began, I give this empty vessel to the moonlight. Seraphina, our timeline has fractured. But as long as there are stars above, your significance remains. Let the moonlight guide you to eternal rest, and let the great blue blaze set you free."

With a gentle, devastating push, Malachi sent the barge drifting out into the dark water.

It caught the ocean current, gliding slowly along the shimmering path of moonlight. As the wooden vessel drifted out to a respectable distance from the shore, tears streamed down Casia's face. The past eight cycles had fundamentally shifted her reality. The profound, steady compassion Malachi had shown her throughout their shared grief had touched her heart in ways she never expected, and this quiet, dignified moment on the dock was just another testament to the strength of the man Seraphina had loved.

Malachi turned his frame toward Casia. The moonlight illuminated the solemn gravity in his expression.

"The Rite of the Ancients was granted to Chancellor Olesya sometime around the year 500,020 AD," Malachi stated, his deep voice carrying the absolute, undeniable weight of history. "Now, it has been repeated for Seraphina. But as one ancient rite concludes, another must be finalized."

He stepped closer to Casia, looking down at her. "The Rite of Guardianship begins here, under this moonlight. I will honor Seraphina's final command. Are you truly ready?"

Casia nodded, the tears falling freely now. Malachi reached into his dark robes and withdrew a simple, elegant ring band that had belonged to his wife. With absolute reverence, he lowered his hand, extending the ring to Casia.

Overcome by the sheer magnitude of the sacred mandate, Casia slowly sank to her knees on the weathered wooden dock.

"I accept," Casia whispered, her voice thick with emotion as she took the band. "I will do everything in my power to honor the memory of Seraphina. The bond of the starlight and moonlight passes onto me, and I accept it with absolute humility."

She paused, shifting her emerald eyes to the young Morlock who had grown so close to her over the agonizing week. "But only if you accept me, Evaria. You know that this ancient law means I am to be your mother. I cannot even begin to replace the profound bond you had with my best friend. I can only offer you my absolute devotion. So, I ask you... do you accept?"

Evaria looked down at the woman kneeling before her. Fresh tears spilled from her amber eyes, but her sharp mind understood the logical and emotional necessity of this union. She offered a small, brave nod, a genuine smile breaking through her sorrow to bring a sudden, beautiful warmth to the solemn dock.

"I accept, Auntie Casia," Evaria said softly. She immediately caught herself on the familiar title, letting out a small, playful laugh that carried a spark of pure, unburdened joy. "I mean... you were my mother's best friend. But now, you are to be my mother, and my family."

Casia let out a breath of profound relief, a soft, watery laugh escaping her as she looked up at the thirteen-year-old. Beside them, Malachi felt a deep, healing warmth settle into his chest.

With their fractured family finally and formally bound together under the stars, Malachi turned back toward the dark ocean. He withdrew his crystalline data-pad and keyed in the final, localized thermal sequence.

Evaria looked between Casia and her father. "Father, should I press the button?" the thirteen-year-old asked, her voice trembling but resolute. "I have read about the Rite in the historical archives. The duty of the final ignition falls to the First Born. I should be the one to press the rune."

Malachi looked down at his daughter, his sharp yellow eyes filled with profound pride. He nodded slowly, honoring her intellect and her bravery, and handed her the device.

Evaria gripped the smooth glass, looking out at the wooden barge drifting along the silver path of the water. "Goodbye, Mother," she whispered into the cool ocean breeze. "You will always be my starlight."

She pressed the ignition rune.

There was no sudden explosion. Instead, an intense flash of pure, hyper-concentrated blue pyrotechnic fire erupted from the base of the barge. It was scientifically flawless—a localized, absolute thermal incineration that burned vastly hotter than any red or orange flame. The majestic blue fire flared upward, consuming the dark wood and Seraphina's physical form in a towering column of sapphire light.

It looked exactly like a piece of a star had fallen directly into the ocean.

Malachi stood at the edge of the water, the intense blue light reflecting in his tears. Beside him, Casia reached out and securely pulled Evaria into her arms, both of them weeping quietly as the beautiful blue star slowly burned down into the gentle, lapping waves of the Southern Sea.

The Premier Historian had kept his vow. He had given her the stars.

Chapter V — The Truth Of Stone

How Malachi became "Hollow" (689,789 AD)

Two years had passed, and the absence of Seraphina had fundamentally altered the architecture of Malachi's life. In the time since he had returned her to the starlight on the Southern Sea, he had immersed himself entirely in the forgotten, lower strata. His recent excavations within these unstable, collapsed ancient ruins had yielded a vast wealth of historical data for the Morlocks. He had uncovered irrefutable proof of an endless, cyclical loop—a continuous, devastating rhythm of wars and natural disasters that had locked the Eloi and Morlocks in a shared struggle for survival for hundreds of thousands of years.

Each Aeterna stone he had recovered from the dark during those two years held the frozen voices of his ancestors. There were desperate messages from ancient laborers, calculated records from forgotten scholars, and decrees from fallen Chancellors. To Malachi's formidable, encyclopedic mind, each stone was not just a relic; it was a fractured piece of a massive, terrifying jigsaw puzzle.

He sat alone in the dim shadows of his subterranean office; his sharp yellow eyes fixed on a trio of holographic projections hovering just above the surface of his desk. The first was a capture of a fractured past: himself, Evaria, and Seraphina, frozen in a moment of unblemished joy.

The second projection displayed Evaria as she was now. At fifteen years of age, her biological maturation was undeniable. She was growing into the exact image of her mother, possessing the same dark hair and the same compassionate, luminous yellow-green eyes.

The final image was a testament to their survival. It featured himself, Casia, and Evaria, captured exactly one year ago during a rare visit to the Horticulture Gardens to sample the enclave's latest engineered hybridization: Appleberries. The horticultural specialists had successfully extracted dormant genetic material from two distinct specimens within an ancient subterranean seed vault—a nectarine and a baseline apple. By meticulously splicing the chromosomal sequences together, they had engineered a resilient new fruit with a uniquely tart, vibrant flavor profile.

A profound, grounding pride swelled in Malachi's chest as he studied his daughter's face. Despite the looming biological threat of the disease, her intellect remained undeniably sharp. She consistently asked him the exact, analytically precise questions regarding his historical excavations. For Malachi, sharing his deep-earth discoveries with Evaria and Casia before anyone else acted as a vital emotional release valve, venting the agonizing pressure of his grief and keeping his mind grounded in the present.

His sorrow still surfaced in unpredictable waves, most often tethered to the memory of Seraphina. In those moments, Casia was the perfect partner. Because she had been Seraphina's closest confidante, she inherently understood him and the complex architecture of his grief. She was a profoundly wise choice for his soulmate, a living testament to Seraphina's foresight; his late wife had somehow known that Casia would be the exact person necessary to keep Malachi from becoming *Hollow*.

Scattered among the holographic projectors and Aeterna stones lay physical remnants pulled from the deep earth. One was the delicate, fossilized imprint of an ancient avian—what the forgotten world might have called a starling. Malachi, however, possessed no linguistic reference for that term. To his analytical mind, it was simply the structural fossil of a winged creature once capable of atmospheric flight.

Beside it rested a far heavier relic: the fossilized remains of an ancient man. Homo sapiens. It was a remarkably preserved, dark brown skull that he kept at the corner of his workspace, mathematically dated back exactly 687,759 years to roughly the era of 2030 AD. He often marveled at its structural density. The cranium was neither Eloi nor Morlock; it was something entirely different, an unmutated baseline. It sat on his desk as a quiet, physical reminder of what the planet's surface once cultivated long before the splintering of their species.

Malachi shifted his focus from the fossilized remains to the worn, woven satchel resting near his feet. Reaching inside, he retrieved two Aeterna stones, carefully extracting the newest acquisition and placing it onto the illuminated surface of his desk.

He leaned in, his sharp yellow eyes meticulously examining its exterior. He immediately noted several deep, jagged micro-fractures webbing across the dark casing, prompting his analytical mind to calculate its exact historical age. With deliberate precision, he pressed a specialized diagnostic tool against the stone's flank. A faint, erratic blue pulse flickered to life.

Aeterna stones were masterworks of ancient engineering, typically composed of dense obsidian and piezoelectric quartz, interwoven with microscopic resonance circuitry. As the blue light sputtered, his desktop scanner registered a critical power depletion. He gently transferred the relic onto an induction charging pad. Recognizing the extreme physical fragility of this specific stone, he manually adjusted the console to a low-voltage regulatory setting to prevent a catastrophic thermal overload of the ancient circuits.

Just as he finalized the charging sequence, the heavy doors to his workspace hissed open. Casia stepped into the dim light of the office, carrying a thermal container holding their mid-cycle meal.

"Casia, what a pleasant surprise to see my beautiful wife," Malachi greeted her, his voice uncharacteristically warm.

She paused just past the threshold, a gentle, genuine smile touching her lips as she registered his demeanor. While he certainly navigated the natural ebbs and flows of sorrow like anyone else, today his features were entirely unburdened, reflecting a steady, focused energy. As she stepped fully into the workspace, her emerald eyes immediately drifted toward the low-voltage induction pad on the edge of the desk.

"You found another Aeterna stone, I see."

Malachi nodded. Casia took the seat across from him, efficiently unfolding a small, woven cloth over a cleared section of the metal desk to prepare their meal.

"I have," Malachi said, his gaze returning to the pulsing blue light of the relic. "And this one might hold the exact historical data I have been searching for. If the logs are intact, it could provide Dr. Klorioa with the chemical baseline necessary to discover a superior treatment—or perhaps a permanent cure—for the PCR mutation once and for all."

As he spoke the words, the underlying tone of his voice shifted. The confident historian gave way to the anxious, desperate father. Casia heard the fragile hope straining against his forced composure. They both knew the terrifying biological reality: after two years of artificial stability, Evaria was beginning to experience renewed episodes of cognitive shear. Evaria was now taking the maximum allowable dosage of Regrestat, yet the Stage One glitches were returning. It was a silent, undeniable alarm that the experimental drug she relied on was finally reaching its absolute biological limit, a reality that deeply concerned Malachi, Casia, and Dr. Klorioa.

"There are thousands of stones scattered in the deep earth. How can you be certain this specific one is a medical archive?" Casia asked, her tone gentle. "I am only curious, my beloved. You know I would never disrespect the precision of your work."

As she spoke, she began dividing a portion of the newly engineered Appleberries and ancient Peachberries onto his plate.

"I saw this resting on a solitary shelf next to the hybridization pods in the enclave," she explained, her emerald eyes reflecting the smooth, dark skin of the fruit. "This is the genetic secret behind the new berries. It is just like my redberries, Malachi. Ancient, completely unmodified by the centuries, and yet perfectly sweet."

Malachi studied the deep crimson skin with quiet awe. He had previously only seen holographic projections of the recovered fruit in the agricultural reports; witnessing the physical reality of it resting on his desk was remarkable.

"They are slowly being phased into the food chain across all the Morlock regions," Casia added.

She sat back in her chair, a look of quiet satisfaction on her face, and ate a few of the bright redberries from her side of the cloth. Then, with a quick, fluid motion, her pale fingers darted across the woven fabric, casually claiming a small handful of the redberries from his side as well.

Malachi paused, his sharp yellow eyes tracking her hand. He offered a small, amused smirk, noting her sudden, intense appetite, but his highly analytical mind entirely missed the deeper biological implication. He simply assumed she had developed a profound fondness for the fruit, completely unaware of the true reason behind her sudden cravings.

"To answer your previous question," Malachi said, his tone shifting back to the analytical precision of a historian. He carefully lifted the fragile Aeterna stone from the low-voltage pad and rotated it toward the dim light. "This specific casing bears a distinct insignia."

He pointed a pale finger at a faint, deliberate etching near the base of the fractured obsidian. It was a simple, equidistant cross-like design, worn smooth by the friction of hundreds of thousands of years.

Casia leaned forward, her luminous eyes tracing the faint geometric lines in the stone. She recognized it immediately. Even after eons of historical decay and societal collapse, it remained the universal, foundational symbol for medical science. She gave a slow, understanding nod.

"Malachi—I hope this has the answers we need for Evaria, and for all the others who suffer from PCR," Casia said, her voice faltering slightly. "I know the weight of it is hurting both of us. The glitches are getting worse."

She hesitated, her pale hand instinctively coming to rest against her lower belly.

"Yet... there is something else I need to tell you. I am not sure how you will react. I know how heavily you feel the burden of things we cannot control."

He glanced up at her; his sharp yellow eyes filled with profound compassion and concern. He saw the physical toll the anxiety was taking on her, mistakenly attributing all of her nervous tension to their shared terror over Evaria's declining mind.

"I know," he sighed, his gaze dropping heavily to the meal between them. "Evaria could succumb to the disease at any time. That is exactly why I shifted the entire focus of my excavations a year ago to hunt specifically for these medical stones. Yes, Casia, it is mathematically like looking for a needle in a silkworm stack. Still, I must believe there is a biological variable left behind that can help her. A missing piece of historical data that can solve the PCR mutation before Evaria's mind completely shatters."

Casia lowered her head, absorbing the heavy truth of his words. The vow she had taken to him, to Evaria, and to Seraphina's memory was the commitment she prized above all else. Now was not the right moment to share her news; his entire intellect and emotional capacity were completely consumed by Evaria's survival.

She desperately wanted to tell him about the new life growing inside her, but she did not know how the revelation would impact his fragile psychological state. Malachi was a profoundly loving husband. He operated on a paradigm of absolute equality and had never compelled her to do anything against her own volition. In Morlock society, the Rite of Guardianship was often exploited; many males took the sacred oath for granted, treating the bonded Guardian as little more than a domestic servant to manage the household and care for their existing children.

Malachi was entirely different. He divided the domestic labor flawlessly, caring enough to assist with the daily upkeep of their home even when he returned utterly exhausted from historical excavations. He respected her physical autonomy and intellectual viewpoints to a degree she had once thought impossible. In his eyes, and in the physical reality of their home, she was never a replacement for Seraphina; she was his absolute equal. She knew, undeniably, that many female Morlocks who bound themselves to the Rite were not so fortunate.

"Well, is it fully charged? May I share this moment with you?" she asked, clearing the remaining meal from the area and watching her husband study the artifact for a few more seconds. He carefully attached a secondary device—a specialized diagnostic sleeve—around the stone to protect the fragile casing while simultaneously stabilizing the data extraction.

"Absolutely," he replied.

He held the sleeve gently. The induction pad hummed, and the faint, flickering hologram of a male Morlock physician materialized above the desk. A crisp temporal timestamp materialized beneath him, reading: 555,879 AD.

Malachi's breath hitched. It was the exact same year as the haunting stone he had discovered two years prior—the recording of a grieving Morlock whose courier wife had been murdered by Eloi experiencing violent chemical withdrawals.

"I am Doctor Voldern, and I must record the absolute truth for whoever finds this archive," the hologram spoke, his audio feed degraded but legible. "The base substance, Chacoidine, required to synthesize Calvenine is entirely depleted, and we have fundamentally exhausted every scientific avenue to engineer a viable substitute. We never intended to weaponize this compound. It was the Eloi who abused it, demanding continuous synthesis to numb their emotional burdens and escape the natural struggles of life. They chose a manufactured, docile oblivion over the biological necessity of experiencing existence. It was a devastating paradox: by avoiding the pain of living, they forgot how to survive."

"Now, the supply is gone. The sudden chemical withdrawals have shattered their fragile minds, forcing them to brutally confront a reality they are no longer equipped to navigate. They are slaughtering us. The Golden Age is over."

Malachi nodded grimly. The terrifying context of that first stone from two years ago was now fully, undeniably corroborated by a medical professional of the era.

"Furthermore, I am one of the few medical scientists to discover a chilling biological reality. The continuous synthesis and environmental exposure of the drug—which the Eloi exploited for several centuries—had an unstable, unintended secondary effect. It has caused Gene 1543 in the Morlock genome to mutate. If this new war with the Eloi does not eradicate us, this genetic degradation eventually will, by regressing our intellects and turning us into feral savages. I—believe—the cure... lies within the blood of the Eloi."

The audio abruptly cut out, the projection collapsing into a dead, static hum.

Malachi looked up at Casia, his sharp yellow eyes wide with absolute astonishment. He was no longer shocked by the Calvenine withdrawals—that grim history was now a confirmed fact—but the medical revelation entirely staggered him.

"So that is the key?" he repeated, his voice a sharp mixture of profound excitement and deep, analytical frustration that the data stream had terminated so suddenly. "The blood of the Eloi. Something in their biological makeup holds the exact formula to reverse the PCR mutation? This could save Evaria... and the entirety of our species."

Casia stood from her chair and offered a slow, affirming nod, her hand once again resting subconsciously against her lower belly. Malachi's vivid yellow eyes were entirely locked on the dead stone; his formidable intellect completely missed the physical gesture. His mind was already calculating the next logical steps, but his immediate protective instinct for his daughter quickly resurfaced. Even with this newfound hope, the undeniable reality of Evaria's declining condition remained a present danger. He did not like leaving her alone in their quarters, despite her absolute capability to care for herself.

"Go home, Casia, and keep a close eye on Evaria," he instructed gently, finally looking up from the desk. "I will be home in a few hours for the evening meal. I just need to finish processing a few more things here."

She nodded in agreement. Walking around the desk, she leaned down and pressed a soft kiss to his cheek. He smiled warmly at her, entirely oblivious to the fact that she was carrying his unborn child. Casia desperately wanted to tell him the truth, but her logic dictated that this was still not the correct moment. The discovery of the Eloi blood requirement was too massive for his mind to process alongside anything else right now.

Perhaps during the evening meal, she thought quietly to herself, turning and leaving the dim light of his office.

Once the heavy office doors sealed behind Casia, Malachi exhaled into the quiet room. He gently lifted the medical stone and secured it back onto the charging pad to preserve Dr. Voldern's invaluable data. Then, his sharp yellow eyes shifted to the second relic he had excavated from the deep strata.

He picked up a handheld micro-optic magnifier and leaned over the desk to study the second dark casing. Unlike the fragile, age-worn micro-fractures of Dr. Voldern's medical log, this artifact bore a single, severe, jagged fissure running directly down its center, stopping mere millimeters from the holographic sensor emitter. The delicate component was miraculously intact and unfractured. As the lens magnified the internal structure, Malachi drew in a sharp breath. This was no ordinary civilian or medical archive. The underlying lattice was woven with a hyper-dense, luminescent mineral. It was a Royal Aeterna Quartz recorder—a tier of technology strictly reserved for the absolute highest echelons of the ancient Morlock political class.

He knew instantly the gravity of what he was holding. These specific quartz recorders were engineered with exceptional structural integrity, designed to preserve vital state secrets through extreme environmental or societal disasters. Furthermore, his desktop scanner provided a rapid radiometric date: the stone's casing was forged in the year 555,879 AD. That made it exactly 133,910 years old. What mathematical or physical force could have possibly possessed enough raw kinetic energy to crack such a heavily fortified artifact?

Desperate for answers, Malachi carefully connected the fissured Royal stone to his diagnostic interface, holding onto a thin margin of hope that the internal memory core was still viable. As the system initiated its delicate bypass protocols to stabilize the relic, he raised his hand and tapped the smooth face of his circular communications device, opening a direct, encrypted frequency to Dr. Klorioa.

The circular screen on his desk flickered to life, projecting the sharp, analytical features of Dr. Klorioa. As her piercing eyes met his, she immediately registered the tense posture of his shoulders. For a brief, terrifying second, her clinical mind braced for the worst. As Evaria's primary physician, she knew the clinical reality: her patient's Regrestat dosage was now at its absolute biological maximum. The acceleration into Stage Two PCR could trigger at any moment, a reality she was desperately trying to prevent with little success. She was currently developing a secondary experimental drug to help stabilize the condition, but its early success rate was incredibly grim.

"Malachi, is Evaria alright?" she asked instantly, bypassing any standard greeting. "How can I be of service to you? Have you found any more stones that could help?"

"For now, my daughter is stable," Malachi answered, his voice steady but carrying the heavy weight of his exhaustion. "She has experienced a few more glitches, but Casia and I have been able to ground her and help her snap back out of them. Thank you, Doctor, for everything you have been doing to buy us this time. But I have news for you. Can you come to my subterranean office right now, even though it is not a standard work cycle?"

He watched the hologram closely and saw her eyes widen, a rare spark of genuine enthusiasm breaking through her usual clinical stoicism.

"I can be there in fifteen minutes," she replied firmly.

Malachi offered a brief, appreciative smile before the connection severed, leaving the office quiet once again. He immediately shifted his focus back to the diagnostic terminal, where the heavily damaged quartz recorder was beginning to yield its initial decryption stream.

"Chancellor Olesya?" he whispered quietly to the empty room as the digital signature translated across his screen.

If this Royal Aeterna stone truly belonged to Chancellor Olesya, or originated from her direct administration, it was a staggering historical find. It held the potential to finally bridge the massive, undocumented gaps concerning the Golden Age. The historical records between the initial Calvenine collapse in 555,879 AD and the era of 500,000 AD were profoundly inconsistent—a vast, silent expanse of missing data. He stared at the fractured casing, his mind calculating the chronological possibilities. Which era actually contained the true peak of the Golden Age? Was it the 400,000s or the 500,000s? And more importantly, what else had occurred during that massive stretch of missing history besides the Eloi's Calvenine withdrawals?

What unknown historical event possessed enough raw kinetic energy to crack such a heavily fortified Chancellor's stone?

Seeking the exact truth, he carefully activated the diagnostic bypass. The heavily fractured stone hummed, emitting a harsh burst of static before projecting a degraded, flickering hologram. The temporal timestamp locked in: 500,020 AD. The regal figure of Chancellor Olesya appeared, her small, holographic projection materializing directly above the desk in his dim office.

Malachi knew from the historical archives that 500,020 AD was the exact year of her death—the year she was granted the Rite of the Ancients. Observing her now, the physical reality was undeniable. It was not merely the degraded static making the transmission look terrible; her features were profoundly aged and physically exhausted, bearing the devastating weight of a collapsing civilization. This had to be a final, desperate recording made just before the end.

"I am Chancellor Olesya," the audio hissed, the frequency barely stabilizing. "If this—you. Ian—failed in his attempt—twenty years earlier—to stop—Eloi aggression. Time Travellers—three—failed."

With a sharp, terminal screech, the quartz core overloaded. The audio cut entirely, and the projection collapsed into total darkness.

Malachi winced, recoiling physically from the sudden auditory feedback. He sat perfectly still in the silence of his office; his piercing yellow eyes fixed on the dead stone. He placed a pale hand firmly over his mouth, his breathing shallow as his formidable intellect immediately began dissecting the fragmented variables.

Time travel? he thought, his strict mind grappling with the sheer magnitude of the concept. The stone was recorded in 500,020 AD. She stated the attempt occurred twenty years earlier. That mathematically places this temporal event exactly in the year 500,000 AD—the precise epicenter of their missing historical record. Did the arrival of these Time Travellers fracture the era itself?

He played the remaining words over in his mind. *Time Travellers. Three.* The audio was heavily degraded, but the structural logic was undeniable: three distinct individuals had successfully traversed time, arriving in 500,000 AD in a failed attempt to stop the Eloi aggression.

He systematically searched his encyclopedic memory for the name Ian, but yielded zero historical matches. To be absolutely certain, he quickly queried his primary archival console, running a global search to see if the designation had ever been recorded by any other historian across the Morlock enclaves. The system returned zero hits. His strictly linear logic deduced the only possible conclusion: they must be rogue Morlock scientists from a distant, undocumented future who had jumped backward to alter the collapsing trajectory of their species. While Chancellor Olesya's log confirmed they had arrived in 500,000 AD, he had absolutely no mathematical way to calculate where they had come from; their true temporal origin point remained a baffling blank. The undeniable historical truth that three unknown entities had fundamentally altered the timeline left him completely confounded.

Furthermore, the specific phonetic structure of the name Ian presented an entirely different anomaly. It was uncharacteristically brief, completely lacking the polysyllabic resonance typical of Morlock nomenclature. He ran a secondary, deliberate mental query through his knowledge of ancient linguistics, but the historical database yielded nothing.

If this individual was truly a Morlock scientist from a distant, undocumented future, why did his name sound so fundamentally alien? Could it be an acronym? A highly classified military or temporal designation rather than a biological birth name?

He frowned; his gaze locked on the dormant quartz stone as his thoughts cycled relentlessly through the fragmented data.

Before he could process another chronological theory, a sharp electronic chime echoed through the quiet subterranean room, physically breaking his intense concentration. He reached across the desk and tapped the interface console to disengage the primary seal. The heavy metal doors hissed apart, revealing the sharp, clinical figure of Doctor Klorioa standing in the threshold.

"Malachi, what have you found?" Doctor Klorioa asked as the heavy metal doors sealed behind her. Her piercing eyes immediately registered his intense, calculating posture in the dim light of the workspace. "You are deeply focused. You clearly possess something of historical importance to share with me."

Malachi bypassed standard pleasantries. He smoothly transferred the diagnostic interface back to the medical Aeterna stone he had previously reviewed with Casia, securing the fragile obsidian onto the low-voltage induction pad. With a precise tap of his console, he activated the decryption sequence.

The degraded hologram of Doctor Voldern materialized once more. Klorioa watched in absolute silence as the ancient physician broadcast the tragic biological history of the Calvenine depletion, the subsequent mutation of Gene 1543, and his desperate, final hypothesis regarding the blood of the Eloi.

As the projection collapsed into static, Doctor Klorioa remained perfectly still. Her sharp, clinical mind rapidly processed the ancient variables. The biological logic was staggering, yet mathematically sound. Over the hundreds of thousands of years of parallel evolution, Morlock and Eloi DNA had drastically deviated. While the subterranean Morlocks suffered the cascading genetic damage that triggered PCR, the surface-dwelling Eloi had maintained an entirely different evolutionary trajectory.

"Malachi? Do you realize the implication?" she asked, her features initially brightening with more hope than she had felt since Regrestat was released to the public two years ago. "This changes everything. The blood of the Eloi contains the unmutated baseline of Gene 1543."

But then her piercing eyes lowered, the clinical reality tempering her excitement. "However, raw Eloi blood alone will not cure Evaria. It merely provides the healthy genetic blueprint. To actually splice that baseline correction into our degrading DNA, we require the missing catalyst Dr. Voldern mentioned: Chacoidine."

She looked back up at him, her analytical mind rapidly connecting the ancient data. "I have studied the chemical profile of chacoidine in the medical archives. It was the delivery system—the precise chemical catalyst required to bind genetic repairs into the mind. We need the Eloi blood to provide the natural, undamaged copy of the gene, but without Chacoidine, the blood alone is useless. And as Dr. Voldern stated, it is entirely depleted."

She paused, her clinical mind calculating a fragile, secondary contingency. "Unless a surviving sample of the actual drug still exists. If we could somehow procure an ancient, preserved vial of Calvenine, the Chacoidine would still be synthesized within it. Furthermore, the fact that the ancient world simply 'ran out' of the base substance suggests it was dependent on a specific, harvestable derivative—perhaps something botanical."

Her jaw tightened with clinical resolve. "It is a massive historical long shot. But if you can somehow convince the Eloi to donate samples of their blood, I will tear apart every botanical and chemical archive we possess to find a modern substitute for that catalyst."

Malachi began to shake his head yes, and then no—a flicker of indecision crossing his face. Yes, he knew it had to be done to save Evaria and thousands of other Morlocks, but no—he knew the political reality. Asking the Eloi for blood samples to cure PCR would trigger an immediate, hostile rejection.

"I understand the logic, but the Eloi will not," he replied, his voice heavy with the gravity of the situation. "Can you imagine me talking to Minister Xenora of the Eloi Senate? She is the worst of them all. To her, this request would be an insult."

He paused, his brow furrowing as he considered the alternative.

"Not unless... I talk to... let me try. I have to." He realized he might actually have an ally within the Eloi. *Fena.*

"Talk to who else?" Klorioa asked, her brow furrowing as she processed the logistical weight of his suggestion.

"Someone who granted me the rite to give a befitting send-off to Seraphina," Malachi answered, his voice low and measured. "There are a few among the Eloi who do not wish to engage in the degrading tactics enforced by the Eloi Elites. It is a long shot, I know. She might be able to help, but I do not know for certain."

Klorioa went silent, her analytical mind likely calculating the severe risks of such a request. The barrier between their two species was not just political; it was built on generations of systemic resentment. Malachi watched her, waiting for the clinical assessment of his desperate plan, the silence in the office deepening.

"You realize that if this 'friend' helps you, they could be killed by their own—or worse, you could be?" Klorioa's gaze was fixed on him, her expression devoid of clinical detachment. It was pure, unfiltered concern. She knew the volatility of the surface politics better than most.

"If I do not try, who else will?" Malachi retorted, the agitation in his voice betraying his usual historian's composure. He turned away from the desk, pacing the narrow width of the office. "I have been dealing with the Eloi for at least sixteen to eighteen years, and I am surprised they have not attempted to stop me already."

He stopped, his sharp yellow eyes darkening as he recalled the countless hours wasted in their legislative chambers. "I have stood before their Senate, presenting empirical data, only to be met with derision. Every time I bring them a historical breakthrough, they mock me, labeling me the 'Fabricator of History.' They treat the Morlock perspective as a delusion rather than a record of events."

He turned back to her, his posture rigid. "They dismiss my findings because they refuse to acknowledge the reality of our shared past. But if I reach out to Fena, it is not a debate about history. It is a request for a cure. I know the risk, Klorioa. I have lived under the threat of their dismissal for nearly two decades. If they are willing to ignore the evidence of their own existence, perhaps they will ignore me long enough to make this contact."

"Perhaps I could come with you to the surface Eloi Senate Chamber and confirm your findings?" Klorioa suggested, her piercing eyes narrowing as she mentally mapped out the political landscape. "Maybe they will listen to me? Then again, they have always ignored the medical profession of the Morlocks. Hatred and revulsion are all they have ever shown us. They treat our profession like we are crackpots or charlatans, even though our healing methods are ninety-five percent identical to theirs. They still treat us like we are savages."

She spoke with a biting, controlled frustration, the exhaustion of years of professional dismissal evident in her tone.

Malachi stopped pacing and turned to face her, his expression softening. He reached out, his hand hovering briefly near the console before he lowered it, signaling his genuine respect for her expertise.

"If the Senate were a court of logic, Klorioa, I would take you without a second thought," Malachi said, his voice level and devoid of any condescension. "Your clinical verification would be the final piece of proof. But you know as well as I do that to Minister Xenora and her peers, your credentials do not matter. To them, the science is irrelevant because the messenger is a Morlock."

He looked at the dead Aeterna stone one last time before powering down his terminal. "If we walk into that chamber, they will dismiss you as a 'savage' pretending at science, and they will dismiss me as the 'Fabricator of History.' We would not get a hearing; we would get a dismissal."

He met her gaze, his vivid yellow eyes burning with the determination he had felt since finding the stone. "That is why I cannot use official channels. I need Fena. If there is a crack in their ideology, she is the only one I trust to navigate it. I need you to stay here, Klorioa. Monitor Evaria. Keep the stabilization protocols running. If I make contact, I need to know you are ready to receive the samples the moment they are in my hands."

Dr. Klorioa nodded, the sharp, angular movements of her head reflecting a sudden, hardening resolve. She was right to accept the burden. In this moment, she had become the critical line of defense for the future of their species, positioned to either contain the PCR or shepherd the cure. The weight of that responsibility was absolute, but it was rooted in an ancient oath—a fundamental covenant of medicine that had survived for six hundred thousand years. Even in this fractured era of 689,789 AD, the oath remained the silent, binding bridge between the Morlock and Eloi medical fields, untouched by the vitriol of the Senate or the surface-level hatred. She would honor it, even if she had to operate in the shadows of their politics to do so.

"I will be ready," Klorioa said, her voice devoid of its previous agitation, replaced by the calm, rhythmic cadence of a doctor preparing for a critical procedure. "Do not worry about the stabilization protocols. Evaria will be monitored. I will maintain her levels at the absolute limit allowed by the current guidelines. Make the call, Malachi. Contact Fena. Secure those samples."

Malachi exhaled, the tension in his shoulders finally beginning to dissipate as he realized he had the one partner who truly understood the stakes. He stepped toward his communication console, his fingers tracing the cold, metallic surface as he prepared to initialize the encrypted channel to the surface.

"I will update you the moment I have an answer," he promised, though he knew the reality of Eloi politics could turn a brief transmission into an hours-long negotiation.

Klorioa offered a final, resolute nod and turned toward the exit of his office.

Once the heavy doors sealed shut behind Doctor Klorioa, Malachi turned his full attention to the glowing interface of his console. He was about to initiate a contact that carried massive biological and historical weight. It could either secure the genetic key needed to cure Evaria and ensure the biological continuation of the Morlock species, or it could be the immediate catalyst for his own termination. He harbored no grand illusions of being a savior, nor did he naively believe this single transmission would suddenly erase hundreds of thousands of years of entrenched generational hatred to unify the surface with the underground. He simply wanted his daughter to live, and his species to survive.

He brought up the secure communications matrix and meticulously inputted the complex encryption key required to bypass the standard Senate surveillance grids, establishing a direct, untraceable line to Eloi Minister Fena.

He took a deep, stabilizing breath, his fingers hovering over the input surface, and began to type out the most critical transmission of his life.

Minister Fena,

I have excavated an ancient medical Aeterna stone dating back to the historical depletion of Calvenine. The recorded data provides empirical proof that the PCR anomaly—the degradation of Morlock Gene 1543—was a direct biological consequence of synthesizing that drug for your ancestors.

Furthermore, our top medical personnel have reviewed the data and confirmed the stone's final hypothesis: the genetic baseline required to reverse this mutation and cure the disease lies within the unmutated blood of the Eloi.

I am requesting your assistance. I need you to help secure a meeting, or perhaps a more discreet avenue, to convince members of the Eloi to provide us with viable blood samples. I am fully aware of the immense political magnitude and the delicate nature of this request.

Additionally, our clinical analysis indicates that splicing this genetic baseline into our degrading DNA requires a specific chemical catalyst originally found within Calvenine. Historical records state that the global supply of this compound was entirely exhausted hundreds of thousands of years ago. However, if there is even the slightest mathematical probability that a single, preserved vial of Calvenine survived within an isolated Eloi archive or vault, I respectfully ask you to search for it. A viable sample of that drug, combined with the unmutated blood, is the exact biological formula required to finalize the cure.

The mathematical trajectory of this disease is undeniable. If we cannot cure the PCR, our intellect will permanently collapse. If the Morlocks become feral, your society will inevitably suffer the devastating consequences. Our survival is mutually dependent.

You showed me grace during Seraphina's passing. I am respectfully asking for your help once again.

Warm regards,

Malachi

He reviewed the text once to ensure every detail was absolute, then executed the transmission command. The screen flashed briefly as the encrypted data packet launched toward the surface. He leaned back in his chair, staring at the static display.

While waiting in the quiet isolation of his office, Malachi accessed the central historical database. He initiated a comprehensive query on Chancellor Olesya, pulling up every surviving Aeterna log and fragmented text associated with her administration. The recovered data from that heavily degraded era confirmed only a few absolute truths: Olesya had remained in power as the Morlock Chancellor for nearly sixty years. She was highly regarded by the Morlocks of her time, and, significantly, she too had advocated for unification with the Eloi.

However, the chronological gaps surrounding her tenure were massive. The database indicated only that a fragile peace was brokered by her administration during or immediately preceding the year 500,020 AD. Beyond that, the archive was a silent void. There was absolutely no recorded documentation of Time Travellers, no explanation of what exactly happened to fracture the era, and zero mentions of an individual named "Ian".

He stared at the sparse, incomplete data, the fragmented words from the quartz stone echoing in his mind: *Three. Failed.* His linear intellect returned to the only logical deduction he could formulate: the three individuals had to be Morlock scientists from a distant, undocumented future who had jumped back to assist Olesya, only to fail in their temporal objective. He pondered the missing variables; his sharp yellow eyes locked on the screen.

Suddenly, the communications console chimed sharply, breaking his intense concentration. The encryption matrix stabilized, and the holographic projection of Eloi Minister Fena illuminated the dim room. Her expression was serious, yet devoid of the typical surface-level arrogance.

"Malachi, it is good to see you," Fena said, her voice carrying a quiet urgency. "I have already started the process to secure a meeting between you and one of our top medical physicians. You need not worry about her discretion; she can be trusted. I am making arrangements for you to travel to a secure location under the cover of night."

She paused, transmitting a data packet that materialized on his secondary screen.

"You will need to conceal your physical identifiers. Wear a heavy hooded garment, light-dampening ocular shades to hide your eyes, and coverings for your hands. Nothing that would attract surface attention. In fact, I have just uploaded the schematics of the civilian clothing you should procure for yourself before you arrive. I will provide the exact time and coordinates shortly."

Malachi studied the data, the sheer logistical reality of her support settling over him.

"You just need to provide the exact medical data of what you have found and why you need Eloi blood samples," Fena continued, her holographic eyes meeting his. Then, her voice dropped to a tense, terrified whisper. "And Calvenine? Malachi, are you serious? That word is absolutely forbidden here. To even speak it is treason. But... I believe there might be a way to secure just one vial from a restricted historical museum. I cannot even guarantee if it is fake or real, given the hundreds of thousands of years that have passed, but I will try to acquire it."

She leaned forward slightly, her tone brimming with a quiet, dangerous bravery. "I want to help. These past two years have opened up doors for me.

I have made many new friends who think as I do, and as you do. Unification is not merely an impossible ideal; it could happen, though it will not be overnight."

Malachi held her gaze, a profound respect settling over his analytical mind. In a society entirely dictated by historical hatred, her logical compassion was an absolute anomaly.

"Thank you, Fena," Malachi replied, his voice steady and devoid of its usual clinical detachment. "I will procure the necessary garments and await your coordinates. Stay safe."

"You as well, Malachi," she said.

The encryption matrix collapsed, and the hologram faded, plunging the subterranean office back into its standard, dim lighting. Malachi sat in the silence for a long moment, processing the sheer magnitude of Minister Fena's treason against the Eloi Senate. He had intentionally bypassed standard diplomatic protocols; formally requesting Eloi blood and the extinct Calvenine would have been instantly condemned by the surface as an act of biological warfare. By securing an Eloi minister's complicity in the shadows, he was exploiting the secretive nature of both governments to save his daughter. The trajectory was set.

Moving with deliberate precision, he unhooked the diagnostic sleeves from both Aeterna stones. He carefully secured the fragile obsidian and quartz relics inside a heavily insulated containment lockbox beneath his desk, ensuring the historical and medical data remained protected. He then powered down his primary console and initiated the physical lockdown sequence for the office doors.

It was time to go home.

He stepped out into the quiet, metallic corridors of the Morlock enclave. The standard work cycle was winding down, the artificial lighting dimming to simulate the passage of evening. As he walked the familiar route toward his residential quarters, his strict intellect continued to run through the logistics of the upcoming surface infiltration. He cataloged the materials he would need to assemble his disguise and calculated the optimal subterranean routes that would bypass the Senate's security grids.

Yet, beneath the heavy tactical planning, his primary motivation remained sharply in focus. He was going home to have the evening meal with Casia and Evaria. He had secured the tangible hope they desperately needed. He just had to maintain the fragile stability of their lives long enough to execute the plan.

Malachi turned the final corridor, approaching the heavy, sealed door of his family's quarters. He reached out to disengage the entry chime, completely unaware that the fragile stability he was relying on was already beginning to fracture.

Chapter VI — Catatonic Decline

Malachi stepped through the heavy, sealed doors of his family's quarters, the metallic hum of the enclave fading behind him. Evaria walked over to greet him, her pace measured and calm—a stark contrast to the frantic, running embraces of her childhood. Two years had passed since the tragedy on the Southern Sea, and the thirteen-year-old girl he remembered had definitively grown into a fifteen-year-old young adult. Her dark hair flowed smoothly against her light blue-gray skin, and her luminous yellow-green eyes shined as brightly as stars in the ambient light of their home.

Malachi smiled, a profound warmth breaking through his deep exhaustion, and pulled her into a long, grounding hug.

Arm in arm, they walked toward the dining area. Casia emerged from the cooking station, carrying a large thermal serving bowl. Malachi halted in his tracks, a spontaneous, rare laugh escaping his chest. Casia was wearing a newly procured apron emblazoned with bold text: *Redberries for Life*. He had never seen it before, and the sheer domestic absurdity of it instantly lifted the heavy political weight he had carried from his office.

"Tonight, I have made a delicious Redberry bowl," Casia announced, setting the dish down on the table with a dramatic flourish. "It is a take on the traditional Peachberry bowls, but it is entirely my own recipe."

Malachi and Evaria exchanged a stunned, synchronized look. The last time Casia had experimented with her own recipe, the household had been fiercely divided—Evaria claiming it was overwhelmingly sweet, and Malachi arguing it was aggressively tart.

"Are you absolutely sure this one is going to be good?" Malachi teased, his vivid yellow eyes crinkling at the corners.

Evaria broke into her usual, highly contagious giggle, the bright sound filling the room.

"For goodness' sake, I am cooking for four—I mean, three of us," Casia began to protest, trying to suppress her own laugh as her pale cheeks flushed slightly. She quickly waved a hand over the bowl to dismiss the verbal slip.

But the laughter in the room hitched. Evaria's sharp intellect caught the mathematical error instantly. She stopped giggling and looked at Casia, her yellow-green eyes wide with immediate, intense curiosity.

"Did you just say... cooking for four?" Evaria asked.

Malachi stood perfectly still. The brilliant, analytical mind that had spent the entire afternoon dissecting the complexities of Aeterna stones and Eloi genetics instantly snapped an entirely different set of variables into place. He remembered the lunch they had shared just hours ago in his office. He remembered Casia claiming an unusually large share of the bright redberries. And then, the final, undeniable data point locked in: the subconscious, protective way she had kept resting her hand against her lower belly while he was fixated on the hologram.

The mathematical equation of their family had changed. A profound, overwhelming realization washed over his face as his sharp yellow eyes darted from his daughter to his wife, his mouth opening slightly as the truth finally registered.

"I meant three. Just a verbal slip—I must be losing my edge. Come on, sit, both of you," Casia protested, trying to laugh it off as a slight flush crept up her cheeks.

Malachi just stared at her, his yellow eyes wide. He wasn't upset; instead, a profound, undeniable joy flooded through him at the revelation. *Another daughter*, he thought to himself, the possibility expanding in his chest. *Or a son.*

"Are you pregnant?" Malachi finally breathed.

Instead of answering directly, Casia simply sat down and began ladling the redberry mixture into their bowls.

"Come on, Mali... We have Evaria. Isn't she enough for us?"

Evaria let out a soft giggle, catching her mother's eye. She knew she was enough for them. But the cold logic of her PCR diagnosis remained a dangerous countdown. If the disease took her, her father risked suffering a catatonic decline—becoming a *Hollow*, a shell of bitterness. Looking at the warmth returning to Malachi's face, Evaria realized a new sibling wasn't a replacement. It was a lifeline to save his soul.

"Mother?" Evaria prompted, still giggling as Casia pointedly took a bite of her food.

Malachi met his daughter's gaze, a conspiratorial smile spreading across his face. "Looks like Casia might want to drag this out a bit. Maybe we should play along, Evaria? Though, I for one would be absolutely overjoyed if she is carrying a child."

Evaria laughed even harder, the sound bright and genuine, as she and Malachi finally dug into their bowls alongside her.

"I think it will be a boy," Evaria declared, scooping up the last of her redberries. "And if it is, we are absolutely not naming him after Uncle Salvess. I refuse to have a brother named Salvess."

Casia laughed, shaking her head. "Well, since I am carrying the child, I suppose I should have the final say on the name—"

She froze, her eyes widening as she realized what she had just confirmed. She tried to backtrack, stammering, "I mean... I meant if I were to be pregnant, obviously. It was just a thought."

Malachi and Evaria burst into laughter, their joy filling the room. Casia groaned, effectively defeated, and covered her face with her hands, her light blue-gray skin flushing a deeper, embarrassed shade. "Oh, fine. You two are impossible. You caught me."

Malachi grinned, leaning back in his chair with a look of pure, unadulterated happiness. "The mathematics of your appetite, my love. It never lies."

Later, as the ambient lights of their quarters dimmed to signal the rest cycle, the energy in the home settled into a quiet, peaceful rhythm. Malachi sat on the edge of Evaria's bed, pulling the heavy, woven blankets up to her shoulders. He smoothed a stray lock of dark hair away from her forehead. In the doorway, Casia leaned against the frame, a contented smile lingering on her face as she watched them, her hand resting instinctively and protectively over her lower belly.

"Father," Evaria said, her voice dropping to a comfortable, sleepy tone. She lifted her hand and pointed toward his waist. "You have a redberry stain right on your purple sash. You will need to wash that before your morning rotation."

Malachi looked down at the bright red smudge on the fine purple silk and let out a quiet chuckle. "I suppose I was a bit distracted tonight," he said, looking back up with a smile. "Goodnight, Evaria."

She did not answer.

Her hand, which had just been pointing at his sash, was now frozen in mid-air. Her luminous, yellow-green eyes were locked forward, staring blankly past him at the wall. She did not blink. Her chest continued to rise and fall with quiet, steady breaths, but the bright, giggling teenager from the dinner table was gone, replaced by a terrifying, rigid stillness.

From the doorway, Casia's smile didn't just vanish; it withered. She surged across the room, falling to her knees beside the bed. "Evaria? Evaria, look at me!" Casia's voice was desperate. She grabbed her daughter's shoulders, shaking her gently, waiting for the familiar, subtle twitching—the fight that the Regrestat usually triggered to snap her back.

There was nothing. Just a vacant, terrifying rigidity.

"She's not fighting it," Casia choked out, the reality making her stomach churn with a sudden, sickening dread. "This isn't like the other times, Malachi. She's... she's not twitching. She's gone; she's just gone!"

"Get Doctor Klorioa! We need to bring her in now!" Malachi commanded, his deep voice raised in a desperate shout as he fought to remain calm, his hands hovering frantically over his daughter's rigid form.

Casia fumbled for her circular metallic wafer, her hands trembling so violently she nearly dropped it. She punched the frequency for Klorioa's private office, hoping for a direct answer, but a sterile, automated voice answered instead. "You have reached the office messaging system for Dr. Klorioa. Please leave a request after the tone..."

Casia looked up at Malachi, tears spilling from her emerald eyes as panic overwhelmed her. "It is her recording message; she is not picking up!" she cried out. "I will call the Enclave immediate help desk!"

She didn't wait for the machine to finish. Knowing the private office line would be too slow to mobilize a team, she needed the facility's active response unit. She slammed her thumb against the metallic wafer, switching channels to the Enclave's main emergency triage desk.

"Medical Enclave, triage," a steady Morlock voice finally answered, cool and professional against the backdrop of the chaos.

"This is Casia! I am invoking Malachi's priority override!" she barked, her voice cracking but authoritative. "Evaria is completely rigid. The Regrestat isn't triggering a break. I need an emergency transport dispatched to our quarters immediately, and patch this frequency directly to Doctor Klorioa's trauma team!"

There was a frantic clicking of keys on the other end. "Understood. Transport is mobilized. Patching you through now. Get her to the corridor loading zone!"

Casia shoved the metallic wafer into her pocket. Malachi didn't wait. He scooped Evaria up, her body unnervingly stiff against his chest. His movements were frantic but precise. They burst out of their quarters, the heavy doors sealing behind them as they raced toward the sector's transit corridor, the crushing weight of the unknown closing in on them.

"Evaria, come out of it!" Malachi pleaded, gently shaking his daughter's frozen arm as they reached the staging area. A single tear escaped Evaria's eye, tracing a slow, agonizing path down her cheek. Casia choked back a sob just as the emergency transport screeched to a halt beside them. Medics instantly swarmed out, taking Evaria from Malachi's arms and loading her into the cabin. Malachi and Casia climbed into the transport right behind them, refusing to leave her side as the vehicle sped toward the Medical Enclave.

A standard trip across their sprawling subterranean city to the Medical Enclave would normally take fifteen to twenty minutes, but the emergency transport engaged a dedicated bypass network—a high-speed transit artery suspended above the bustling lower districts, strictly reserved for critical response. The harrowing journey took less than six minutes.

Casia sat weeping in the cramped transport cabin, helplessly watching the medics rapidly attach diagnostic sensors, confirming that Evaria's physical vitals remained eerily stable despite her terrifying catatonic state. Suddenly, her metallic wafer vibrated. The triage patch had finally gone through; the encrypted channel to Doctor Klorioa was connected.

Casia lifted the device, her voice breaking into a hysterical sob. "Doctor Klorioa, please! She is completely locked up. It might be Stage Two of PCR! Please, you have to help us! I... I think I am pregnant, and all this stress—" She choked on the words, her terrified mind fracturing under the weight of the crisis. She wasn't just agonizing over the unresponsive teenager on the stretcher; she was terrified for the fragile new life growing inside her, and she knew with absolute certainty that losing Evaria would completely hollow Malachi out. "We cannot... I cannot lose Evaria!"

Seeing Casia fully fracturing under the sheer weight of the panic, Malachi reached over and gently but firmly took the wafer from her trembling hands.

"Doctor! She is completely frozen and not showing any signs of breaking out of it!" Malachi shouted into the device, his deep voice fighting to be heard over the deafening wail of the transport's sirens as they echoed off the towering stone architecture of the underground metropolis.

"Put us on open broadcast," Dr. Klorioa commanded, realizing Malachi was struggling to hear her over the blaring sirens.

She could hear the sheer chaos inside the transport. Fortunately, she lived only a single sector away from the Medical Enclave and had already rushed into the triage bay the moment the emergency alert triggered. Ever since she witnessed Seraphina's tragic death and Casia's sacred vow of Guardianship two years prior, Dr. Klorioa had made Evaria's survival her absolute personal and professional priority.

Malachi tapped the smooth surface of the circular wafer, instantly projecting the doctor's voice throughout the cramped cabin.

"Listen to me carefully," Dr. Klorioa's voice cut through the noise with steady, clinical authority. "I am already at the center, and the trauma suite is prepped. I will do everything in my power to pull Evaria out of this. Casia, you must breathe. I am going to take care of Evaria, and I will examine you the moment you arrive to ensure the baby is safe. Just hold on. We are ready for you."

Following the doctor's command, Casia forced herself to draw a slow, shuddering breath, wrapping her arms protectively around her lower abdomen.

Malachi looked between his rigid, unresponsive daughter and his terrified wife. *I have to be their strength,* he told himself, forcefully locking away his own rising panic.

His brilliant mind raced, cycling rapidly through a flood of desperate variables. The most critical among them was Eloi Minister Fena. If the covert meeting on the surface succeeded—if Fena could actually procure the unmutated Eloi blood samples—there was a tangible, biological probability they could reverse the PCR.

And if she truly manages to secure a viable vial of Calvenine from that museum, he realized, a fierce hope sparking in his chest, *it will provide the exact catalyst Dr. Klorioa needs. Evaria could be saved. The entirety of our species could be saved.*

He winced, his hands curling into tight fists. He refused to calculate the catastrophic outcomes that could await them all if those samples were not secured.

A few agonizing minutes later, the transport screeched to a halt. The deafening sirens finally cut off as the heavy doors flew open. The medical team instantly pulled Evaria's stretcher from the cabin, rushing her toward the triage area. Malachi and Casia scrambled out right behind them, immediately spotting Doctor Klorioa waiting at the entrance. The doctor's hair was visibly disheveled, pulled hastily into a knot after being roused from a deep sleep, but her posture was rigid and completely focused. Seeing the brilliant physician already taking charge, a wave of profound relief washed over Casia's light blue-gray face, her emerald eyes welling with fresh tears.

Once inside the secure trauma suite, the chaos shifted to clinical precision. Klorioa swept a soft, amber diagnostic light across Evaria's unresponsive, staring eyes, purposefully utilizing a spectrum that would not agitate sensitive Morlock vision. She rapidly scanned the hovering vital displays, her fingers flying across the glass interface of her medical console. Malachi and Casia stood frozen near the doorway, watching the doctor work with a calculated, efficient intensity as she tried to confirm the terrifying biological reality.

"Computer," Doctor Klorioa ordered, her voice sharp and commanding. "Display the protein degradation of Gene 1543 for patient Evaria. Compare current levels to her baseline from thirty days ago. Then, cross-reference the data with all known Stage Two markers of PCR."

The sterile glass of the medical console flared to life, casting a harsh, pale light across the darkened trauma suite. A massive, three-dimensional projection of Evaria's DNA and RNA helix strands materialized in the air. As the computer processed the command, the projection rapidly magnified, isolating the exact structural representation of the 1543 Gene.

Klorioa stared at the floating data, her piercing eyes locking onto the genetic breakdown. For the past two years, the doctor had utilized specialized scans to meticulously track how this specific gene fractured, mapping its exact visual descent from a healthy state to full degradation. Now, she could see the edges of Evaria's chromosomal lattice severely fraying, the healthy proteins almost completely eroded. The system flashed a silent, definitive crimson warning across the glass:

- **STAGE TWO-A MARKERS PRESENT**

- **STAGE ONE TETHER STILL INTACT.**

- **SUB-STAGE RARITY CONFIRMED: CASE 101.**

It was a devastating, yet profoundly baffling clinical designation. Over the years, Doctor Klorioa had tracked hundreds of PCR cases across the subterranean enclaves. For the vast majority of Morlocks, the mutation was ruthlessly efficient, dragging the victim from the catatonic lock of Stage One directly into the feral aggression of Stage Two with alarming speed. But Evaria was not falling instantly. She was the 101st documented case of a rare physiological anomaly—a Morlock actively fighting the genetic shear. Her biology was desperately clinging to the Stage One tether even as the Stage Two markers began to manifest, forcing the disease into a prolonged, agonizing sub-stage. How these rare individuals managed to physically slow the mutation's ruthless advance remained an absolute medical mystery, but the genetic fraying meant she was actively teetering on the cusp. If she broke through that final threshold, the cognitive shear would trigger hostile, unpredictable aggression—a horrifying precursor to the primal madness of Stage Three.

Klorioa slowly shook her head. No. The absolute, undeniable reality of the mutation threatened to completely crush her clinical composure. She did not want to accept that the Regrestat had finally failed, but the cold science rotating before her was undeniable. Evaria's mind was slipping into the abyss.

The silence in the room felt suffocating. Klorioa closed her eyes, the agonizing burden of delivering this terminal news to Malachi and Casia pressing heavily onto her shoulders. Her brilliant mind frantically searched for a lifeline, her thoughts instantly snapping back to the dim light of Malachi's office just hours earlier. The ancient Aeterna stone. The blood of the Eloi.

She opened her eyes, catching Malachi's distressed, desperate gaze in the reflection of the glass console. She silently prayed that he had successfully initiated the covert transmission to Minister Fena. Because if he had failed, the glowing, mutated helix rotating above her terminal was not just a diagnosis—it was an absolute death sentence.

"Malachi... Casia... I am so sorry," Dr. Klorioa whispered. She lowered her gaze, shaking her head, though her rigid posture refused to accept defeat. "Evaria has crossed the initial biological threshold. She is in a sub-stage we classify as Stage Two-A."

Malachi's brow furrowed, his analytical mind grasping for the unfamiliar medical term. "Two-A? What does that mean, Doctor?"

"It is an extreme rarity," Klorioa explained, her voice steadying into a compassionate, clinical cadence. "For almost every Morlock, the mutation drags them straight from the catatonic lock of Stage One into the hostile aggression of Stage Two. But Evaria is not falling instantly. Her biology is actively fighting the genetic shear. She is only the one hundred and first documented case of this anomaly. Her body is frozen, but she can likely still hear us. We simply have not isolated what is keeping her from slipping into the feral hostility of true Stage Two, or worse, the complete primal madness of Stage Three."

Casia's legs gave out. She collapsed to the cold stone floor, her body trembling uncontrollably as a broken sob tore from her throat. Malachi instantly dropped to his knees beside her, wrapping his arms around her shaking frame. He knew the sheer, crushing weight of this reality was threatening to break her. She had honored the ancient Rite of Guardianship flawlessly, loving Evaria as her own flesh and blood, and acting as the absolute soulmate and lifeline Malachi desperately needed to prevent himself from *Hollowing* out.

"Wait! Listen to me," Klorioa commanded, her voice suddenly sharpening with desperate clinical authority. "I have a highly experimental neuro-stimulant. It is completely untested for this stage. If it works, it may artificially bridge the degraded synapses. She might regain marginal verbal function—speaking slowly, like a child learning to form words for the very first time."

The doctor paused, the grim reality of the science hardening her features. "But if her biology rejects it... there will either be zero response, or the neural shock could severely accelerate the mutation directly into the primal aggression of Stage Three. It is a massive risk. I need to know what you want to do."

Casia looked up at Malachi, her tear-streaked face pale in the clinical light, desperately searching his vivid yellow eyes. In a moment completely devoid of hope, she needed his unyielding logic to guide them through the nightmare.

"Doctor, the absolute last thing we ever wanted was for this to reach Stage Two," Malachi said. He paused, looking down at Casia, his deep voice softening with a fragile, desperate hope. "But the fact that she is actively fighting it—that her biology is holding onto this Stage Two-A anomaly—is a miracle. It is a devastating reality to face, Casia, but she is still fighting for us."

She was wiping her emerald eyes, fiercely fighting the overwhelming sadness, frustration, and sheer anger of being completely helpless to save her adoptive daughter she loved. Yet, honoring the sacred vow she had taken under the stars, she forced herself to stand up. She physically braced her posture, desperately needing to be the unyielding lifeline Malachi required in this fractured moment.

"If we administer this stimulant," Malachi continued, his deep voice heavy with the grim calculus of the disease, "how do we keep everyone safe should the medication fail and throw her directly into Stage Three?"

"Malachi?" Casia gasped, her eyes widening in sheer horror. "If she jumps to Stage Three, the Enclave protocols mandate her immediate termination! How can we even contemplate risking that?" The absolute horror of the feral, primal aggression of PCR's final stage—and the Enclave's unforgiving, lethal solution to it—threatened to completely shatter her newly found composure.

"Two years ago, Zeangol showed me exactly what happens in the lower wards," Malachi said, his deep voice thick with dread as he turned to Casia. "I saw the Amber Area. I saw how they warehouse the Stage Two patients to monitor their decline. I absolutely will not allow my daughter to be locked in one of those rooms." He shifted his sharp yellow eyes to Doctor Klorioa, his expression heavy not with anger, but with the crushing, exhausted frustration of a father running out of options.

"Things have changed, Malachi," Doctor Klorioa replied calmly, maintaining her steady, clinical composure. "We no longer utilize that setup. Because Regrestat successfully stabilized the majority of the population over the past two years, the Enclave has updated its containment protocols. We now have the resources to offer isolated, private care for Stage Two patients."

Malachi frowned, his analytical mind struggling to reconcile this with the horrors he had witnessed. "I do not understand. You used to keep multiple unpredictable patients in a single containment cell."

"We did," Klorioa nodded, the grim reality of the disease softening into scientific hope. "But our longitudinal studies have yielded a new biological fact. A catatonic Stage Two patient does not easily escalate to the hostile, feral aggression of Stage Three unless their neural pathways are overstimulated. We discovered that if we eliminate external stimulation—placing the patient in absolute, isolated quiet—the PCR progression effectively stalls. We do not fully understand the exact genetic mechanism yet, but the empirical science supports it. If she stays here, she will have her own secure room, entirely isolated from the other patients."

"This is definitely a different outcome," Malachi murmured, his brilliant mind racing. "She has a chance—if—"

He abruptly stopped himself. The words *Eloi Minister Fena* and the blood samples nearly slipped from his lips, but he forcefully swallowed them down.

"Absolutely no to this experimental treatment, Malachi!" Casia pleaded, her voice trembling as she gripped his arm. "We cannot risk pushing her into Stage Three!"

"Doctor, my wife is right," Malachi agreed, gently wrapping his hands over Casia's to calm her rising terror. He shook his head slowly. "The risk level is far too high for Evaria. We will not administer the stimulant."

Dr. Klorioa offered a firm, respectful nod, instantly accepting their decision. "Understood. We will proceed immediately with the Stage Two isolation protocols. I am transferring her to a secure, absolute-zero sensory suite in my private wing. My former assistant, Zeangol—who is now a fully credentialed Doctor—will be personally overseeing Evaria's care alongside me. We will monitor her vitals around the clock. She will be kept entirely safe, calm, and comfortable. You have my word."

Malachi and Casia stared at the lead physician in profound astonishment. Klorioa was actively bypassing standard subterranean medical protocols, offering them a level of personal sanctuary far beyond her required clinical obligations. A deep, genuine wave of gratitude washed over them both. They knew with absolute certainty that Evaria would be fiercely protected by the exact same brilliant mind who had stabilized her two years prior. Furthermore, hearing that Zeangol had finally achieved her full medical credentials brought a rare, piercing spark of joy into the bleak reality of the trauma suite. It was the ultimate, undeniable bond of trust.

Malachi exhaled, a fraction of the crushing weight lifting from his shoulders. He looked down at Casia, gently lifting her chin so her emerald eyes met his. "She is in the best possible hands, my love. I know Doctor Zeangol well. She understands the devastation of this disease intimately, and I trust her completely. Now... we must ensure that you and the baby are safe."

Klorioa didn't waste a second. She guided the exhausted, weeping Casia to a secondary diagnostic bed across the trauma suite. With practiced, clinical grace, the doctor retrieved a sleek medical scan wand and passed it gently over Casia's lower abdomen.

A soft, rhythmic thrumming sound suddenly filled the sterile room. It was a rapid, steady heartbeat.

Casia gasped, her hands flying to her mouth as fresh, joyous tears spilled over her cheeks. On the secondary console, a new genomic lattice materialized. Klorioa's piercing eyes scanned the scrolling data with intense scrutiny, looking for any micro-fractures or anomalies in the fetal DNA and RNA helix strands.

"The fetal development is perfectly normal," Doctor Klorioa announced, a rare, genuine smile breaking through her clinical armor. "And more importantly, the baseline for the 1543 Gene sequence is entirely stable. There is absolutely no sign of the mutation. Your baby is healthy, Casia."

The doctor tapped a secondary readout on the glass console, noting a minor chemical elevation. "I am also detecting unusually high serum levels of anthocyanins in your bloodstream. It is merely a harmless botanical compound, likely from a heavy dietary intake of the enclave's new red-berries. It is clinically insignificant for the pregnancy, but I prefer to be completely thorough with my diagnostics."

Casia broke down into a profound, breathless sob of pure relief. She kept her emerald eyes locked on the rhythmic pulse of the monitor, completely captivated by the fragile new life growing inside her.

Standing a few feet away in the dimmer shadows of the room, Malachi felt a sharp, distinct vibration against his chest.

He carefully withdrew his circular metallic wafer, angling the screen away from his wife. The encryption matrix dissolved, revealing a secure, priority text from Minister Fena:

"The physician is secured and possesses the unmutated blood samples you require. I also have something else I must give you in person—an item of absolute necessity. Surface Access Grid, Sector 4. 2:00 AM. Come alone and unseen."

Malachi's jaw tightened. He wiped the screen blank and slipped the wafer seamlessly back into his dark robes. He could not tell Casia.

I despise doing this to her, he thought, a bitter ache rising in his chest. *She values absolute truth above all else, and I am about to look her directly in the eyes and lie.* But the sheer stress of knowing he was about to walk directly into hostile Eloi territory—and that Minister Fena was actively committing high treason against her own Senate to open the door for him—would completely shatter the fragile peace Casia had just found. He had to carry this immense burden alone to protect them both.

Across the room, Casia remained entirely focused on the rhythmic pulse of the fetal heartbeat, her tear-streaked face shining with relief. Taking advantage of her distraction, Malachi stepped quietly over to Doctor Klorioa. He touched her arm, gently pulling the physician a few steps away into the dimmer shadows of the trauma suite.

"Fena just messaged me," Malachi whispered, his deep voice barely audible over the hum of the medical machinery. "She has the unmutated blood samples waiting, and there is a high probability she secured the Calvenine as well. The mission is a go. I must leave for the surface immediately."

Klorioa's piercing eyes widened for a fraction of a second in realization. She stepped slightly closer, dropping her voice to a strict, clinical murmur. "Does Casia know?"

"No," Malachi replied, the heavy factual reality of his decision anchoring his tone. "And she cannot know. I firmly believe I will be back, but for now, she must be kept entirely unaware of the extreme risk I am taking. If I am gone for more than six hours without making contact, then you must tell her everything."

Klorioa gave a firm, subtle nod, an ironclad pact sealing between them. "Understood. I will keep Casia and Evaria entirely safe in the subterranean dark while you hunt for the cure. Return safely to your family, Malachi."

"Casia," Malachi said, his voice smooth and perfectly controlled as he stepped back into the light. "I need to return to our quarters. Since Evaria will be in isolation here, I must gather enough clothing and personal necessities to make her comfortable. I also need to notify my excavation team that I will be taking a brief leave of absence until our family is settled."

Before Casia could respond, the heavy metal doors of the trauma suite hissed open. A female Morlock in pristine medical robes stepped inside. Casia immediately recognized the vibrant orange eyes of Doctor Zeangol, remembering the profound empathy the young physician had shown at Seraphina's bedside two years ago.

"Right on time," Doctor Klorioa announced, a reassuring warmth returning to her clinical tone. "Doctor Zeangol will be stationed in this suite tonight to personally monitor both Evaria's neurological stability and the health of your baby."

Zeangol offered a warm, comforting smile as she approached, carrying a remarkably large, sealed ration pouch of fresh redberries. As she stepped closer to the secondary diagnostic bed, her sharp gaze flicked to the illuminated medical monitor. Seeing the rapid, steady rhythm of the fetal heartbeat scrolling across the screen, her bright eyes widened in genuine delight.

"Oh, Casia, congratulations!" Zeangol beamed, her exhaustion momentarily vanishing as she looked at the expectant mother.

Casia offered a tearful, grateful smile, but her emerald eyes quickly drifted down, locking entirely onto the massive pouch of vibrant fruit in the doctor's hand. Despite the crushing weight of the situation, a sudden, undeniable pregnancy craving spiked through her. Casia was inherently generous and always preferred to share, but the biological demand was intensely overwhelming.

Noticing the fixated stare, Zeangol chuckled softly, the gentle sound providing a brief, desperately needed fracture in the room's heavy tension. She looked down at her own massive ration, then back up at Casia.

"I brought these to survive the night shift," Zeangol said, her tone playful and sincere as she extended the large pouch forward. "But seeing as you are currently eating for two, I think your biological requirement officially supersedes mine. Please, take them."

Casia flushed slightly, her generous nature warring with her immediate craving. She reached out to accept the pouch. "I can share them with you, Doctor. It is a very large pouch."

"Absolutely not," Zeangol laughed warmly, pressing the fruit fully into Casia's hands. "Consider it my first official prescription for the baby."

Watching the exchange from the primary terminal, Doctor Klorioa shook her head, a rare, genuine smile breaking through her strict clinical mask. "Wow... you both really like the redberries."

A deep, genuine laugh broke from Malachi, completely shattering the suffocating dread in the room.

"Doctors, you have no idea how much my wife loves redberries," he interjected, his vivid yellow eyes crinkling with amusement as he looked affectionately at Casia. "Even before she was eating for two, she regularly attempted to commandeer my share of them at every meal."

Casia flushed a deeper shade, clutching the pouch protectively against her chest while laughing along with him. A soft, genuine wave of laughter rippled through the sterile suite, completely breaking the tension. Even Malachi found himself deeply grounded by the moment, profoundly grateful for this brief, authentic warmth before he faced the dark reality of the surface.

A profound sense of security washed over Casia as she held the pouch. "Thank you, Doctor. I will stay right here with them. Please hurry back, Malachi."

"I will," Malachi promised, his deep voice carrying a trace of lingering amusement as he stepped over to press a tender kiss to Casia's forehead.

He then moved across the trauma suite to the diagnostic bed where Evaria lay trapped in her rigid state. He leaned down, placing his hands gently on either side of her face. Bringing his lips close to her ear, he dropped his voice to a whisper meant only for her.

"If the mathematics of tonight hold true, you will be healed," he whispered, his deep voice thick with devotion. "I am going to the surface. Just hold on a little longer, my brilliant girl."

He slowly pulled back, entirely missing the single, silent tear that pooled in the corner of her unblinking yellow-green eye and slipped down her light blue-gray cheek. Though the Stage Two-A mutation held her physical form in a rigid, catatonic lock, her cognitive awareness remained completely intact. She had heard every word of his hushed conversation with Klorioa before Zeangol arrived. She understood the absolute, terrifying risk her father was taking for her and their entire species, carrying a deadly secret that her mother remained entirely oblivious to.

Unable to offer him a word of caution or comfort, Evaria could only watch from behind her frozen gaze as he stood up.

Malachi did not look back down. He gave the room one final, sweeping glance, his sharp yellow eyes lingering on his family and Doctor Klorioa. He committed them to his flawless memory, the heavy silence carrying the profound weight of what could be a final goodbye.

Then, he turned away. The heavy metal doors of the trauma suite hissed open, and the Historian stepped out into the cold, sprawling corridors of the subterranean metropolis, heading toward the darkest, most dangerous night of his life.

Chapter VII — The Handoff

Malachi left the sterile, clinical chill of the Medical Enclave behind, stepping out into the ambient, heavy warmth of the subterranean transit corridors. He bypassed the civilian arteries, his long, calculated strides carrying him toward the restricted access grid that housed the surface elevators.

These massive vertical transports were heavily guarded and strictly regulated. Ascending to the surface was absolutely forbidden to the general Morlock population unless an individual was directly involved in the physical delivery of subterranean goods, or possessed high-level political clearance. As the Premier Historian, Malachi held exactly the right credentials. His position within Morlock society carried such immense weight that he possessed the rare, unquestioned authority—and risk—to travel above ground entirely at his own discretion.

This rigid segregation, however, was an ironclad mandate enforced entirely by the surface dwellers. For hundreds of thousands of years, the Eloi Senate had cultivated a deeply entrenched superiority complex. Despite the Morlocks' brilliantly advanced civilization, the Eloi arrogantly viewed them as nothing more than a subclass of laborers. It was a vicious, unbreakable cycle—every logical Morlock attempt to argue for societal reunification was met with immediate, visceral conflict. The Eloi wanted them kept in the dark, contained beneath the earth.

But tonight, Malachi would use his specific clearance to bypass the subterranean gates, only to don a covert disguise the moment he reached the surface. He was stepping into their territory under the cover of darkness not to deliver a secret, but to secure one: the unmutated Eloi blood samples, and possibly the extinct Calvenine catalyst, required to cure PCR. He was undertaking this massive risk to save Evaria, but also to guarantee his species' absolute right to exist. As a Historian, he understood the factual, devastating calculus of their codependency.

If the Morlocks succumbed to the disease, he could envision one horrific scenario where the surface world would inevitably starve and collapse with them. The subterranean facilities produced virtually everything the Eloi relied upon. While some surface dwellers retained the knowledge to manufacture their own goods, they lacked the raw materials. To secure those resources, the Eloi would be forced to venture underground, directly into the pitch-black tunnels teeming with feral, cannibalistic Morlocks—the final, horrific outcome of the mutation. Without a cure and the eventual reunification of the two species, their shared lineage was hurtling toward total extinction—a grim, primitive regression that would spell the absolute end for both the surface and the underground.

"Historian Malachi?" one of the lift guards asked, her voice laced with genuine surprise. Even beneath the heavy, shadowed hood of his surface cloak, his tall, familiar frame was unmistakable.

The guard, a woman clad in the dark green uniform of the subterranean security force, looked up at him. Her eyes shone with a vibrant orange, contrasting sharply with his own piercing yellow, and the subtle inflection in her voice marked her from one of the distant, outer sectors of the underground.

"I have urgent business with the surface this late in the night," Malachi stated, his deep tone calm but unwavering. He did not need to explain himself further; his official clearance as Premier Historian spoke for itself.

The guard offered a respectful nod, gesturing toward the digital security ledger. While a standard biometric hand scan was sufficient for daily travel within the subterranean sectors, ascending to the surface demanded a highly restricted, encrypted authorization code. An unauthorized border crossing into Eloi territory would instantly trigger a catastrophic diplomatic nightmare. Malachi quickly keyed in his signature and stepped past her into the cavernous, metallic elevator tube.

As the heavy doors sealed shut and the lift began its massive, silent ascent, the physical isolation immediately pressed in on him. His mind flashed back to the horrifying image of his daughter, her hand rigidly pointing at the stain on the purple sash he wore—the very sash Evaria had given him—her mind entirely locked in time. He forcefully blinked away the burning tears, his thoughts drifting to Seraphina. Two years had passed since her death, yet the heavy reality of it still echoed in his mind. He wondered what his late wife would think of the desperate lengths he was going to tonight. He knew that Casia was flawlessly upholding the Rite of

Guardianship, stepping into the permanent void Seraphina's passing had left to act as the lifeline his family needed.

I despise the lie I just told Casia, he thought, a bitter guilt twisting in his stomach. *She values absolute truth above all else, yet I looked her in the eyes and deceived her.* The memory of the tender kiss he had pressed to her forehead in the trauma suite suddenly carried a devastating weight. *If I fail tonight, the Eloi will kill me, and that kiss will be my last.* But he had to take the risk. He was stepping into hostile Eloi territory, relying on the fact that Minister Fena was actively committing high treason against her own Senate to open this door for him.

But above all, his focus shifted to Casia and the fragile, unmutated heartbeat they had just heard in the trauma suite. The absolute, factual relief that the PCR had not infected his unborn child fueled his ironclad resolve. The biological stakes of this mission were absolute, and failure was simply not an option.

As the lift continued its massive ascent, Malachi's mind turned to the Eloi Minister waiting for him in the dark.

She is risking her very life for us tonight, he thought, the stark reality of her actions settling heavily in his chest. *She is nothing like the typical Eloi politicians I am accustomed to dealing with. Where the Senate is usually cold-hearted, arrogant, and rigidly prejudiced, Fena has shown me genuine respect over the past two years. She has quietly contributed to my historical research, risking her political standing just to help me confirm the authenticity of various Aeterna stones.*

He leaned his tall frame against the cold metal of the elevator wall, his yellow eyes fixed on the passing subterranean levels.

But stones are one thing. Unmutated Eloi blood is an entirely different, incredibly dangerous threshold, along with a secured Calvenine sample that may or may not exist! Malachi thought. *This entire day feels like an escalating, surreal nightmare. Tonight, her own kind would not hesitate to execute her if they discovered she was handing over their sacred biological material to a Morlock.*

Malachi knew the absolute, unforgiving calculus of the Eloi Senate. He was walking into a situation where discovery meant a swift, guaranteed death for both of them. He deeply feared for her safety, desperately not wanting to see anything happen to the one surface dweller who had proven herself a true friend. Yet, the survival of his daughter—and his species—required them both to step directly into the fatal crosshairs of the Senate tonight.

The massive vibration of the lift began to ease as it finally neared the surface. Malachi reached into his dark robes and retrieved his shades, sliding them on to completely conceal his piercing yellow eyes. He pulled his heavy hood forward and tightly adjusted his gloves, ensuring not a single fraction of his Morlock physiology was visible before stepping into Eloi territory.

Will there be guards stationed directly outside these doors? he thought, his muscles tensing in calculated preparation. *They usually do not waste the military resources unless they want to make a point.*

He knew the Eloi only heavily secured the access entryways when they wanted to send a direct, intimidating message to the subterranean population. The Senate would deploy the military to the grids strictly to enforce government edicts, using the guards as a harsh, physical reminder to keep the Morlocks in their place whenever the surface leaders felt they were stepping out of line. But currently, the geopolitical status quo was flat. The agreements from two years ago had established that PCR was exclusively a Morlock disease and posed absolutely no cross-species threat. He was banking on the fact that without a manufactured political crisis to enforce, the Eloi's arrogance would leave the entryway completely unguarded tonight.

Surface Access Grid, Sector 4. 2:00 AM. Come alone and unseen. The words repeated on a continuous loop in Malachi's mind as the heavy lift doors finally hissed open.

A sudden, bracing rush of crisp surface air washed over him, completely devoid of the sterile, recycled metallic scent of the subterranean metropolis. He immediately scanned the perimeter. Just as his logical deduction had projected, the access entryway was entirely unguarded. Malachi allowed himself a single, tightly controlled exhale of relief.

He withdrew his circular metallic wafer from his heavy robes, his gloved fingers swiftly keying in the exact geographical coordinates Minister Fena had provided for their meeting.

He stepped fully out of the lift. Above him, a brilliant, unhindered canopy of stars shined down, casting a pale glow over the towering, impossibly advanced architecture of the Eloi cities. The surface world was undeniably impressive, alive with the factual, organic reality of nature—the rhythmic chirping of nocturnal insects and the distant calls of night-hunting avian creatures.

He closed his eyes beneath the heavy hood, inhaling the fresh, unfiltered air of the surface. For a brief, unguarded moment, his thoughts drifted back through time. He remembered the devastating loss of Seraphina, but alongside that grief was the profound, genuine beauty of his wedding night on the Southern Sea. He recalled the gentle sway of the barge and the deeply romantic vows he had exchanged under these very stars to marry Casia. It was a union forged in absolute love and dignity—a sacred Rite of Guardianship that Seraphina had miraculously awoken from her coma to bless, and one that young Evaria had embraced with her whole heart.

But Malachi had no time to admire the view or linger in the past. His absolute priority was securing the blood samples. Seeing that the immediate vicinity was completely devoid of any Eloi presence, he secured his wafer, melted into the deep shadows of the towering structures, and began his rapid, silent advance toward Sector 4.

Minutes bled away as Malachi navigated the sprawling, silent architecture of Sector 4. The surface streets were entirely devoid of citizens, yet a cold prickle of paranoia crawled up his spine.

I am being watched, he thought, his heightened Morlock senses straining against the quiet night. His logical mind calculated that he was wholly alone in the sector, but the visceral, underlying feeling of eyes locked onto him refused to fade.

He pushed the sensation down, his concealed eyes scanning the darkness until he finally spotted a familiar silhouette.

Minister Fena was waiting in what appeared to be a vast, cultivated surface park. She was dressed for evasion, wearing a sleek black and yellow blouse and trouser combination that blended into the shadows far better than her usual Senate regalia. As she turned her head, the ambient starlight caught the sharp, distinct point of her Eloi ear.

Spotting his cloaked form, Fena raised a hand and quickly motioned for him to approach her position near the edge of a large, glassy lake.

Malachi moved silently toward the stone bench area. As he closed the distance, he confirmed Fena was not alone. Standing rigidly beside her was another Eloi male. The stranger was dressed entirely in black, the dark fabric broken only by the stark, undeniable presence of a red medical cross positioned over his chest. It was the physician. The individual holding the unmutated key to Evaria's survival.

Malachi's steps slowed slightly, his sharp yellow eyes narrowing in the darkness. His formidable mind immediately flagged the discrepancy. In their final encrypted communication, Fena had explicitly stated she was securing a trusted female Eloi physician for the transfer. The fact that a male doctor now stood in her place deeply unsettled him.

What is going on? he calculated silently, the heavy dread of a potential trap spiking through his chest. *Why the sudden substitution?*

"Malachi, this is Doctor Dalvin. He is carrying the unmutated blood samples and the Calvenine within his medical case," Fena whispered, gesturing to the silent male beside her. "But before we proceed with the biological transfer, I have something else for you. An artifact for your historical archives—an item you must take."

She reached into her pocket and withdrew a small, glass-like stone. It was shaped like a multi-faceted, triangular pyramid—smooth and jet-black, with deep veins of blue embedded across each of its five distinct sides. It was compact, only slightly larger than his circular communications wafer.

"Why are you risking everything for me? For the Morlocks?" Malachi asked, his voice low as he carefully slipped the compact stone into the secure, zippered pocket of his dark robes for safekeeping. Despite its dark, solid appearance, it felt strangely light, almost as if something were suspended deep within its core.

"Because everything you have ever said to me is entirely factual. I did the research, I found the truth, and I made some friends who believe in reunification," Fena replied, her tone hushed but fierce. "If our two species are going to survive, we absolutely have to overcome this hatred."

Standing directly beside her, Dalvin remained perfectly still. He did not shift his weight or check his surroundings. His ice-blue eyes were locked on the exchange, his posture utterly devoid of the subtle, empathetic movements of a medical professional. He said nothing.

"I am grateful, Fena, but I thought you were bringing a female physician?" Malachi asked, his gaze shifting to the man standing so closely to his friend.

There is something deeply wrong here, Malachi thought, an unsettled, visceral coldness washing over him. *Something is completely off.* He studied Doctor Dalvin, his mind trying to pinpoint the exact source of his rising alarm, but the logical deduction slipped just out of reach.

"Each time I cross-reference your historical finds," Fena continued, missing Malachi's concern as she drew his attention back, "I uncover buried articles and Senate edicts designed specifically to rebuff your claims to the public masses. I even found sealed records showing they systematically buried the diplomatic efforts of your father, Ambassador Mordechai, and others before him."

At the mention of Mordechai, the silent physician's ice-blue eyes snapped toward Fena, then locked onto Malachi. It was a stare of such profound, freezing hostility that it immediately triggered Malachi's survival instincts. He caught the icy glare instantly, his analytical mind flagging the aggressively un-medical reaction, but he forced himself to brush it aside for a split second to listen to Fena.

She remained entirely oblivious to the lethal shift beside her. "The leadership lies to us," Fena pressed on, her voice thick with conviction. "Not all Eloi think like the Senate, Malachi. We just want to exist, the same as you. To live with our families and friends, enjoy the simple comforts of a day's work, and exist in peace."

And still, Doctor Dalvin remained silent, an unnerving, statuesque observer watching the treason unfold right beside her in the dark.

"I agree with you, Fena, but you said you were bringing a female doctor," Malachi pressed, his deep voice dropping to a grave, urgent register. He felt the factual parameters of the meeting fracturing.

"Hundreds of thousands of years of division between the Morlocks and the Eloi. It is a continuous, systemic conflict that seems to have no logical end in sight for either of us," Fena said, cutting him off, oblivious to the fact that Malachi was asking a sincere, critical question.

He looked past Fena, locking his shielded gaze onto the silent physician standing right beside her. The stranger's ice-blue eyes seemed to slightly narrow in on Malachi.

"As a Historian, I know there was another species before us, Fena," Malachi continued, speaking with absolute certainty, using the science to test the stranger. "An intelligent progenitor race. *Homo sapiens*, they once called themselves. Something catastrophic happened to them, causing a mass extinction, and both of our species biologically branched out from their surviving genetic foundation. Doctor Dalvin, as a medical professional, you must agree with the baseline DNA and RNA findings, do you not?"

He waited for the physician to respond.

Yet, to his horror...

A heavy, suffocating silence fell over the dark park. Dalvin stared at Malachi. His ice-blue eyes were entirely devoid of emotion. He did not look at the Historian as a sentient equal, but rather as a diseased, feral animal that had wandered too far from its subterranean cage.

He then shifted his cold, hateful gaze to Minister Fena.

"Doctor?" Fena asked, her voice dropping to a tense whisper, finally registering the absolute zero of his demeanor.

The false medical persona vanished instantly, replaced by the rigid, lethal posture of the Eloi secret police.

"Did you honestly believe the Senate would remain blind to this festering treason, Fena?" Dalvin hissed, his voice a flat, freezing blade of absolute arrogance. "That we would permit you to contaminate the pristine lineage of the Eloi to save a race of subterranean parasites? And for what? To hand over Calvenine—the forbidden narcotic they weaponized against our ancestors to render us docile over a hundred and thirty-three thousand years ago? You are willingly giving the biological lifeblood of our species to this feral abomination. You are a disgusting, pathetic stain on the Senate."

Fena stumbled backward, the color instantly draining from her face. Her fierce idealism shattered into sheer terror as the reality of the betrayal finally crashed over her.

The female physician—the true Reunification ally I secured for this tra nsfer... Fena's mind spun with the paralyzing, icy dread of her own catastrophic mistake. *Dalvin must have intercepted Doctor Giena,* she thought. *He told me she could not make it, and that he was strictly assigned to accompany me for the safe drop of the samples.* The fatal geometry of his deception finally clicked into place, making horrible sense to her. And she had believed him. She had brought the Eloi Secret Police directly to the exchange. Her desperate hope to save the Morlocks had just cost her her life.

"Dalvin, no—" Fena gasped, raising her trembling hands in a desperate plea.

It was at that exact moment Dalvin pulled an object from his black medical coat. It was not a storage vial of blood. It was a sleek, featureless white cylinder—a molecular phase-shifter.

A weapon, Malachi realized, the fatal geometry of the trap suddenly locking into place in his highly analytical mind. *He is not a physician.*

"Fena!" Malachi screamed, his deep voice cracking with desperation as he surged forward.

He was a fraction of a second too late. Dalvin aimed the cylinder and engaged the firing mechanism.

There was no beam of light, no explosive sound. Instead, the cylinder emitted a localized, devastating frequency that instantly severed the molecular bonds of Fena's body. In a microsecond, her physical form was converted into a catastrophic, blinding burst of hyper-white photonic energy.

The flash was absolute. It pierced straight through the polarized shielding of Malachi's shades. He instinctively threw his gloved hands over his sensitive Morlock eyes as his vision was instantly overwhelmed by a stark, disorienting brilliance. The displaced air rushed into the vacuum where Fena had stood with a sharp, concussive crack.

When Malachi's vision finally began to tearfully resolve into harsh, blurry shapes, there was no body. No ash. No blood. Minister Fena had been completely, sterilely erased from existence.

Dalvin stood perfectly still, turning the featureless white cylinder directly toward Malachi's chest.

"Let me make myself entirely known to you, savage," Dalvin's cold voice cut through the ringing in Malachi's ears, thick with spite. "I am not a doctor. I am the Senate's absolute authority—the Secret Police, tasked to purge collaborators from our society. And you have just seen exactly how we enforce the boundary. We leave no trace."

Malachi braced his tall frame, his mind rapidly calculating the inescapable geometry of his own death. He was entirely unarmed and visually compromised. *This is the end,* he thought, bracing for the fatal flash.

Dalvin held the weapon steady, his ice-blue eyes gleaming with sadistic amusement. "You thought you were getting blood samples tonight, did you not?" Dalvin asked, his voice dripping with aristocratic mockery. "To save your pathetic subterranean race? Perhaps... a diseased loved one?"

Malachi's jaw clenched, refusing to give the executioner the satisfaction of his terror.

Dalvin took a slow, arrogant step forward. "Blood is one thing. But she crossed the ultimate, unforgivable line, Morlock. She attempted to smuggle the forbidden Calvenine catalyst into the dark. That alone mandated her immediate, absolute eradication."

Dalvin's gaze shifted to the secure pocket of Malachi's robes, and a low, chilling laugh echoed from his throat. "And the supreme irony of her pathetic treason? She died for absolutely nothing. All you received for her life was a useless stone relic."

It was a sound of pure, spiteful fascination as the Secret Police agent watched the Historian prepare to die in the dark. Dalvin held the weapon steady for a harrowing second more, then slowly lowered it, a sickeningly calm dismissal in his eyes.

"Go back to the underground soil in which you toil," Dalvin ordered, his voice echoing with cold, dejected hatred in the empty dark. "Run! Go back to where you degenerates are dying anyway! You did not see a thing tonight."

Pure survival logic overrode Malachi's horror. *If I die tonight, Casia is alone. Evaria dies. The Morlocks die.*

Unarmed, his vision swimming with bright afterimages, and completely outmatched, Malachi had only one factual option. He spun on his heel and sprinted into the deep shadows of the Eloi architecture, his blurred sight straining desperately to navigate the sprawling layout until he finally reached the unguarded access grid.

He threw himself into the elevator, slamming his palm against the descent controls. As the heavy metallic doors sealed him inside and the descending lift began its long plummet back into the earth, the adrenaline finally broke.

Malachi leaned his tall frame against the cold wall, his chest heaving as hot tears spilled from his piercing yellow eyes. *I left her there,* he thought, the crushing weight of the grief settling over him. *Fena sacrificed everything, and I failed. The mission is lost.*

The vibration of the lift slowed, and the doors hissed open to the subterranean Morlock sector.

The same female guard in the dark green uniform was stationed at the ledger. Her vibrant orange eyes widened in alarm as she saw the Premier Historian step out, his breathing ragged, his demeanor completely shattered.

"Historian Malachi? What happened up there?" she asked, stepping forward with genuine concern.

Malachi forcefully wiped his face, struggling to recompose his official bearing. He slowly peeled the heavy surface gloves from his trembling hands, the physical act helping to ground him back in the safety of the subterranean air. With a bare hand, he unzipped the secure pocket of his dark robes, instinctively seeking the only piece of Fena he had left. He reached inside and grasped the small, black-and-blue pyramidal Aeterna stone.

The moment his bare skin made contact with the relic, registering the unique bio-electric signature of his Morlock physiology, the stone flared to life.

A soft, blue holographic projection illuminated the dim corridor between Malachi and the guard. Minister Fena's voice echoed clearly from the multi-faceted glass.

"Malachi, if you are hearing this, it means my darkest suspicions were correct. Doctor Giena successfully extracted the cargo and delivered it to me, but she did not arrive for our final escort to the park. A stranger was sent in her place. Fearing the Senate had compromised the handoff, I could not risk leaving the true cargo in the medical case. I secretly transferred the items into this stasis stone. Inside, I have preserved the unmutated Eloi blood samples. And something else... a fully preserved vial containing the absolute last sample of the Calvenine drug. Save your daughter, my friend. Save our future."

The hologram faded, leaving the corridor in stunned, breathless silence.

The guard stared at the pyramid resting in Malachi's bare hand.

She actually secured the Calvenine, Malachi thought, his analytical mind reeling from the sheer biological impossibility resting in his palm. The drug had been extinct for thousands of years. But Fena had previously mentioned infiltrating a highly restricted, classified museum on the surface. The exact logistics of her heist remained an absolute enigma, but the irrefutable, physical proof was now glowing right in his grasp. Furthermore, her tactical brilliance in deceiving the Secret Police by hiding the biological matter within a historical relic had flawlessly outmaneuvered the Eloi Senate.

"What is this? An Eloi message?" the guard whispered. She was utterly stunned by the Eloi Minister's compassion and the deeply personalized, sacrificial nature of the recording addressed to Malachi. Her vibrant orange eyes widened with disbelief as the absolute reality of Fena's words set in. She looked up at him, completely astounded. "I think I need a new line of work. That... that could be the PCR cure?"

Malachi's heart hammered against his ribs. The devastating failure on the surface had just transformed into the ultimate salvation. He looked at the guard and gave a single, fierce nod.

He did not say another word. He bypassed the security checkpoint entirely, his long, calculated strides breaking into a dead run toward the Medical Enclave.

Minutes later, the heavy doors of the trauma suite burst open. Inside, the sterile environment was a hive of quiet, focused activity. Doctor Zeangol stood diligently beside the diagnostic bed, actively monitoring the neurological readouts above Evaria's motionless form, while Casia sat close by, gripping her daughter's hand. Across the room, Doctor Klorioa was already stationed at the primary lab console, calibrating the biochemical synthesizers and centrifuges in absolute, factual anticipation of Malachi's return.

Klorioa spun around at the sudden intrusion. Seeing Malachi step through the threshold, a profound, hidden sigh of relief escaped the lead physician's lips. He had returned just before their strict six-hour deadline expired, sparing her the agonizing duty of breaking their pact and revealing his deadly secret to Casia.

Malachi crossed the room in seconds. He bypassed protocol entirely, pressing the black-and-blue pyramid directly into Klorioa's hands.

"Doctor," Malachi commanded, his deep voice thick with absolute, undeniable hope. "I have the blood samples. And I have the Calvenine."

"What?" Casia asked, her emerald eyes widening in pure confusion as she looked up from the bed. "You said you were going to our quarters to gather Evaria's things."

"Casia, I am deeply sorry for the deception," Malachi confessed, his deep voice trembling slightly. He looked up at the digital chronometer on the trauma suite wall; it read exactly 5:55 AM. The entire night had bled away in a nightmare of betrayal and death, but he had beaten the six-hour window.

If I had told you the truth, the sheer stress would have endangered you and the baby, he thought, the bitter guilt settling heavily in his chest.

"I went to the surface tonight to meet with an Eloi Minister," Malachi stated, finally giving his wife the absolute truth.

Casia gasped softly.

He swallowed hard, his tall frame shaking slightly as the sterile, horrific memory of Fena's execution flashed behind his eyes. "Do you remember Minister Fena?"

Casia offered a slow, stunned nod. She distinctly remembered the one Eloi politician Malachi trusted. Fena was the only surface dweller who had shown them actual empathy two years ago, using her political power to secure the sacred Morlock Rite of Burial for Seraphina.

"She agreed to help me get the unmutated Eloi blood samples, and she personally secured this Calvenine drug," Malachi explained, his voice breaking. "But—she was killed tonight. In cold blood. Right in front of me."

"What?" Casia said. She looked at her husband as if his logical mind had finally fractured, yet she offered a small, disbelieving smile, reassuring him that despite the sheer, factual insanity of what he had done behind her back, she was still with him.

"I am sorry. I had to try. Everything happened so fast. Here, look."

He placed the black-and-blue pyramidal Aeterna stone onto the metallic medical tray, his bare hand lingering on the glass just long enough for the bio-electric charge to activate it again. It projected Fena's final holographic message in front of Casia, Doctor Klorioa, and Doctor Zeangol.

As the Minister's brave, doomed words filled the sterile suite, tears welled in all of their eyes. The profound weight of Fena's sacrifice settled over them in absolute silence.

Then, a sound shattered the quiet.

It was a strained, agonizingly slow whisper. Malachi and Casia snapped their heads toward the diagnostic bed.

Evaria remained physically frozen in time, her body locked in the rigid paralysis of Stage Two-A PCR. Yet, a single, fresh tear breached the corner of her unblinking eye, sliding down her pale cheek. She was fighting the neurological lock with every ounce of her willpower, proving she could hear and comprehend exactly what Fena had done for her.

"Fat—ther," Evaria forced the fractured syllables through her paralyzed vocal cords. "Eloi... Hero."

The combined diagnostics confirmed Evaria was still firmly locked in the physical paralysis of Stage Two-A, but her neurological activity was spiking wildly. She was actively fighting the disease. This was the first absolute confirmation that something entirely different was happening within Malachi's daughter.

She is defying the biological progression of the mutation, Malachi thought, leaning tightly over the diagnostic bed as he analyzed the readings alongside the physicians.

Just minutes before Malachi had arrived, Doctor Zeangol and Klorioa had inserted an intravenous tube into Evaria to extract fresh blood samples and provide nourishment, as she could not eat in her catatonic state. They had administered a heavy peachberry solution. The doctors had noted the high chemical levels in the readout, but neither Klorioa nor Zeangol made the connection that the high concentration of anthocyanins in the peachberries was exactly what had given Evaria the biological edge to fight the paralysis and speak those three miraculous words.

"This is completely unexpected," Doctor Klorioa stated, her clinical tone fracturing with disbelief as she looked over at her colleague. "Zeangol, are you seeing this?"

"I am," Zeangol confirmed, her voice hushed with scientific awe. "Evaria is still physically in Stage Two-A, but the cellular and neural scans are isolating a completely new gene marker. It is unlike anything in our documented research."

Klorioa turned her scanner so Malachi and Casia could see the erratic, overlapping waveforms on the screen.

"The bio-electric signature is bifurcated, but I cannot determine the exact nature of why this is happening," Klorioa explained, her scientific mind struggling to categorize the sheer impossibility of the data. "It is as if she is anchored here in this room, yet simultaneously existing somewhere else. Biologically, she is caught between two distinct, distorted times."

"Time travel?" Malachi asked, his analytical mind immediately trying to process the implications.

Doctor Klorioa shook her head, her piercing eyes fixed entirely on the scanner's output. "No. It is not active transit. Think of it more as a temporal prison. She is trapped, constantly trying to break out into the present flow of time but unable to cross the threshold. It is as if she can see the opening—she is actively pushing toward us—but she physically cannot bridge the gap to reach where she needs to go."

On the diagnostic bed, Evaria's rigidly pointed finger began to sway—up and down, then left and right. She was fiercely trying to break out of the condition.

"Doctor, look!" Casia gasped, pointing at Evaria as if the young woman might break through the invisible wall and return to them at any second.

"Listen to me, I am going to run the samples Fena gave you into the medical AI mainframe right now," Klorioa said, her voice tight with adrenaline. "I cannot promise anything, but her neurological resistance is astonishing."

Moving with precise urgency, Doctor Zeangol extracted a fresh blood sample from Evaria's rigid arm and immediately handed the localized vial to Klorioa.

Klorioa grabbed the two vials of unmutated Eloi blood from the tray. The glass casings were etched in flowing Eloi script: one read *Universal*, the other *Baseline Non-Universal*. Running entirely on the desperate, adrenaline-fueled momentum of the crisis, both physicians made a critical oversight. They secured the blood, completely bypassing the small stasis vial of Calvenine. It remained sitting untouched next to the Aeterna stone on the metallic tray.

They programmed the AI mainframe to isolate the 1543 Gene within the Eloi blood, cross-referencing it with Evaria's fresh sample, and binding it directly to Klorioa's experimental Morlock peptide formula.

Five agonizing minutes passed. To Malachi and Casia, the wait felt like an eternity. They stood helplessly by the bed, watching Evaria blink, shed silent tears, and strain against her invisible prison all at once.

Finally, the sterile voice of the medical computer chimed through the suite.

- **POSSIBLE STAGE THREE OVERRIDE SYNTHESIZED.**
- **WARNING: THIS IS NOT A CURE.**
- **BASELINE SEQUENCE: UNSTABLE**
- **MISSING CRITICAL PROTEIN STRANDS.**
- **TEMPORARY NEUROLOGICAL STABILITY AT 51%**
- **OPTIMAL ANCHOR REQUIRES 98%.**

"Fifty-one percent might be just enough to pull her back," Klorioa breathed, making a desperate medical calculation. She swiftly extracted the newly synthesized serum into a pneumatic injector and pressed it directly against Evaria's neck, administering the dose.

For three harrowing seconds, nothing happened.

Then, the rigid temporal lock shattered. Evaria gasped, a massive intake of air filling her lungs as she slumped forward.

Malachi caught her instantly, pulling his daughter into his arms. Evaria sobbed, burying her face into his dark robes before reaching out to pull Casia into the desperate embrace.

"Mother! Father!" Evaria cried, her voice finally her own. She looked over Malachi's shoulder at Klorioa, a tearful, exhausted smile breaking across her face. "Doctor... thank you."

Evaria pulled back from her parents, taking a deep, shaky breath. She turned, lifting her foot to take a step toward the physicians.

Her foot never hit the floor.

Mid-stride, Evaria's eyes went wide. The tear on her cheek stopped rolling. Her body locked entirely in place, perfectly balanced on one leg, utterly trapped in time once more.

The suite plunged into a devastated silence.

"What went wrong, Doctor?" Malachi asked, his deep voice heavy with a crushing, quiet disappointment. He wasn't angry; as a man of science, he understood the brutal reality of variables.

"Why did it stop?" Casia asked, gently resting her hand on Evaria's frozen arm.

Dr. Zeangol immediately ran the handheld scanner over Evaria's rigid form, her vibrant orange eyes dimming in shock and profound sadness. She checked the neural interface, her voice tight. "Her synaptic pathways have completely locked down again, Doctor Klorioa. The neural spike has flatlined back to the baseline."

"The 1543 Gene stabilized the temporal anchor for a brief window," Klorioa explained, her tone shifting from sudden disappointment to a fierce, factual determination. "But without those missing protein strands the AI warned us about, the sequence collapsed. The formula could not hold the connection."

She looked up at Malachi and Casia, her piercing eyes unwavering. "We are stuck back at Stage Two-A, but we will not surrender to this. Evaria is entirely stable and in no pain. We will maintain the exact same isolation protocols and watch her carefully until we finally crack the code of the 1543 Gene. We are closer now than we have ever been; we just need to return to the drawing board."

"I will secure her vitals and initiate the sensory protocols immediately," Zeangol added softly, stepping up to take the active watch so Klorioa could tend to the parents.

Malachi slowly nodded, wrapping his arm around Casia to pull her into a comforting embrace. But the hold was rigid and *hollow*. A creeping, unsure coldness had begun to settle heavily over his analytical mind, fracturing his emotional core.

Casia could instantly feel the unnatural stiffness in his touch—a chilling, embracing detachment that was entirely unlike him. But her emerald eyes remained so desperately locked on the frozen form of their daughter that her grief overshadowed the warning signs. She leaned into him, too devastated to fully process the profound shift happening within her husband.

Fena was murdered for nothing, Malachi thought, his analytical mind shutting down into cold, sterile logic. *I risked everything, she gave her life, and I still failed them all.*

He slowly pulled away from the embrace. *An Eloi who overcame prejudices to help me and my fellow Morlocks... Senseless death.*

"I must leave," Malachi stated, his deep voice entirely flat, stripped of its usual warmth. "I have to contact Eloi Minister Xenora."

Casia, Doctor Klorioa, and Doctor Zeangol all briefly glanced at him, but the sheer emotional exhaustion and the immediate crisis of monitoring Evaria's vitals completely overshadowed this second, glaring warning sign. His tone was far too cold and clinical for a father who had just watched his daughter relapse, but none of the women possessed the clarity through their grief to recognize the *Hollowing* taking root.

Turning away without another word, Malachi moved with a detached, stiffness. He stepped back from the diagnostic bed and approached the metallic medical tray. He reached out and retrieved the small, black-and-blue obsidian pyramid, slipping the Aeterna stone back into his pocket. His intellect was so clouded by the trauma of his perceived failure that he did not even look at what else was resting mere inches from his hand.

He walked directly toward the heavy trauma suite doors. The warmth of Malachi wanting to look back—to assure Casia and the physicians that he still held onto the hope of a cure—was entirely gone. The heavy doors hissed open, and he simply stepped through.

He did not pause. He did not look back.

He vanished into the dark subterranean corridor, entirely consumed by the *Hollow*. Casia stared at the empty doorway, a sudden, chilling spike of dread finally piercing through her grief.

Left behind under the sterile white lights of the trauma suite, the small stasis vial containing the absolute last sample of ***Calvenine*** continued to sit silently on the metallic tray, completely forgotten.

Chapter VIII — The Hollow Mockery

Malachi's physical frame had reached its absolute biological limit. The creeping coldness of the *Hollow* now dictated his movements—a devastating, detached hyper-fixation that entirely stripped away his analytical reasoning. He was completely consumed by the perceived, permanent loss of his daughter to the PCR, his logic so broken and clouded by grief that he no longer cared about anything outside of Evaria, Casia, and the absolute survival of the Morlocks. His mind was so fractured he was not even thinking about his wife's unborn baby. This cold, illogical state masked the severe exhaustion that threatened to collapse his legs.

Deep within the pocket of his dark robes rested the small, obsidian pyramid. He utilized the subterranean movable walkway, his piercing, heavy yellow eyes bloodshot from a severe lack of sleep, staring blankly ahead as he navigated the route back to his private office.

Upon unlocking the heavy doors, he crossed the room and sank into the chair behind his desk. Operating on pure, illogical focus, he programmed his chronometer for an 11:00 AM wake cycle. As the setting locked in, the last physical remnants of his adrenaline vanished. He simply laid his head on the cold desk, wrapping his arms over his face as deep, heavy sobs wracked his exhausted frame. Within moments, he wept until his consciousness abruptly shut down.

However, the emotional suppression he relied upon while awake immediately failed the moment he fell asleep. Malachi found himself trapped in a vivid, agonizing dream state, pulled right back to the surface. He was entirely paralyzed—a helpless observer locked outside of his own body. He was forced to watch his past self and Minister Fena as the exact events of her assassination began to unfold in real-time.

Turn around! Malachi screamed within his mind, fighting desperately against the invisible restraints. *He is not a doctor! Dalvin is secret police!* But his thoughts made no sound. Fena could not hear him, and his past self remained oblivious to the approaching threat. He could do absolutely nothing. He was forced to watch, in excruciating detail, as Dalvin executed the Minister. He felt the phantom surge of panic as his past self tried to react, instantly followed by the blinding, searing white light of the weapon that swallowed the surface in total darkness.

This is pure insanity, Malachi thought, his mind struggling to process the sheer, senseless brutality. *Fena posed no threat to anyone, yet she was executed simply for providing blood samples and the Calvenine to help cure a disease.*

He thought about the broken words Evaria had forced out while locked in the rigid paralysis of Stage Two-A. *Eloi... Hero.* It was a biological anomaly that had completely puzzled Doctor Klorioa, but to Malachi, the statement itself was absolute fact.

She is a hero, his thoughts continued, *but this act descends into the realm of deep insanity. The Eloi are killing their own kind just because she refused to conform to their hateful dogma of treating Morlocks as subservient. She overcame the stigma.*

The horrific imagery of the surface abruptly faded, and he found himself standing entirely alone in the dark.

Then, a brilliant, piercing light ignited in the darkness. For a fraction of a second, Malachi instinctively raised his hands to shield his face. Intense light always had a blinding, effect on the sensitive yellow eyes of a Morlock. But as the glare washed over him, he realized his vision was rapidly adjusting. He was able to process the illumination without the familiar burning sensation.

Grounded in the realization that he was still dreaming, Malachi lowered his hands. As a man of science, he was not religious, nor did he spend time theorizing about an afterlife. However, he had always reasoned that if such a plane of existence were real, its nature would be far beyond anything his mind could ever imagine. *Was this it?* he thought, watching intently as a silhouette began to emerge from the center of the brilliant light, moving steadily toward him.

Malachi widened his heavy eyes. As the silhouette solidified, his breath caught in his throat.

It was Seraphina.

She approached him, her light blue-gray skin with its familiar, beautiful hint of green practically radiant in the ambient illumination. She reached out and gently touched his cheek. The physical sensation was absolute. As a single tear rolled down his face, he felt the warmth of her fingers brushing it away. He wanted to protest, suddenly ashamed; he did not want his late wife to see him in this broken, *Hollow* state. So many conflicting data points were running through his analytical mind. He knew with absolute certainty that this was a dream, yet the environment around him, the gravity of her presence, felt entirely real.

"Malachi, I see it," Seraphina said, her voice echoing with profound, infinite empathy. "The *Hollow* is consuming your spirit, and you must fight it. Your heart is shattered, but this moment is not what it seems. Casia loves you. Evaria needs you. And you must stay strong for the fragile, unborn life Casia carries. Trust me. I stand entirely outside of time. I see the truth of what is to come, but I cannot reveal the path. You must simply refuse to let the dark take you."

Malachi trembled uncontrollably, shaking his head in absolute denial. "No! No!" he protested, his deep voice cracking. "You are dead. You are not real." Yet, he hesitated, momentarily disarmed by the warmth of the brilliant light—a light he could somehow process without being temporarily blurred or blinded as a Morlock. Still, he forced himself to reject the comfort she was offering. The factual reality of his failure was too heavy.

"Evaria is locked in a catatonic state!" he screamed, his deep voice fracturing under the immense weight of his guilt. "She is totally dependent on twenty-four-hour care! I failed! And Fena... the Eloi will know what happened to Fena. I have the proof right here! I have the final message, and Eloi Minister Xenora will have no choice but to address it nationally! I will make a fool out of her! They have to change their ways! They cannot treat our species, the Morlocks, like trash anymore! No more!"

Malachi shouted the last words, trembling with such profound, blinding anger that it prompted Seraphina to step forward. She reached out to embrace him, desperate to absorb his pain and stop his spiraling agony.

But Malachi physically recoiled. He backed away from her, the cold detachment of the *Hollow* rejecting the emotional connection.

"No! No!" Malachi shouted, his grief hardening into absolute fury. "I am finished being mocked by the Eloi! History has to change! The stagnation of this hateful status quo has to stop! They will listen, or both the Eloi and the Morlocks will die. Resources are at critical levels! If we cannot reunify with the surface and secure new resources by exploring the nighttime stars, then both our species will face extinction! Can't you see that, Seraphina? Our history is dying! I have studied it, and I have lived it! Why can't you understand it???"

Tears finally spilled from his piercing yellow eyes as he cried out to her. But before Seraphina could answer, her form abruptly dissolved into the light.

The blaring, piercing shriek of his chronometer's 11:00 AM alarm shattered the void, harshly yanking him awake and back into the cold, sterile reality of his subterranean office.

Malachi rose heavily from the desk, the blaring alarm completely severing him from the dream. Moving with a cold, rigid detachment, he walked into his personal restroom. The harsh lighting buzzed faintly overhead as he washed his face in the ice-cold water. He picked up his brush, methodically pulling it through his long hair—a stark white threaded heavily with strands of grey and faint traces of black.

He untied the purple sash from his waist. Retrieving a specialized chemical solvent, he carefully scrubbed away a small, lingering redberry stain from the fabric. Once it was perfectly clean and dry, he wrapped it securely back around his black robes. He knew perfectly well how to tie a standard utility knot, but he deliberately secured the fabric exactly the way Evaria had taught him, choosing her specific method as opposed to his own technique.

Evaria, he thought, his piercing yellow eyes staring into the mirror, anchoring himself to the cold reality of his reflection. *I do what I do now for you, and no one else.* "Casia... please forgive me," he muttered to his reflection, his deep voice barely a whisper in the quiet, sterile room.

He stepped back into his dimly lit office and approached the desk. He reached for his circular communication wafer. For a fraction of a second, his hand hesitated—a final, fleeting surge of his analytical, practical mind trying to stop him. But the *Hollow*'s profound indifference surged forward like a physical chill, entirely overriding his hesitation. He pressed the wafer.

A few seconds passed before the holographic projector hummed to life, casting a stark, bluish light across the dark room. The shimmering image of Eloi Minister Xenora materialized over his desk. Her long blonde hair cascaded over her shoulder, tucking behind one distinctly pointed ear. She looked at him with an expression of puzzled disdain.

"Malachi?" Xenora said, her tone dripping with a disrespectful, cold authority that cut through the heavy silence of the office. "Why are you calling me directly instead of using the established communication protocols dictated by the Eloi-Morlock Accords? What is the meaning of this?"

Malachi stared at her projection, absorbing the blatant disdain. Then, a slow, chillingly icy smile crept across his face—a direct, calculated response to her arrogance.

"Section 2BA-Red," Malachi stated, his voice entirely devoid of emotion. "I declare it."

Xenora's eyes widened in genuine shock, her rigid composure fracturing. The ancient protocol was an inescapable mandate engineered solely to warn of catastrophic, planetary-wide consequences—imminent crises that both the Morlocks and Eloi would be forced to address together.

"You cannot be serious," she hissed, the holographic projection flickering slightly with her sudden movement. "You dare to invoke a Class-Red Disaster Protocol? I have no choice but to call the Senate into order to hear this." She glared at him, her disdain returning, hard and absolute. "Fine. Be at the Senate Antechamber in one hour."

The comm-link abruptly went dead, the hologram collapsing into nothingness and plunging the office back into deep, oppressive shadows.

Malachi's icy smile vanished, replaced instantly by unyielding, sterile focus. He reached into his robe pocket and pulled out the small, obsidian pyramid. In the dim light, he ran his thumb over the diagnostic node to verify its energy capacity. The digital readout illuminated faintly, confirming the charge was steady and holding at ninety-five percent. Satisfied with the factual data, he slipped the absolute proof of Fena's murder safely back into his pocket.

Malachi stepped out of his dimly lit office and proceeded toward the subterranean lifts that would carry him to the surface and into the Eloi Senate Antechamber. His heart was completely cold.

As he passed through the upper tiers of the Morlock business sector, he glanced at the colossal public projection screens. The local media networks were already breaking into their regular broadcasts, flashing the severe, crimson alerts that a Class-Red Disaster Protocol had been invoked.

A chilling, confident smile touched his lips. He logically calculated that today, the Eloi would finally be forced to accept Reunification. The sheer public unrest that would ignite over the undeniable proof of Minister Fena's murder would leave them with zero political leverage. He believed his strategy was absolutely airtight.

The Hollow inside you... you must fight it!

Seraphina's desperate warning echoed in the back of his mind, a fleeting ghost of empathy trying to breach his cold defenses.

Malachi simply shook his head, physically discarding the thought as he stepped into the lift. He buried the echo under heavy layers of indifference. He believed he was in total control, entirely unaware that his usually flawless rationality was now secretly spiraling into chaos, completely hijacked by the *Hollow*.

The heavy transit doors sealed shut, and Malachi began his rapid subterranean ascent toward the surface. Reaching the upper staging level, he walked with rigid precision through a long, dark access corridor and stepped onto the central circular platform of the Senate Antechamber, gripping the metallic railing tightly.

Deep within his black robes, his circular holo-wafer began to chirp. He withdrew the device and looked at the flashing display. It was Casia.

Not now, Malachi thought, his mind processing the interruption with cold, sterile detachment. *I do not want to deal with this.*

He felt nothing. He did not open the connection. Operating entirely detached from his surroundings, he put the device on silent and slid it back into his pocket just as the heavy gears engaged and the circular lift began to rise.

High above him, the heavy iris doors of the Senate floor unsealed. Blinding, pristine surface light poured down into the shaft. Instantly, the platform's localized environmental systems engaged, enveloping Malachi in a cylindrical, tinted protection field to shield his sensitive eyes from the harsh brightness of the chamber.

He rose through the floor, coming to a halt in the exact dead center of the colossal amphitheater. Towering tiers of seating completely surrounded him. Nearly four hundred Eloi stared down at him from the heights of the room—over two hundred regional Senators were physically present, while a hundred and seventy high-ranking politicians from the far reaches of the planet were projected onto small digital screens that rounded the amphitheater's perimeter. They were draped in pristine yellow and white garments, bathed in continuous illumination, while Malachi stood isolated below them in a column of artificial shadow.

The deafening murmur of the vast assembly echoed down to the floor. Then, the sharp, authoritative crack of a gavel cut through the noise. On the digital interface pad bolted to Malachi's circular stand, Minister Xenora's face materialized.

"This is a 2BA-Red Protocol, initiated by the Morlock Historian, Malachi," Xenora's amplified voice boomed across the vast chamber. "The protocol must be heard by all members of the Eloi Senate without further delay."

A profound, absolute silence immediately fell over the hundreds of politicians. Because it was reserved only for matters of planetary survival, the invocation of a Class-Red disaster forced an immediate, inescapable resolution, completely bypassing months of bureaucratic delays.

Malachi scanned the towering tiers of light, his piercing yellow eyes analyzing the hundreds of faces looking down at him. Within the protective shadow of his cylinder, he formulated his rhetorical strategy with calculated precision.

First, I will present the undeniable, factual necessity of Reunification, he reasoned, his mind operating sequentially. *I will detail exactly why our mutual survival demands it now. When they laugh and mock the data—which historical probability dictates they absolutely will—I will deploy the secondary variable.*

His hand subtly brushed the heavy fabric of his pocket, feeling the sharp, obsidian edges of the Aeterna stone.

I will play Minister Fena's final recording. They will be forced to react to the factual evidence of her murder. They will have to listen to her final assessment. Out of nearly four hundred Eloi in this chamber, surely one of them possesses enough fundamental logic to agree that hundreds of thousands of years of systemic cruelty must end so a new era can survive.

"Distinguished members of the Eloi Senate, and representatives of the far reaches of the surface," Malachi began, his deep voice projecting up into the blinding light with cold, unwavering clarity. "I come before you once more to present an undeniable factual crisis. Planetary resources are rapidly approaching absolute depletion. The subterranean manufacturing infrastructure required to sustain your surface lifestyle will suffer a complete, mathematical collapse within 1,200 Grid-cycles. In your measurement of time, that is exactly one hundred years—"

Immediately, the colossal amphitheater erupted into chaos. Deafening jeers and laughter echoed down from the blinding tiers.

Malachi arched his shoulders forward, physically anchoring himself against the railing of his platform. He did not yield to the noise, nor did he shout in anger. He simply amplified his voice, cutting through the unified mockery with chilling, sterile precision.

"If you cannot overcome your systemic hatred for the Morlocks, both of our species will face total extinction," Malachi stated firmly, his piercing yellow eyes locked on the digital interface pad. "I do not deal in fabrications. These figures are absolute. We must begin the process of Reunification immediately."

Minister Xenora shook her head, a sneer of complete, arrogant annoyance crossing her pristine features. She had heard this exact apocalyptic rhetoric countless times before. She was entirely used to Malachi constantly warning that resources were running low, just as she had been used to his father, the former Ambassador to the Morlocks, preaching the exact same message. To Xenora, a deeply entrenched elitist who cared only for her own absolute power, personal luxury, and the maintenance of the subjugated status quo, the data was meaningless. It was not his message that infuriated her; it was the sheer, audacious annoyance that a Morlock had dared to weaponize the sacred 2BA-Red Protocol to force her to listen.

She struck her gavel so harshly that the deafening room fell quiet immediately.

"Silence!" Xenora's voice boomed through the chamber, overpowering the remaining echoes. She glared down at the shadowy column isolating the Morlock. "One hundred years is a distant hypothetical, Historian! It is not considered an immediate planetary emergency! And your delusional talk of Reunification is absolutely not grounds for a 2BA-Red Protocol!"

Her venomous dismissal acted as a catalyst. The hundreds of Eloi politicians became further infuriated by his presence, unleashing a renewed wave of intense jeering and savage name-calling raining down into the center of the chamber. They were so caught up in their own luxury and their lifestyle of subjugation that they physically could not view the Morlocks as equals.

Malachi nodded his head in cold disdain. A chilling, icy smile touched his lips as he realized his logical calculation was entirely correct—they were reacting exactly as he had predicted. He reached deep into his robes and withdrew the black-and-blue obsidian Aeterna stone.

Instantly, the deafening jeers died down to a tense, hushed murmur. Every Eloi in the chamber recognized the ancient, pyramidal technology—it was a personal stasis journal, the surface world's equivalent of a last will and testament.

He pressed the activation sequence. The digital interface pad on his stand synchronized with the chamber's massive screens, forcefully overriding the Senate's localized feed. In a matter of seconds, the broadcast was transmitted across the entire surface world and relayed deep into the subterranean Morlock grid.

The shimmering, unmistakable holographic image of Minister Fena materialized for both species to see.

"Malachi, if you are hearing this, it means my darkest suspicions were correct," Fena's voice echoed through the amphitheater. *"Doctor Giena successfully extracted the cargo and delivered it to me, but she did not arrive for our final escort to the park. A stranger was sent in her place. Fearing the Senate had compromised the handoff, I could not risk leaving the true cargo in the medical case. I secretly transferred the items into this stasis stone. Inside, I have preserved the unmutated Eloi blood samples. And something else... a fully preserved vial containing the absolute last sample of the Calvenine drug. Save your daughter, my friend. Save our future."*

Minister Xenora stared at the undeniable image of her murdered colleague. She attempted to maintain her political mask, though her pristine features twitched with panic. "Historian Malachi, what is the meaning of this?" she demanded, her false calm rapidly fracturing. "Calvenine is a forbidden substance! It was banned hundreds of thousands of years ago! It started a planetary conflict with you savages who drugged us!"

Xenora lost all composure, her voice breaking into an angry shout.

Unexpectedly, Malachi nodded. A chilling, humorless smile crossed his face. It was the calculated expression of a man holding the absolute, undeniable truth.

"I possess the historical records of that era," Malachi stated, his deep voice booming through the chamber with piercing, sterile clarity. "I have the factual proof that Morlocks did not intentionally drug you. PCR was an unintentional, devastating biological side effect that altered the Morlock genetic marker 1543!"

He leaned forward over the railing, shouting over the rising panic in the room. "The Eloi had no reservations about consuming Calvenine! You gladly took it until the specific chemical ingredients required to manufacture it were entirely depleted and the drug could no longer be synthesized! How dare you accuse the Morlocks of drugging you! You started a global war because you were suffering from biological withdrawals!"

"How dare you!" Xenora shrieked, her face twisting in pure malice as her foundational lies were broadcast to the world.

She slammed her hand onto her master control console. Instantly, Malachi's audio feed was abruptly severed. But she did not stop there.

Driven by pure spite, she bypassed the platform's environmental controls and deactivated his safety shield.

The tinted cylindrical field vanished.

The unshielded, blinding brilliance of the surface-level amphitheater slammed down onto Malachi. He withered instantly, a raw scream tearing from his throat as the intense light blinded his sensitive yellow eyes like a sudden camera flash going off in the absolute darkness, brightly illuminating his blue-green gray skin without physically burning it.

"Get out of here!" Xenora screamed, hitting the master descent sequence.

The heavy gears engaged with a jolt, and Malachi's platform abruptly dropped, pulling his agonized, blinded form back down toward the dark subterranean depths.

"You are all savages and liars! All of you!" Xenora roared into her microphone.

She slammed the master kill-switch. In an instant, the massive screens in the Senate went dark. Across the sunlit surface, and deep within the illuminated subterranean cities, every single media feed abruptly snapped to absolute, dead black.

Malachi wept in the protective shadows of the descending lift. While his body was utterly exhausted, he was not in any systemic physical pain; rather, his sensitive yellow eyes were blurry for several minutes from the lingering optical shock of the amphitheater's brilliance. His analytical mind, unable to process the sheer weight of this absolute failure, finally collapsed into the cold, sterile indifference of the *Hollow*.

Reaching the bottom of the shaft, he stumbled off the platform and walked down the long, dark transit tunnel with a cold, numb stiffness. Deep within his robes, his circular holo-wafer began to vibrate and chirp incessantly. This was Casia's second attempt to reach him, but he flatly refused to answer. He let the device ring against his chest, entirely consumed by the hurt, the unexpected humiliation, and the freezing grip of the *Hollow*.

Her desperate, unanswered calls were the direct result of a terrifying sequence of events that had begun unfolding hours earlier.

At exactly 9:00 AM, long before the Senate broadcast had hijacked the airwaves, Doctor Klorioa awoke from a brief, heavy sleep in the adjacent on-call quarters. The subterranean trauma suite was entirely silent. She quietly checked the recovery room. Casia was sleeping in the same bed as Evaria, refusing to go home to an empty house while Malachi attended to his mysterious business with the Eloi Senate.

Satisfied that Evaria's vitals were stable, Klorioa returned to the main lab. By 9:15 AM, she was already pacing before the diagnostic monitors, reviewing the data streams with deep, clinical frustration.

Something is missing, she thought, her mind running through the chemical equations. *I did everything right. The unmutated Eloi blood stabilized the Stage Two-A shift, but the genetic markers are only paused, not reversing. What did I miss? How can I completely eradicate this terrible disease for Evaria and the others?*

Just before 11:00 AM, thoroughly exhausted, she finally sank into the chair behind the primary terminal. She let out a quiet sigh, leaning back and stretching her stiff arms over her head to relieve the tension in her neck.

At that exact moment, Doctor Zeangol stumbled out of the on-call quarters. Her usually sharp neurological focus was completely blurred by sheer exhaustion. She rubbed her vibrant orange eyes and walked toward the primary terminal, entirely failing to calculate her distance to the metallic surgical tray sitting exactly where Malachi had left it the night before.

Her hip collided hard with the steel edge.

The tray rattled harshly. A small stasis vial tipped over and rolled perilously toward the edge.

Zeangol let out a sharp gasp of panic, her reflexes suddenly firing as she lunged, catching the glass vial just a millimeter before it plummeted to the floor. She let out a breathless exhale, clutching it to her chest. "I am so sorry, Klorioa. My spatial awareness is statistically zero right now."

Klorioa did not reprimand her. Her piercing eyes widened in absolute, factual shock as she stared at the object resting in her colleague's hand.

"Zeangol... what are you holding?" Klorioa asked, slowly standing up.

Zeangol blinked, looking down at the compact casing. "It is the... the Calvenine."

"THAT IS IT!" Klorioa shouted, the sudden burst of volume making the exhausted neurologist jump. "The Calvenine! It is the missing base ingredient! In the sheer chaos of Evaria crashing last night, we completely forgot to integrate the primary catalyst!"

Moving with sudden, frantic energy, the two doctors rushed to the primary diagnostic terminal. Zeangol inserted the sample into the centrifuge while Klorioa initiated a high-speed AI molecular simulation. Her fingers flew across the holographic keys to calculate exactly what the Calvenine base would do to the mutated 1543 Gene. As the analyzer began tearing down the extinct drug's chemical profile, the initial readouts flashed across the screen, hinting at a highly complex, botanical derivative.

As the simulation ran, Casia suddenly awoke in the adjacent recovery quarters. It was exactly 12:12 PM. Seeing the empty space where her husband should have been, a sharp spike of anxiety hit her. She grabbed her circular holo-wafer and immediately initiated a direct call to Malachi. She listened to the outgoing chime ring incessantly, but he did not answer. After several agonizing seconds, the connection timed out and went dead.

Casia stepped hurriedly into the main lab, gripping the wafer tightly.

"Doctor, Malachi is not answering his comms—"

Before Klorioa could respond, or the AI could output the final simulation result, every digital monitor in the lab suddenly flickered. The medical data was abruptly shoved aside as a planetary override command hijacked the screens.

It was exactly 12:15 PM.

The audio blasted through the quiet lab. "This is a 2BA-Red Protocol, initiated by the Morlock Historian, Malachi..."

Casia stood paralyzed before the main laboratory monitor, her emerald eyes wide in horror as she watched her husband on the colossal feed. He stood contained within the sheer walls of the central enclosure circle—isolated in a stark column of shadow, entirely surrounded by the blinding, oppressive tiers of the Eloi Senate.

Seeing his rigid, anchored posture within that confined space and hearing his cold, flat delivery, the missing variables finally clicked in Casia's mind. The chilling, cold detachment she had felt in his embrace earlier wasn't a lack of love. It was the *Hollow*. He had intentionally shut off his emotional core because he knew he was stepping into the most dangerous, hostile political cage on the planet to fight for their daughter's life.

"Doctor, look," Casia whispered, her anxiety peaking.

She knew her husband better than anyone. As she listened to his escalating tone, she recognized the *Hollow* for what it truly was—a profound, melancholic depression. It was a severe state of mind where true rationality became impossible because he was entirely consumed by the trauma and the compounding problems plaguing their family. The sterile detachment he had weaponized for the trial was fracturing under the sheer weight of his own despair. As he grew genuinely angry on the screen, losing his grip on the cold facts, she realized his silence on the comms minutes earlier was intentional. He had shut her out because his traumatized mind could only focus on surviving the hostile political cage he had just stepped into.

Doctor Klorioa and Doctor Zeangol briefly tore their eyes away from the primary terminal to glance at the broadcast. Beside them, the AI centrifuge hummed at maximum capacity, its processors rapidly running the complex molecular cycles.

"No," Doctor Klorioa muttered, her clinical gaze locked on the screen.

She could see Malachi was already half gone. As one of the top neurologists in the subterranean grid, Zeangol stepped up beside Klorioa, her expression grave. They both understood the *Hollow* was far more than just profound melancholy; it was a severe, cascading neurological trauma response. His erratic, rigid behavior on the broadcast wasn't a calculated political strategy anymore. They knew exactly what they were witnessing—an analytical mind actively experiencing a public nervous breakdown under the crushing, impossible weight of grief and exhaustion.

"Doctor! Look!" Casia gasped, her voice trembling as she pointed at the monitor.

On the colossal feed, Malachi had just withdrawn the obsidian Aeterna stone. A moment later, Minister Fena's unmistakable holographic image materialized, her doomed words echoing across the global override. But it was what Malachi did next that sent pure, suffocating terror gripping through Casia. Using Fena's holographic confession as the catalyst, Malachi boldly shouted the true, damning historical origins of the Calvenine withdrawals.

She realized with sickening clarity that her husband had just broadcasted the Eloi Senate's darkest, most guarded historical secret to millions of viewers across both the surface and the subterranean grid. He had cornered the most powerful, ruthless politicians in the world on a live, inescapable feed, placing himself in immediate, fatal danger.

On the screen, Minister Xenora shrieked. She slammed the master kill-switch. In an instant, the colossal screens in the laboratory abruptly snapped to absolute, dead black.

"Casia, get a hold of Malachi! Keep trying his communicator right now!" Klorioa ordered, her voice sharp with panic.

Casia gasped in pure terror. Frantically, she raised her holo-wafer and dialed Malachi's comm-link a second time, praying he would answer. She held it tightly, listening to the agonizing, endless ringing as the line went completely ignored.

But just as the second connection timed out, a sharp, crystalline chime cut through the heavy dread in the lab.

The primary diagnostic terminal hummed back to life. The high-speed AI molecular simulation was complete.

The sudden shift in lighting instantly pulled the two doctors' attention away from the political disaster and back to the illuminated data of the cure. A crisp, green block of text scrolled across the holographic display, rendering the complex biology into absolute fact:

- **BASELINE:** CHACOIDINE CATALYST SYNTHESIZED.
- **EFFICACY RATE:** 99.9% **(0.1% DEVIATION).**
- **BIO-CHEMICAL MECHANISM:** HIGH-CONCENTRATION ANTHOCYANINS **(DELPHINIDIN/MALVIDIN)** REQUIRED TO CROSS BLOOD-BRAIN BARRIER.
- **CLINICAL NOTE 1:** REDBERRY **(PELARGONIDIN)** DERIVATIVES ACTED AS TEMPORARY STAGE 2-A INHIBITOR.
- **CLINICAL NOTE 2:** PEACHBERRY INTRAVENOUS SOLUTION CREATED TEMPORARY SYNAPTIC SURGE.
- **CRITICAL CATALYST REQUIREMENT:** ANCIENT BLUEBERRY FRUIT DERIVATIVE.
- **STATUS:** RECENTLY RESEQUENCED. AVAILABLE SOON FOR MASS DISTRIBUTION FROM HORTICULTURE ENCLAVE.

Doctor Klorioa stopped breathing. She stared at the flashing letters, her analytical mind racing to process the data as the massive biological puzzle finally locked into place.

"The Chacoidine..." Klorioa breathed, absolute scientific clarity washing over her. She stared at the flashing text, flawlessly bridging the ancient history with modern botany. "The extinct base catalyst Malachi found in the archives... it is not some lost synthetic compound. It is simply a hyper-concentrated derivative of anthocyanins." She slowly turned her head, her piercing eyes locking onto Casia.

Standing right beside the terminal, completely consumed by her terrifying anxiety over Malachi's unanswered calls, Casia was nervously chewing on a redberry she had absently pulled from Casia personal rations. She froze mid-bite as both doctors suddenly stared at her.

"The redberries Evaria has been eating contain just enough of the pelargonidin chemical to act as a hidden biological shield," Klorioa explained, her clinical tone breaking into sheer disbelief. "That is exactly why her mutation locked into Stage Two-A instead of progressing to Stage Three! She was unknowingly medicating herself for the last two years!"

Klorioa paused, a sudden spark of realization hitting her. "Wait..." she muttered, her fingers flying across the holographic interface to access the subterranean medical registry. She rapidly cross-referenced the dietary logs of every Morlock patient currently paralyzed in the Enclave.

Her piercing eyes widened as the data aligned. "It is a statistical absolute," she announced, looking back at Zeangol and Casia. "Every single patient currently stabilized in Stage Two-A has maintained a high-pelargonidin diet heavy in redberries and peachberries! Their diets are the exact, factual reason they have not succumbed to the final stage of the disease!"

Klorioa pointed sharply at the fifth line of the readout. "And the peachberry intravenous drip we gave Evaria this morning—it flooded her system with enough raw anthocyanins to temporarily bridge the neural gap! That is how she found the strength to force out those words—Eloi... Hero!"

Zeangol stared at the complex holographic data, her exhaustion momentarily forgotten. "So, the missing anchor to fully cure the disease wasn't some highly complex synthetic chemical..."

Doctor Klorioa stopped breathing. She stared at the flashing letters, her analytical mind racing to process the data as the massive biological puzzle finally locked into place.

"The Chacoidine..." Klorioa breathed, absolute scientific clarity washing over her. She stared at the flashing text, flawlessly bridging the ancient history with modern botany. "The extinct base catalyst Malachi found in the archives... it is not some lost synthetic compound. It is simply a hyper-concentrated derivative of anthocyanins." She slowly turned her head, her piercing eyes locking onto Casia.

Standing right beside the terminal, completely consumed by her terrifying anxiety over Malachi's unanswered calls, Casia was nervously stress-eating from the massive ration pouch of redberries Doctor Zeangol had surrendered to her earlier. Her hand was halfway to her mouth when she froze, a vibrant redberry trapped between her fingers, as both physicians suddenly whipped around to stare at her with wide, intense eyes.

Casia swallowed hard, her protective instincts warring with her sudden embarrassment. "I... I told you I could share them," she offered weakly, fully believing the doctors were judging her voracious pregnancy craving.

"The redberries you and Evaria so frequently consume contain just enough of the pelargonidin chemical to act as a hidden biological shield," Klorioa explained, her clinical tone breaking into sheer disbelief, entirely ignoring the apology. "That is exactly why her mutation locked into Stage Two-A instead of progressing to Stage Three! She was unknowingly medicating herself for the last two years!"

Klorioa paused, a sudden spark of realization hitting her. "Wait..." she muttered, her fingers flying across the holographic interface to access the subterranean medical registry. She rapidly cross-referenced the dietary logs of every Morlock patient currently paralyzed in the Enclave.

Her piercing eyes widened as the data aligned. "It is a statistical absolute," she announced, looking back at Zeangol and Casia. "Every single patient currently stabilized in Stage Two-A has maintained a high-pelargonidin diet heavy in redberries and peachberries! Their diets are the exact, factual reason they have not succumbed to the final stage of the disease!"

Klorioa pointed sharply at the fifth line of the readout. "And the peachberry intravenous drip we gave Evaria this morning—it flooded her system with enough raw anthocyanins to temporarily bridge the neural gap! That is how she found the strength to force out those words—Eloi... Hero!"

Zeangol stared at the complex holographic data, her exhaustion momentarily forgotten. "So, the missing anchor to fully cure the disease wasn't some highly complex synthetic chemical..."

"No!" Klorioa exclaimed, shaking her head as the profound scientific reality set in. "We do not need to synthesize the Calvenine at all! The Calvenine was never the cure—it was the root cause of the genetic damage! When our ancestors manufactured that narcotic for the Eloi over a hundred and thirty-three thousand years ago, they had no factual data indicating its synthesis created a highly volatile, undetectable neurotoxin. It acted as a molecular particulate—like breathing in invisible, toxic dust over generations. It systematically attacked our ancestors' synaptic memory proteins and permanently scarred our genetic baseline, mutating the 1543 Gene!"

Klorioa pointed fiercely at the botanical data. "And the Chacoidine—the extinct catalyst Malachi has been searching for—was originally derived from the ancient Azureberry. It possessed a low-level baseline of anthocyanins that helped manage the genetic breakdown. When that fruit went extinct thousands of years ago, the Chacoidine was lost, and the disease was allowed to ravage our species! We only managed to unknowingly stall the final stages of the mutation a century ago when our botanists hybridized the Peachberry and Redberry, inadvertently reintroducing a weak strain of those protective chemicals into our modern diet!"

She looked at Casia and Zeangol, her piercing eyes burning with absolute, undeniable triumph. "But the AI just handed us the ultimate missing link. The Horticulture Enclave recently utilized the ancient seed storage banks to resurrect the extinct Blueberry! The botanical data is absolute: the Blueberry's delphinidin concentration is massively higher than the ancient Azureberry or our modern Peachberries. It is the purest, most hyper-concentrated form of Chacoidine in existence! We just have to extract its specific compounds to engineer the permanent cure and flush out that inherited toxicity!"

Doctor Zeangol blinked her vibrant orange eyes, slowly looking from the world-altering data on the screen to the lead physician. "Tell me I am understanding this correctly, Klorioa," Zeangol said, her tone dropping in sheer disbelief. "We are going to cure a catastrophic, planetary genetic plague... with a fruit salad?"

Klorioa let out a sharp, breathless laugh, the factual absurdity of it breaking through the suffocating tension in the room. "A highly concentrated, molecularly targeted fruit salad, Zeangol. But factually... yes."

Casia's emerald eyes widened as she read the stark green text over the doctor's shoulder. The absolute finality of the data finally broke through her paralyzing terror regarding the Senate broadcast. For the first time since Evaria had slipped back into a catatonic state, profound, happy tears began to flow freely down Casia's face.

But Doctor Klorioa did not pause to celebrate. Operating on pure, clinical adrenaline, she was already tapping the comm-link on her own holo-wafer, bypassing standard channels to establish a direct emergency line to the Horticulture Enclave.

"This is Doctor Klorioa with a priority medical override," she ordered, her voice crisp and commanding. "I need direct, raw samples of the resequenced blueberry fruit derivative sent to the primary trauma suite immediately. Load it into the Tunnel Vac."

The Horticulture Enclave was physically located three to five minutes away by standard subterranean transit, but Klorioa saw no logical reason to delay the process. Evaria was stable in her catatonic state, but the doctor was determined to pull the young Morlock out of the dark as quickly as possible. She utilized the Tunnel Vac system, a hyper-pressurized, zero-friction vacuum conduit that interconnected the critical subterranean sectors, capable of moving physical matter at blistering speeds for high-priority requests.

We have the baseline, we have the blood, we just need the catalyst, Klorioa thought, staring intently at the wall alcove.

They stood in hopeful, quiet anticipation for less than sixty seconds. Then, a sharp, automated beep echoed through the lab, instantly followed by the heavy, rushing hiss of rapid depressurization.

The sleek, cylindrical vacuum enclosure dropped perfectly into the receiving port. The transparent hatch slid open with a soft click, revealing a sealed containment tray holding the dark, organic cluster of the ancient blueberries—the exact missing variable required to cure the mutated 1543 Gene.

Doctor Klorioa extracted the raw blueberry derivative and transferred it directly into the AI's primary synthesis centrifuge. She locked the chamber, integrating the ancient organic catalyst with the unmutated Eloi blood and the tiny stasis vial of the Calvenine base. The heavy machinery hummed, reverse-engineering the complex cellular structures at a microscopic level.

Klorioa watched the diagnostic feed with profound relief as the AI mapped the data.

"We will never need the forbidden drug or another drop of Eloi blood again," Klorioa whispered to Casia, her scientific mind marveling at the synthesis. "Minister Fena's unmutated sample and the Calvenine merely acted as our biological Rosetta Stone. The blood only served to show the

AI exactly what a healthy, uncorrupted gene should look like. Now that the system has permanently recorded that structural blueprint, the physical blood sample is entirely obsolete. The AI can synthesize the genetic corrections purely from the anthocyanins. Moving forward, the blueberries are the absolute only resource we need to mass-produce the cure. There will be zero biological dependence on the surface—we will never need another sample from the Eloi again."

Within moments, the centrifuge hissed open, revealing a specialized cylinder syringe filled with a stable, bioluminescent blue liquid.

Klorioa lifted the syringe, her clinical mask faltering for just a fraction of a second. She turned to her friend.

"Casia, the AI calculated a 99.9% efficacy rate, but that still leaves a 0.1% deviation," Klorioa warned, her voice heavy with factual caution. "This has to work. If it does not..."

Casia swallowed hard and nodded, fully understanding the mathematical risk.

They moved into the recovery quarters. Evaria lay perfectly still, her heavy yellow eyes open but completely vacant, trapped in the catatonic grip of Stage Two-A PCR. Klorioa approached the bed, carefully sterilizing the injection site before administering the brilliant blue compound directly into the young Morlock's bloodstream.

Then, Evaria took a sharp, sudden breath. Her heavy yellow eyes fluttered rapidly. The vacant, empty stare shattered, replaced instantly by conscious clarity. She blinked against the harsh ambient light, her gaze finally focusing and finding her mother.

"Mom?" Evaria whispered.

Casia let out a choked sob, leaning down to pull her daughter into a desperate, tear-filled embrace.

But Evaria gently pulled back, her heavy yellow eyes wide with a sudden, frantic urgency. "Mom, I heard and saw everything on the monitors," she gasped, her voice raspy but gaining rapid strength. She looked past her mother, acknowledging the two stunned physicians. "Thank you, Doctors. But... my father! He looked so cold! Mother, you have to find him! I am okay this time, I think."

Doctor Klorioa and Doctor Zeangol did not step back to celebrate; they immediately began a rigorous medical examination. Zeangol monitored the sudden surge of healthy neurological responses on her tablet, while

Klorioa scanned the genetic markers for a solid five minutes, ensuring this was not a brief, temporary pause like the night before.

Finally, Zeangol lowered her tablet, a massive, genuine smile breaking across her face. She looked at Klorioa and nodded.

"The mutation is actively reversing," Klorioa announced, her voice trembling slightly with the weight of the historical moment. "The cure is absolute."

Operating on pure efficiency, she turned back to her holo-wafer, rapidly backing up the synthesized data and transmitting the finalized cure schematic to every subterranean medical region across the globe. The plague was officially broken.

As the global upload completed, Evaria squeezed her mother's hand. The sheer terror of what she had witnessed while trapped in her paralyzed state anchored her focus.

"You do not have to stay to protect me, Mother," Evaria urged, her voice steadying. "Even though I could not move, my mind was awake. I saw what he did. I know the danger he is in. Go get my father. I will stay here with the doctors, if they allow it."

Doctor Klorioa let out a short, exhausted breath that was half-laugh, half-sigh. She stepped forward, her clinical demeanor returning, though softened by profound relief.

"Allow it? Evaria, you are not leaving this bed," Klorioa stated with dry, factual humor. "I am a scientist, which means Doctor Zeangol and I still need to run about fifty more genetic and neurological panels on you. I need to be absolutely certain this cure is not a fluke before I let you walk out of here. You are going to be our captive for just a bit longer."

Casia let out a tearful breath of gratitude, giving her daughter one last, desperate hug. She stood up, her emerald eyes hardening with fierce determination.

Before she could turn toward the heavy doors of the trauma suite, Doctor Zeangol gently cleared her throat. The young physician held up the small containment tray. Resting inside was a single, pristine ancient blueberry.

Zeangol's vibrant orange eyes sparked with gentle amusement. "Considering your current biological requirements... do you want to try it?"

Despite the overwhelming weight of the night, a brief, genuine smile broke across Casia's face. She reached out and carefully took the world-altering fruit. She popped it into her mouth, the unfamiliar, sharp sweetness providing the exact burst of energy she needed for what came next.

"Thank you!" Casia said, her voice full of absolute resolve. "These definitely will go good with the redberries."

She turned and rushed out the heavy doors, racing to intercept a completely broken Morlock—a husband whose desperate hope for Reunification had just been entirely shattered by a world that refused to listen.

Chapter IX — The Departure

Malachi was experiencing a complete psychological fracture. The cold, sterile detachment of the *Hollow* that had sustained him through the Senate trial had subsided, shifting instead into a heavy, suffocating melancholy. It was a state of severe, profound depression where the external world simply ceased to matter, leaving his analytical mind fragmented and unable to process the sheer trauma of his failure. A harsh shudder wracked his physical body with every step. He struggled to pull in oxygen, his chest heaving with erratic, shallow breaths as he stumbled onto the subterranean movable walkway that would carry him back to his private office.

His sensitive yellow eyes were severely bloodshot and aching from the sudden optical shock of unshielded surface light, causing his vision to blur as he looked at the few Morlocks on the walkway staring at him. Operating on a desperate, failing instinct to maintain social order, he tried to force a reassuring smile between his ragged gasps and shuffling steps to convey he was okay.

I have to maintain control, he thought, but the factual reality of his physical state completely overrode his rationality.

The walkway was sparsely populated, sparing him from a dense crowd. No one approached him to ask if he required medical assistance, even though his external symptoms were undeniable: the Morlock Historian was in the middle of a severe, fully escalated panic attack.

He finally gripped the metallic handrail, using it to physically anchor his trembling form as the walkway arrived at his office enclave. Stepping off the platform, his aching, bloodshot eyes focused on a large, illuminated digital billboard mounted on the sector wall. The bright text read: "The Newest Sensation to join the Peachberry and Redberry... Coming soon: The Blueberry!"

A faint, trembling smile touched his face. The advertisement sparked a fragmented, genuine memory of Casia's joy whenever she ate redberries. For a fraction of a second, that warmth fought through the severe depression of the *Hollow*. But his exhausted mind still struggled to remain rational, and the crushing melancholy quickly swallowed the brief moment of connection.

He reached his private office and placed his hand against the biometric lock. The heavy doors slid open, and he stumbled inside. He navigated the dim room toward his desk, but his motor skills were failing under the sheer physical toll of the panic attack. As he attempted to sit, his legs gave out prematurely. He collapsed awkwardly, missing the center of the seat and falling halfway out of the chair.

From the open corridor, the ambient audio of a local news broadcast echoed into the room.

"...the Historian calculated that resources would be depleted for the Eloi in exactly one hundred years," the commentator's voice announced over the public sound system.

Malachi winced at the undeniable, factual reminder of his failed broadcast. Gripping the armrests with shaking hands, he pulled himself up, finally dragging his exhausted body fully into the chair just as the office doors sealed shut, plunging the room back into absolute silence.

He stared at the small collection of his family on his desk—a faintly illuminated holographic projection of Seraphina resting right next to a physical, framed photograph of Casia, Evaria, and himself. In the hologram, Seraphina's blue-green gray skin softly illuminated the dim room. Operating under the crushing weight of his depression, he began to speak to her image, his analytical mind momentarily fracturing as if his deceased wife could actually hear him.

"Seraphina, you always knew what to do," Malachi whispered, his deep voice trembling as he reached out to trace the edge of the holographic projector. "You knew how to calm my fears. How to ground me and keep me focused... sensible... respectable. But now, look at me. Listen to what I have done."

He paused, a profound, aching guilt bleeding into his voice. "I cannot burden Casia with this anger within me. I love her just as deeply as I loved you, and Evaria, and our unborn child. Her playful, yet profoundly serious soul is exactly the reason you entrusted her with the Rite of Guardianship before you died. She was your closest friend, and she has been the absolute pillar of this family. But I have failed to truly grasp how to mourn your death after two years. I shut Casia out today because I believed her vibrant spirit could not comprehend the cold, sterile monster I feel I had to become to face the Senate. I pushed my soulmate away because I am broken."

On his desk console, the automated news feed continued to play the unedited audio of the Senate disaster, tracking the global broadcast.

"One hundred years is a distant hypothetical, Historian!" Minister Xenora's sharp, mocking voice blasted through the office speakers, immediately followed by the recorded, deafening jeers of nearly four hundred Eloi politicians laughing at him.

Malachi flinched, the sound physically compounding his humiliation. The rejection of absolute facts was tearing him apart. The mathematical certainty that the subterranean infrastructure would completely collapse in 1,200 Grid-cycles was undeniable, yet the Senate had treated the extinction of both species like a delusional joke.

"Seraphina, my only objective was to present the undeniable data!" he shouted at the shimmering image, a sudden surge of bitter, absolute anger breaking through his tears. "One hundred years! I wanted to convey that without Reunification and a unified push to reach the nighttime stars for new resources, both of our species will face extinction! I just needed *one* Eloi—just a single, rational affirmation from anyone in that chamber—to look up at the stars and see the resources we need to survive! But they are arrogant fools!"

He slammed his fist onto the desk, the physical impact echoing loudly in the silent room.

"Fena, the only Eloi I ever knew, truly possessed that bravery! She was not poisoned by their systemic hatred! She took a leap of faith to save our daughter, and they murdered her for it! I just wanted to find one more Eloi like her in that room... but I failed. I failed the Morlocks. I failed Evaria. And I failed you."

His voice broke, fracturing under the heavy realization of his own unraveling mind.

"But my reasoning... it failed me. I do not understand why my composure just collapsed. Evaria's illness, the sheer exhaustion... why couldn't I hold the line? When they laughed at our mutual destruction, my anger simply drove me to panic. I played the Aeterna stone. I exposed Fena's murder because I believed the desperate, flawed deduction that her death would force at least one of those malicious elitists to have common sense.

Instead, I gave them the exact excuse to humiliate me and my years of work."

He let out a broken sob, wincing sharply as the horrific memory of Fena's execution flashed behind his eyes. He stared at the hologram, desperate for Seraphina to answer and offer him a factual path forward. But the silent projection provided no guidance, and his console only offered the continuous, agonizing loop of his public failure.

"You are all savages and liars! All of you!" Xenora's recorded shriek echoed off the sterile walls.

The sheer cruelty of the Eloi Minister's words—dismissing his desperate plea for mutual survival as an act of savagery—built up inside him. It validated his absolute failure and drove the melancholic *Hollow* deeper into his psyche. He slammed his hands down on the desk, unable to bear the auditory assault for another second.

"Shut the feed off!" Malachi screamed at the computer, his voice tearing in his throat. "I get it! I understand!"

The console immediately recognized his voice command. The audio snapped off, leaving him completely alone in the heavy, suffocating silence of his office.

He wept. Trembling under the weight of his despair, he shifted his aching eyes away from Seraphina's hologram and looked desperately at the physical, framed photograph of Casia and Evaria, anchored to the tragic reality of what his failed strategy would mean for them.

"I failed," he sobbed, his bloodshot yellow eyes still locked on the physical photograph of Casia and Evaria. The crushing reality of his actions settled over him like a physical weight. He had not just failed his species; he had failed his family. Physically, Evaria was safe—secured in a private medical suite and diligently monitored by Doctor Klorioa and Doctor Zeangol. But biologically, she remained completely frozen in place, locked in the catatonic grip of Stage Two-A PCR. He had just guaranteed that even if she survived the horrific mutation, she would inherit a dying world. The agonizing thought of his and Casia's unborn baby also facing that identical, inevitable destruction tore a jagged hole through his chest. His desperate hope for their growing family had turned to ash because of his ruined Senate appeal. His heart was completely, fundamentally broken.

Searching the surface of his desk for any anchor of rationality, his gaze fell upon a pristine, fossilized *Homo sapiens* skull he kept as an artifact. *What were you actually like?* he thought, the question echoing through his fragmented mind. Relying on his archaeological finds and factual observations, he knew this ancient progenitor species possessed advanced intelligence and infrastructure. Yet, the exact catalyst for their mass extinction remained a complete, unsolved mystery to every Morlock Historian who had ever unearthed their skeletal remains.

A sudden, visceral rage pierced through the suffocating numbness of his depression. He picked up the heavy ancient artifact. The anatomical structure of the *Homo sapiens* skull—the cranial slope, the orbital cavities—bore a striking, factual resemblance to the facial features of the modern Eloi. That undeniable physical similarity became an immediate focal point for his unraveled emotions.

"Were you arrogant, too?" Malachi yelled at the fossilized skull, his deep voice raw and echoing in the confined space. "Did you also engage in class warfare? Subjugation? Did you fight each other over dwindling resources? Was it your own sheer entitlement? What was it that erased you from history?!"

In a sudden, explosive loss of his remaining composure, he hurled the heavy, fully mineralized fossil directly at the stone wall of his office.

A sharp, concussive crack echoed through the room. Malachi froze, his chest heaving as the burst of anger immediately burned out. He walked slowly toward the point of impact. The fragile face of the ancient skull had fractured entirely; the heavy rock-like mandible had separated completely from the upper orbital and nasal cavities, scattering bone-shaped mineral fragments across the floor.

But the ruined artifact was no longer his focus.

The sheer force of the dense fossil had struck a deceptively hollow section of the ancient masonry. Where the skull had impacted, a small, structural fissure had broken open in the office wall. Piercing through the darkness of the crack was a distinct, dim violet light. The sheer impossibility of a concealed energy source radiating from behind what was supposed to be a solid subterranean partition instantly halted his panic, replacing his grief with absolute, scientific astonishment.

Malachi stared at the luminescent fissure. A faint draft of stale, ancient air drifted from the crack, carrying the distinct, metallic scent of a completely undisturbed subterranean pocket. Drawing on his extensive archaeological experience, he recognized the structural anomaly immediately; these hidden voids behind the sector walls often led to the discovery of lost, ancient enclaves deep beneath the crust.

Driven by a sudden, obsessive compulsion that completely bypassed his usual meticulous protocols, he turned to his artifact display wall. He reached up and unhooked one of his most prized historical finds: an ancient, heavy-forged steel fire axe from the *Homo sapiens* era. The original shaft had disintegrated hundreds of thousands of years ago, replaced by a dense, Morlock-crafted handle of petrified wood, but the thick, wedge-shaped iron blade had survived the millennia perfectly intact.

Under normal, rational circumstances, Malachi would never dream of using a priceless historical artifact as a brute-force instrument. But his mind was still fractured by his grief and the overwhelming trauma of his ruined Senate appeal. Gripping the heavy stone-wood handle with both hands, he raised the ancient axe, fully intending to smash his office wall wide open to reach the violet light.

He brought the heavy blade down against the stone. The first strike sent a jagged shard of rock ricocheting sharply past his face, narrowly missing his cheek, but Malachi did not even flinch. He swung a second time, the heavy iron biting deeper into the fissure and spiderwebbing the structural wall outward.

Then, he simply lost control. He battered the stone again and again, swinging the ancient weapon as if he were physically attacking the Eloi Senate, his shattered rationality, and the suffocating weight of his own depression. Each heavy, rhythmic crack of the axe echoed harshly through the sterile office. He kept hacking at the solid rock for fifteen grueling minutes, his muscles burning and his chest heaving with ragged gasps, until the fracture finally gave way entirely.

A large section of the wall collapsed inward in a thick cloud of ancient, stale dust, leaving a jagged breach wide enough for him to pass through. The dim violet light now spilled freely into his office.

He stood before the opening, his bloodshot yellow eyes wide and his chest rising and falling rapidly. He was not thinking about structural integrity, contamination protocols, or historical preservation the way a rational Historian or archaeologist should. His analytical mind was entirely consumed by a singular, desperate compulsion: he just needed to get to the other side of his own office wall.

For a few more seconds, he stood before the jagged breach, letting the thick dust settle. Once the opening was clear, he immediately stepped through it, crossing the threshold from his modern office into an unlit, ancient stone tunnel.

The stale, undisturbed air immediately filled his lungs. Drawing on his extensive archaeological expertise, his focused mind began to automatically categorize his surroundings. The specific composition of the stone cuts and the exact dimensions of the tunnel strongly indicated the distinct architecture of the 500,000 AD era—the time of Chancellor Olesya.

A profound sense of historical astonishment hit him, temporarily overriding the suffocating grip of his depression. He walked slowly down the narrow passageway. After navigating the dark corridor for approximately three hundred yards, his path was abruptly halted by a massive, reinforced door constructed of blended steel and heavy stone.

He leaned in closer, his aching, bloodshot yellow eyes scanning the surface. He could see deep indentations and heavy, blackened scoring across the metal. *Are these seared marks from weapons fire?* he thought, tracing the rough, burned edges with his fingers. It strongly resembled the residual damage of concentrated ancient weapons fire. Yet, he could not make a definitive, factual assessment in the pitch-black environment. His only source of illumination was the faint, artificial light of his circular holo-wafer, which he held up like a makeshift torch against the ruined barricade.

He looked closer at the massive door and noticed a faint, localized illumination beneath the layers of ancient dust. Reaching into a small pocket at his waist, concealed just beneath Evaria's purple sash, he retrieved a small cloth. He carefully wiped the grime away from the illuminated area, revealing a perfectly intact biometric hand scanner.

For a fraction of a second, he hesitated. His deeply ingrained training fiercely fought back against his erratic actions.

STOP! You are not engaging in proper archaeological or Historian protocols for this new find! STOP! his rational mind screamed at him.

But he completely ignored his own training. Operating on pure, desperate compulsion, he placed his palm flat against the scanner.

To his absolute surprise, the ancient scanner worked. Deep within the stone framework, heavy machinery groaned. The door hummed and whined, the unmaintained gears grinding fiercely against hundreds of thousands of years of friction and stagnation. Finally, the massive steel-and-stone slabs shuddered and began to part. They did not open completely, the mechanisms jamming after a few agonizing seconds, but they separated just enough for him—and perhaps anyone else who might follow—to squeeze through the gap.

A thick layer of dust coated the main console. Driven by a desperate, frantic need for any kind of factual solution to the extinction he had just mathematically guaranteed, he brushed the grime away. His fingers moved across the terminal with surgical precision, entering diagnostic commands in the old Morlock dialect until the 500,000 AD system finally responded.

The terminal emitted a sharp, automated voice that echoed through the stone chamber: *"SECURED: MER DNA SCAN COMPLETE. PROTECTIVE DIRECTIVE DISENGAGED."*

He stared at the biometric pad, quickly deducing that the ancient scanner possessed a strict genetic lock requiring Morlock DNA, completely rejecting Eloi biology. Yet, the acronym remained a mystery.

MER? Malachi thought, his brow furrowing in confusion. He recognized the automated pronunciation as an older linguistic offshoot of the Morlock language, but the specific acronym completely eluded him.

The Archway began to come back to life, its energy fields pulsing and flickering as the ancient system struggled to stabilize its power source—a source Malachi could not even begin to identify. On the main monitor, the system initiated a sequence of real-time projections, the dates of the future playing out rapidly before his eyes. Malachi watched in suffocating horror as the screen displayed the undeniable future of the Morlocks. He saw the subterranean infrastructure in a profound state of decay, yet still functional, managed by his species through pure primal instinct rather than intellect. He watched his own descendants—reduced to pale, feral predators in loincloths—hunting the Eloi under the cold light of the moon and stars. The Eloi wandered like naive children led to the slaughter, harvested by his own kind for food. He watched, absolutely astounded, as the feral Morlocks completely controlled the surface world at night.

He was horrified. As a Historian, his analytical mind frantically tried to process the nightmare on the screen: he believed he was witnessing the ultimate PCR evolution of the Morlocks. Rather than dying out, his species had fully succumbed to the absolute, mindless feral state of Stage Three, evolving over the millennia into a society driven entirely by a savage, uncontrollable frenzy. The terrifying revelation completely shattered his remaining rationality. He was staring directly at the brutal reality of 802,701 AD.

WARNING: PARADOX DETECTED.

The projection shifted. A male *Homo sapiens* figure emerged from a primitive machine of brass and quartz. Then, in another flash of the Archway, Malachi saw flames fill the screen—a dark forest at night, Morlocks recoiling amid the trees. Their shrieks echoed through the forest not just from the heat, but from the blinding, agonizing light of the fire mercilessly scorching their highly sensitive eyes, while this unusual temporal anomaly brutally attacked the Morlocks trying to reach him. Amidst the frantic struggle, Malachi clearly saw an Eloi woman being dragged away into the darkness by the Morlocks from right underneath the strange male, completely without the man knowing it.

The sheer weight of the tragedy broke the last remnants of Malachi's restraint. He could not save the Senate. He believed his ruined appeal had condemned his daughter Evaria and countless others to eventual death from PCR. He honestly believed his career as a Historian, and his family's future, was completely over—even though, unbeknownst to him, that was not factually true at all.

Desperate to prevent this feral nightmare, a final, massive calculation clicked in his mind. If he could just reach this temporal anomaly, he could present the factual data and logically reason with the man to stop him from traveling into the future. Even in the absolute depths of his despair, Malachi still considered himself a scholar of logic. He wanted to change the timeline through intellect, not violence; attacking or murdering the man on the screen was an option his rational mind absolutely refused to entertain.

"What is this?" Malachi murmured. As he watched the anomaly fight the feral Morlocks on the screen, a fragmented, highly classified memory of Chancellor Olesya's ancient records surfaced in his mind. *Ian?* he thought. *Could this be him?*

The Archway responded instantly, its automated voice crackling. *"Homo sapiens paradox detected. Quantum anomaly."*

"Origin point? Year?" he demanded. "Where did this man come from, and what year is this happening that I see this?"

There was a brief, calculating pause. *"1894, the male Homo sapiens is from. Future Year of his arrival into the future: 802,701,"* the Archway responded.

Malachi's piercing, bloodshot yellow eyes widened with absolute wonder and scientific curiosity. He did not wait for a full diagnostic.

"Can you transport me to this quantum anomaly? To the point of 1894? Initiate temporal transport to the originating point of the subject's timeline," Malachi commanded the console, his voice vibrating with absolute resolve.

"Authorization accepted," a faint, distorted feminine voice replied from the ancient speakers. *"One-way transfer only. Remove the translation pin from the console and attach it to your clothing."*

A small compartment hissed open. Inside lay a metallic pin—two interlocked rings over a silver-etched symbol of a rising plume. He seized it, pinning it roughly to his dark tunic.

"You may now enter the Archway," the system crackled, its automated voice barely cutting through the deep, oceanic hum of the active vortex.

Malachi stepped up to the pulsing amber light. He did not look back. His bloodshot yellow eyes were locked entirely on the swirling energy, his analytical mind completely consumed by the factual calculation that he was jumping back to the year 1894.

Finding his ruined office moments earlier had filled Casia with a sickening terror that he had taken his own life, sending her sprinting blindly down the pitch-black tunnel. Now, the heavy scrape of metal was entirely swallowed by the sweeping, noise-canceling wave of the temporal hum as she desperately squeezed her way through the narrow gap of the jammed steel doors. Stumbling into the ancient chamber, she had absolutely no idea what this towering, roaring machine was. She only saw her husband standing just paces away, preparing to step into the vortex.

"NO! MALACHI, PLEASE DON'T!" Casia screamed, her voice tearing with absolute, desperate hope. "EVARIA IS AWAKE! THE PCR IS CURED!"

She scrambled forward across the ancient stone floor, but the sheer, unnatural vastness of the swirling portal forced her to flinch back. There was no physical shockwave pushing her away—only the terrifying, absolute uncertainty of the churning displacement. The Archway was locked in an active transmission cycle, blinding the chamber with a swirling storm of amber and light-blue energy. Her sharp intuition recognized that the massive, twisting space was deeply unstable; reaching out for him meant stepping into an unimaginable, frightening void.

"WE HAVE OUR DAUGHTER BACK! MALACHI, STOP!" she shrieked, crying hysterically, her raw pleas breaking against his turned back.

But he could not hear her. The machine emitted no violent frequencies, nor did its volume physically hurt the ears, but its sheer acoustic presence was absolute. The deep, rhythmic *vroom... vroom...* of the temporal energy swelled like a roaring ocean of heavy, swooshing waves. It created a massive, atmospheric barrier of sound—a complete noise-canceling effect that effortlessly absorbed her frantic voice. Malachi stepped into the vortex of the Archway portal, crossing the threshold and vanishing into the light before she could safely get anywhere near him.

SYSTEM WARNING: ARCHWAY MALFUNCTION.

STATUS: POWER UNSTABLE.

CRITICAL: DOORWAY COLLAPSE IMMINENT.

The system hissed in static as the amber vortex rapidly shifted into a blinding light-blue, then snapped back to a brilliant amber light, seamlessly swallowing Malachi whole. Then, the ancient machinery short-circuited. The deep, oceanic hum abruptly snapped off as the power completely failed, plunging the chamber into absolute, deafening silence.

Casia collapsed onto the cold stone floor. In the sudden pitch-black darkness, her weeping echoed for the husband she had just lost. She thought she was entirely alone in the dead, ancient chamber. But as she sobbed on the stone, a faint, deliberate shift in the air just beyond the jammed steel doors revealed the chilling, undeniable fact that she was not.

Epilogue — The Arrival 1897

Malachi stepped into the vortex. His back had been entirely turned to the ancient chamber, his focus consumed by the brutal imagery of the year 802,701 AD playing out within the portal—the raging forest fire and the final clash between the feral Morlocks and the mysterious *Homo sapiens* anomaly. Because of this, combined with the deafening mechanical roar of the Archway coming to life, he had not heard Casia running down the long tunnel.

It was only in the final fraction of a second, just as he crossed the threshold into the temporal stream, that her last, agonizing plea pierced the noise.

"MALACHI! STOP!" she shrieked.

To his absolute shock, Malachi turned around within the swirling energy. Through the fading barrier of the portal, he saw Casia, his second wife, collapsed on the chamber floor, sobbing hysterically.

He had no idea she had come into that chamber looking for him. A heavy, physical ache dropped into his chest, and he brought a hand over his mouth. Seeing her absolute devastation, the factual reality struck him: her presence here was not born of duty or the Rite of Guardianship. It was pure love. It was the profound respect he firmly believed he had entirely lost while standing before the Eloi Senate.

She truly loves me, he thought, his analytical mind struggling to process the agonizing depth of her grief.

But the roar of the machine had swallowed the rest of her frantic message. He did not know that the PCR mutation was cured. He had absolutely no idea that Doctor Klorioa had successfully used the Calvenine drug, or that Evaria was finally awake.

His thoughts descended into absolute chaos. Amber and light-blue streaks of temporal energy entirely engulfed his body, leaving him with the sensation of floating weightlessly, even as he stood perfectly still within the roaring maelstrom of light.

His bloodshot yellow eyes were barely able to adjust to the intense glare. Within the roaring vortex, he began to hear voices bleeding through the temporal stream. One voice in particular was muffled, sounding faintly like a desperate, female voice crying out, *"Help me!"* But he could not be sure. It was heavily distorted, as if time itself harbored a secret tied to that single cry. Other fragmented voices echoed around him in the void. He blinked rapidly against the blinding glare before finally raising a hand to shield his sensitive eyes from the light.

Even with his hand half-covering his eyes against the blinding glare, he could still see everything playing out within the void. Vast cosmic projections—entire planets, their orbital systems, and drifting asteroid fields—swept past him in the stream.

Then came the faces.

First were those of his family. Seraphina's eyes and her gentle smile drifted before him like a living memory. Then came Evaria, his daughter; Casia, his second wife; and the fading visages of friends he once had. To his absolute surprise, other, unfamiliar faces began to materialize in the temporal stream—Eloi, Morlocks, and figures entirely unknown to him. Some appeared as fleeting shadows, while others bore features that were not humanoid in the slightest.

He did not logically understand the physics of what he was witnessing, only that it was undeniably there. Suspended in the transit, he was no longer certain if these images were a genuine function of the Archway, or simply hallucinations fracturing within his *Hollow* mind.

The Eloi are an abomination! Curse them for all of this. My daughter, the Calvenine drug, everything. The absolute subjugation of all Morlocks.

Malachi's thoughts spiraled out of control as he floated in the maelstrom.

I left the year 689,789 using this ancient, lost technology to find this anomaly in time. I must stop this ancient being. He had to have somehow caused all of this. In the year 802,701, he is slaughtering my species—my fellow Morlocks who appear to have completely succumbed to the PCR mutation, yet somehow still exist. I cannot logically understand any of it. But if I can just stop him from traveling through time, maybe none of this ever happens. I will fix what is broken. I finally have a chance to regain my stolen dignity.

In the suffocating grip of his *Hollow* state, Malachi's focused mind had developed a dangerous blind spot. He was a master Historian, not a quantum physicist. Consumed by the desperate need to fix what was broken, he completely ignored the absolute reality of the butterfly effect—the fundamental temporal law dictating that even the most microscopic intervention in the past could trigger massive, unpredictable, and catastrophic alterations across the entire timeline.

His rationality was entirely clouded by grief. He failed to fully grasp the ultimate paradox of his mission: if he actually succeeded in stopping the Time Traveller, the present reality he knew would instantly be erased. The stolen dignity he so desperately sought to regain would never have existed to be restored, because an entirely different, unpredictable future would immediately take its place. But floating helplessly in the roaring maelstrom of the void, Malachi only saw a straight line to his own redemption.

The vortex felt cold to him—or perhaps it was simply the *Hollow* state rendering him cold and indifferent to the magnificent cosmic display he was experiencing. He still firmly believed his daughter Evaria was confined to a frozen, catatonic state. The image of his second wife utterly devastated on the chamber floor, reaching out for him, burned in his mind. He could not undo the moment he had stepped inside the vortex.

Casia, you truly did love me? Malachi thought, the realization echoing in the silent void. *For two years, I thought this arrangement was just to ensure Evaria would grow up with a motherly figure. I thought it was just duty. But it became something more.*

He closed his piercing yellow eyes, the crushing weight of another memory surfacing: Casia, he knew, was with child. He already knew the baby was safe from PCR. Yet, his heart was broken that for the past two years he felt he had no control over anything anymore. Only bitterness consumed him. It was the *Hollow*. He did not realize until this moment that the warning Seraphina had spoken to him on her deathbed was now rooted deep inside him.

The factual reality of his massive error in judgment finally hit him. Casia genuinely needed him, regardless of Evaria's condition. He had walked away from a family that was actively growing. Unable to bear the agonizing weight of his own irreversible actions, he forcefully pushed those thoughts away from his mind.

The maelstrom began to shift and stabilize around him. The temporal transit was ending. Slowly, Malachi felt himself being anchored into a new timeline. The past. The far past of hundreds of thousands of years. The vastness of time.

Filby awoke to a thundering sound in the laboratory.

Heart racing, Filby seized the iron poker, lit the chamberstick, and hastened down the corridor. Drawing his skeleton key, he turned it with precision until the lock yielded.

"Reveal yourself, whoever you are!" Filby demanded.

The room appeared just as it had been left: crates stacked, cobwebs draped across beams. Yet in the far corner, a shadowy figure crouched in the darkness. The intruder emitted a low, gurgling sound as he stirred, raising one hand high to shield his face from the flickering candlelight. Filby could make out long, light grey hair streaked with white, and a black garment cut like a robe with a slim purple sash.

The stranger, still crouched, used his free hand to clutch an old, yellowed newspaper clipping.

"I will not ask again! Who are you?" Filby barked, raising the poker.

The figure's concealed hand moved subtly, tapping a small golden mushroom-shaped brooch pinned to his sash. It flickered faintly.

"I... am a friend... of 'The Time Traveller'..." the figure said haltingly.

Filby's eyes widened. "How is this possible? Ian has been absent for years."

The figure shifted, his robe whispering against the floorboards. "Gone? He... left already?" The syllables rolled awkwardly at first, but he quickly adjusted.

"Yes! If you were truly acquainted with him, you would be aware of this!" Filby snapped. "Have you not read *The Time Machine*?"

"No..." the figure replied slowly, his voice carrying a low resonance. "My interest lies solely in the preservation of time and its history."

At that precise moment, the laboratory doors burst open with a sudden, explosive gust. The force snuffed out the candle, plunging the laboratory into suffocating darkness. Filby felt the bitter cold rush inward as he stumbled toward the door. As he pressed against the frame, a sharp sting shot through his palm—a shard of broken glass. Suddenly, a large dead branch, torn free by the wind, crashed against him, pinning his legs.

In the darkness, the mysterious figure stirred. With surprising strength, he seized the fallen branch and heaved it aside—using only one arm, his other hand never leaving his face.

At last, the wind subsided, leaving only the low moan of the draft through the cracks. Filby fumbled with his chamberstick, striking a match with trembling fingers. The tiny flame caught, and he relit the candle. Its soft light spread shakily across the room, revealing crates, dust, and cobwebs once more.

He looked down at his palm. Blood trickled slowly from the cut, dark against his chilled skin. Wincing, he set the chamberstick on a bench and found the tin first aid kit from 1894. It was lightly dusted from disuse, but the latch gave way with a snap. Inside lay brittle bandages and a small bottle of carbolic antiseptic.

Uncorking the bottle, the sharp, medicinal scent filled the space between them. He dabbed the liquid onto his wound, gritting his teeth as a stinging fire shot through his nerves. He steadied himself, wrapping the hand tightly with a strip of cloth until the bleeding ceased.

"Thank you," Filby said at last, his voice tight as he fastened a spare sheet over the broken pane to block the bitter draft.

"It was of no consequence," the figure replied from the shadows.

"No consequence? I could have been seriously injured," Filby retorted, turning to step closer, determined to see the face of this intruder.

"Stay back," the figure warned sharply, shrinking further into the gloom. "I am not fully well. My skin is sensitive to the light, along with my eyes."

Filby stopped, a cold thought taking root. "Are you contagious?" he asked cautiously.

"No—you cannot catch what I have," the figure answered, the voice low and guttural. "But still... stay back. For the moment, it is safer this way."

Then, leaning forward, the urgency returned to the stranger's voice. "Where is his device? I must find him!"

"It left with him. All I have here are these crates of parts and his schematics," Filby gestured with his bandaged hand to the walls. "But I do not possess the mechanical knowledge to assemble a second machine."

The figure's gaze shifted to the stacked boxes. A hunger seemed to emanate from him. "I need complete access to these parts. The future depends on it."

Filby drew in a slow breath. The man's secrecy was troubling, but if he truly possessed the skill to restore Ian's work, then cooperation was necessary.

"Malachi... is my name," the figure said slowly, testing the syllables on his tongue.

"Malachi, what? Surely you have a last name. I am Alan Filby."

Malachi's eyes flicked to one of the crates behind Filby. Stenciled across its side, in bold black paint, was a single word: HOLLOW. His gaze lingered there for a moment, a faint, calculated smile touching his lips.

"Malachi Hollow... is my name," he declared.

He claimed the title of his own profound melancholy. He surrendered his timeline and a devoted, pregnant wife, completely unaware he had abandoned his miraculously cured daughter, Evaria, alongside the finalized PCR cure saving his people. He had crossed an irreversible void only to entirely miss his target of 1894. Marooned in 1897, the anomaly he sacrificed his life to stop was long gone. Entirely alone, the Historian from 689,789 AD was now permanently trapped. Time was truly distorted, exacting the ultimate, devastating price.

About The Author

I am the author of the *Distorted Time* series, a science-fiction trilogy that explores the intricate intersection of temporal mechanics, speculative history, and the human condition.

My storytelling is deeply rooted in the classic literary traditions of H.G. Wells, Jules Verne, Washington Irving, Charles Dickens, and Edgar Allan Poe. An avid enthusiast of speculative fiction, I draw further inspiration from the complex narratives found in *Doctor Who*, *The Time Machine*, *Star Trek*, *Star Wars*, *The Twilight Zone*, and the original *Quantum Leap* series. Through these influences, I can create stories that challenge the boundaries of what is known and what is lost to the expanse of time.

For updates on the *Distorted Time* series and new releases, please follow and review me on **Amazon**. You can also connect with the author and join the conversation on **Goodreads**.

Distorted Time: Future Forward ***(Goodreads Group)***

Best Journeys,
H.M. Holzman

www.ingramcontent.com/pod-product-compliance
Lightning Source LLC
LaVergne TN
LVHW090606110826
845146LV00001B/276

* 9 7 9 8 9 9 4 9 0 0 8 3 3 *